# NIKETOWN

# BY THE SAME AUTHOR

Seagalogy: A Study of the Ass-Kicking
Films of Steven Seagal

"Yippee Ki-Yay Moviegoer!" Writings On Bruce Willis,
Badass Cinema and Other Important Topics

# NIKETOWN

## a novel
## by Vern

# ONE

# 1

CARTER READJUSTED HIS ASS on the sidewalk and wondered what the hell was taking his brothers so long. Did they forget? He was getting tired of waiting there leaning up against the wall of the Greyhound station. Having exhausted any interest he might've had in watching the young professionals buy coffee across the street, he was now staring at the statue of Jesus on the side of the Verizon First Methodist Church down the block. The Lord's hands were held out as a welcoming gesture to His children, but as pedestrians walked by oblivious Carter thought it looked like He was shrugging at them. Saying *dude, what the fuck? Come into my church. Am I invisible?*

In the street a pigeon pecked at a dried up puddle of vomit that someone had partly covered with a section of newspaper. Another pigeon saw what was going on, rushed over and had a few bites for himself. Apparently happy with what he tasted, the newcomer tried to shove the first bird out of the way. They puffed out their chests and batted their wings threateningly. Just two hungry souls fighting over puke.

Carter laughed. "Ain't that the truth?" he said. The longhair with the frame backpack gave him a suspicious look. As long as he had his attention, Carter asked him what time it was again.

The city was mostly how he remembered it. Seemed bigger, though. Either the buildings had gotten taller since he'd been gone or he just never respected them. When you're walking down the street you keep your eyes at ground level and you forget what's up there.

He would have to get used to these computer phone things that everybody seemed to be fiddling with constantly. Or the ones in the ears. He kept thinking they were headsets, like the guys at the McDonalds drive-thru wear. It seemed like everybody was looking at or talking on a phone – drivers, pedestrians, even bicyclists. But nobody talked to each other. Carter was relieved to see two businessmen crossing the street together having a conversation, but as they passed he realized they were on separate phone calls.

"Afternoon gentlemen," Carter said. Both men looked away, pretended they didn't hear anything. Carter laughed and looked at Backpack.

"You see that?"

The longhair nodded. "I know, nobody can even say hi to each other anymore," he muttered, then looked away again to end the conversation.

It was a city full of distracted people, distant people. People weaving through each other but not talking to each other, not looking at each other or at where they were going. Their bodies traveled between their businesses and homes, but their minds were always somewhere else, their ears listening to headphones, their fingers typing to people who were standing in other places, but who weren't there either. There were people all around, but where *was* everybody? A horrible thought.

As he took a drag on the cigarette he remembered that he had bummed it from a guy in the terminal earlier. Human interaction would always exist as long as people kept running out of smokes. He didn't smoke much, but this was a special occasion. He should be thankful to even be here in the city at all, right? It was a fair point, but it was too late. A wave of depression and panic hit him, a profound feeling that he didn't belong in this world. He was an old scratched up record in the middle of a CD store. But he'd heard that his favorite CD store wasn't there anymore, bulldozed and turned into a bank. He wasn't sure if they even *made* CDs anymore. Even the metaphor for his obsolescence was out of date.

He wanted to reach out to a stranger, make a connection, almost as an act of rebellion. He was so out of practice that when he tried to make small talk with the

4

longhair he just scared the guy. So he kept asking him the time just to fuck with him. He could tell this guy wished his organic hippie code allowed him to get an iPod like everybody else. That would shield him from this sort of trouble.

Finally, a Toyota Corolla pulled up to the edge of the sidewalk, and Carter' older brother Mason was driving. Carter stood up and threw down his American Spirit.

"See ya pal," he said to the longhair, patting him condescendingly on his matted head. Mason looked startled as he turned and saw Carter approaching the car. He stared at him for a moment before the doors came unlocked with a *clunk*.

Carter looked at the empty passenger seat, then the empty back seat, and got in. "Shit, you look *different*, Jimmy," Mason said, calling Carter by the nickname the brothers had used for him ever since learning the name "Jimmy Carter" in elementary school. "I almost didn't recognize you. Who was that guy, by the way?"

"Old war buddy," Carter said. "Where's Mark?"

"Didn't show up," Mason said.

"What do you mean he didn't show up? Did you call him?"

"Not answering. I don't know."

"I'm supposed to stay at his place tonight."

"Well, he'll show up. When'd your bus get in?"

"When I said it was getting in. Couple hours ago."

"Sorry about that."

"Yeah."

"Don't be pissy about it. At least you're out of prison. Man, you should *enjoy* waiting at the bus station. The freedom, man."

"Yeah, thanks."

They didn't talk much as Mason got on the freeway and headed for the suburbs. Of course Carter was mesmerized by the view of the city, the streets, the sky - things he hadn't seen in so god damn long – but the main reason for the silence was that Carter and Mason had never been very close. None of the family were, really, but in recent years Carter had kept in touch with Mark, who wrote him letters, sent him books and even came to visit a couple times. Being the closest in age they had the most in common, they understood each other's humor better, and each other's interests, and they looked out for each other more.

Only Mark could get away with preaching to Carter, corny shit about positivity and walking the straight path and all that. They talked about what a waste this all was, all this over money. Money is important, but is it more important than family, than life? Carter had made bad decisions, and because of that he'd grown away from his brothers, he'd missed the last years of his father's life, the last years of his mother's life. Now he had to go through the rest of his years knowing both of his parents died with one son locked up, a deadbeat.

"Was all that worth it? For money?" Mark had asked him.

Well, it wasn't a fair question, because he didn't *get* the money. If he got the money he wouldn't *be* in jail and he could've visited his parents a couple times a year, none of this would be a problem and *yes* it would've been worth it. Still, he knew his brother had a point. Carter was pretty sure there were things in life that were profoundly more important than money, and that it would be smart to put his energy toward finding them.

The last time they talked was about a week ago, just after their mother's death. Mark had come to break the news personally, and made Carter take a sacred vow. "I'm serious about this, Jimmy," he said, and his eyes backed up that claim. "We're all we have left. Me, you and Mason, the last of the Chases."

"And Dana," Carter corrected.

"Well… okay. I guess."

They both laughed.

"I want you to stay with me for a while. I want us to be a family again. But as long as you're in my house you have to straighten the fuck out. I want you to promise me. No fighting…"

Carter held up his right hand. "No fighting, no stealing, no ill-gotten gains."

"Ill-gotten gains?" Mark laughed. "Where'd you get that?"

"Prob'ly one of those books."

"Oh yeah, do you need any more?"

"Nah, I just started that last Lincoln one you gave me. That should last me."

"Okay. Well, be ready. Be mentally prepared. We'll come pick you up, get you some real food, bring you to the duplex. And I think I'll have a few job interviews lined up. Your record makes it tricky but, you know, a lot of people owe me favors. I think it'll work out. I've been talking to some people."

"I'm lucky to have you, Mark."

"No shit."

"Mom and dad always wanted me to be more like you."

"That's not true. They just wanted you staying out of trouble, for your own happiness. You don't want to spend your life in here."

"Well, I appreciate it Mark. I don't know how I'll repay you."

"Come visit *me* some time. It seems like I always have to be the one to come see you, you lazy fuck."

Those were good talks they had. Without Mark he would've had nothing but bitterness and anger to keep him company in there. And he'd have known a lot less about the Civil War era, because the prison library was shit. Whenever he talked to Mark he really believed he could change. Forget about revenge, forget about money, just work on becoming a good person, finding peace, contributing to society instead of degrading it. If he couldn't do it for himself then he should do it as a gesture to his little brother.

If the prick wasn't gonna show up, though, fuck that.

After about ten minutes Carter broke the silence.

"They had these ads for video games in front of the urinals. At the bus station. So you read it while you're pissing."

"Yeah, I've seen those in places," Mason said.

"Thought that was weird."

The first stop was at Lake View Self Storage, to pick up Carter's shit. After Carter was convicted, Mark and Mason had packed up everything from his apartment and put it in a storage space. Most of it he didn't care about, but he would at least need some clothes for now, and later the furniture would help when he found a place.

"Why'd you pick a place all the way out here?"

"I don't know. I think maybe your friend Dante recommended this place."

"Dante's not my friend."

He'd have to find someone to help him drag all the shit across town. But at least it wasn't all the way out in the suburbs where Mason lived. And anyway he shouldn't complain, it was nice of them to secure his belongings for him. Most of the cons he knew didn't have anyone to do that for them.

Mason looked at his phone as he pulled up to the gate. The security code was saved on there. He typed it into the keypad three times, but it wouldn't work. He pressed the button to buzz the front office.

The guy seemed surprised to have something to do. He let them in and brought them to his office, which looked like a mobile home. He wasn't seeing Carter's name in his computer. He tried under Mason's and Mark's and then Carter's again, and then realized that it *was* on there but he missed it the first time because it was on the right side of the screen in red with the closed accounts.

It said Mason hadn't paid any bills after the initial

8

deposit. The card number on file had been cancelled. This outraged Mason, who started tossing off statistics about how much money he made, but the guy just meant the bank had changed the number on his account, so they couldn't charge it. He said there would've been three warnings sent to him before all Carter's shit was either auctioned off or donated.

"I never got any warnings."

"Well, we would've sent them."

"This is bullshit."

"Well, I'm sorry, I don't know what to tell you, man. This was years ago. I didn't even work here."

"We're long time customers."

"I'm sorry."

Mason tried to stare the guy down. Carter probably could've done it, but he refused to participate. When the guy didn't budge Mason sighed, exasperated. "I want to see the manager." Like he was pulling out the big guns.

Carter had had enough. "What's the manager gonna do? Go to all the Goodwills and ask if any of my pants are still there? Fuck it, let's go."

"We should at least get our money back."

"What money? He says you didn't ever pay them."

"We deserve a coupon or something. One free month storage."

In the car they didn't talk or look at each other.

At about 4:45 they pulled up at the funeral home. "Man, I can't get over how different you look," Mason said. "You're a scary lookin' dude now! I should send you after some of the guys at work, make 'em shit their pants."

"Why are we here?" Carter asked. "Are we doing this *now?*"

"*You're* doing this now. I have to pick up Dana at 5:00. I'm already late."

"That's fine, I'll go with you."

"Carter, this is your responsibility. I did it for Dad while you were in prison. Now it's your turn. You or Mark.

It's only fair."

"You think I wanted to be locked up? Come on, man. I would've been there if I could've."

"Well, you weren't."

Carter shook his head and got out of the car. Shit. He just got out this morning, didn't think he'd have to figure out how to bury his mom quite yet. But he was here, might as well get it over with. As he walked around some shockingly green landscaping to the entrance, Mason pulled up alongside him and lowered his window.

"Here," Mason said, holding out some money.

"Forget it, Mason."

"Come on Jimmy. Take it. I feel bad about the storage space."

Carter sighed. He didn't want to accept it, but the storage debacle had definitely set him back. Whatever he had in his checking account would probably just cover the funeral. He did have a minor loot stash he could check, but somebody could've discovered it by now. He couldn't count on it being there.

He swiped the money from Mason's hand and slid it in his pocket in one quick motion, like they were making an illegal transaction.

"Call me if there's any problems," Mason said.

Carter looked around. "If I can find a pay phone."

"You don't have a phone?"

"I just got out, Mason."

"Well… should've thought of that before you committed a crime." He rolled up his window, turned and put both hands on the steering wheel. After a moment he turned back to look his brother in the eye again. Then he locked the car doors.

As Mason pulled away Carter pulled the money out of his pocket and looked at it. It was a five and three ones.

"Thanks, Mason."

The receptionist took down his name and his mom's

name and made him wait, even though there was no one else to help. Eventually a fat man in a baggy suit came out and shook his hand. "How's business?" Carter asked. The man smiled, but did not answer. He brought Carter into an office with a big window and a soothing view of a garden. The serenity of the place kind of creeped Carter out, but the procedure wasn't as hard as he thought it would be. The guy walked him through most of it.

"Would you like chairs? There is a small fee but we deliver and set them up for you."

"Okay, that sounds good."

"Has the number of guests changed since the reservation?"

"Oh I—I just got out. I'm not really in contact with most of the, uh—shit."

"Oh no sir, we already have a guest list. We talked to…" He ran his finger across his ledger looking for a name.

"My brother."

"Yes, we talked to your brother on the phone, so we already have a list of guests and invitations have already been taken care of. Just let us know if you find out you will be needing significantly more or less than 25 chairs."

"Okay."

"Now," the man said, delicately opening a tablet with a leather cover like a hymnal, "we provide a number of options for the style of burial and marker. You can choose a package that appeals to your family's needs or you can customize it."

"She wasn't picky. Just give her whatever the standard package is, I guess."

"Okay." The man used a stylus to navigate to the proper electronic form. "Would you prefer open casket, or closed, sir?"

"Huh, that's a good question. I'm not sure about that one."

"The cause of death was a traffic accident?"

Carter nodded. "You're right. The car flipped over and

everything. I haven't seen the body, but that sounds like a closed casket all right."

The man checked the box for closed casket, then handed the tablet to Carter with the sections he needed to complete highlighted in yellow.

So Carter finished up the paperwork, all very impersonal, like filling out a survey. He felt like kind of an asshole though, realizing how much about his mom he wasn't really sure about. Religion: Presbyterian, I think, at least she was when we were kids. Church: Not sure. He decided to put down Verizon. *Am I invisible?* That lonely Jesus statue would appreciate the gesture. He went back, deleted the religion part and changed it to Methodist.

When he got to the "sponsorship" section he asked what that was all about.

"Well, it's a quarterly payout. If you choose direct deposit there is no minimum balance. If you choose check it's a minimum of 50 dollars, anything less rolls over until the next pay date. If you don't have the routing information with you just go ahead and put down check for now and we can change it later."

Carter stared blankly, clearly not comprehending. "Unless there's another family member, or an estate. Some people like to choose a charity, it's up to you. Whoever the check should be made out to, you write it there."

"What's—I don't think I understand. What check are you talking about?"

"The earnings. For the affiliate program. You said you wanted the standard—"

"I'm sorry, I don't—I haven't done this before. I was incarce-- incapacitated when my dad died, so..."

"Oh, I see. No problem." The man exhaled and took a moment to gather his thoughts, but not in a condescending way. He seemed to be genuinely searching for the best words to explain it. "Okay, it's like this. We all would like to continue providing for our loved ones after we pass on, but not all of us have wealth to leave behind. The affiliate program is a solution to that problem. Think of it like a sponsorship. There's a small monitor on the monument, below your mother's name and inscription, that shows advertisements. Very subtle, not intrusive at all. You can choose from a list of possible sponsors. You're lucky that this plot has been in your family for so long. It happens to have very good placement, along the main path and between some historical graves. So you have some good choices. You have Pepsi on your list, which is a very high paying sponsor, so I would recommend them. They're required by their contract with us to pay a higher rate to monuments within this particular zone. There's a body sensor near the grave that records how many people pass by and how long they stay within sight range. You get a certain sum for each impression multiplied by the length of the impression. Normally it's only a few cents per hit, but yours would be higher because of the location. Does that makes sense? Do you have any questions?"

"So—they do that now?"

"It's pretty standard these days, pretty unusual for a new grave not to have a sponsor."

"Huh. Okay, I guess that's fine."

He pulled a scrap of paper out of his wallet and copied Mark's address onto the form, since he didn't know where he would be staying. Then he pulled out his Visa debit card. It was bent and the magnetic strip was worn out, he wasn't sure if it would work. Ah, shit. It expired two years ago.

An hour and fifteen minutes later, after learning that his bank had been bought out by Chase and retrieving some cash, a roll of quarters and a temporary checkbook with the help of his thankfully-not-quite-expired passport, Carter returned, paid the bill, signed the tablet. He took a business card from the man's desk and put it in his wallet just in case.

He shook the man's hand and said, "Thanks man. Have a good one."

"I'm sorry for your loss."

"Yeah, you too."

After leaving he wondered if he should've tipped the guy. Probably not. Well, he was pretty much cleaned out anyway.

It was another journey to find a working payphone. Even homeless people had cell phones now, he realized, so there wasn't much business for phone booths. One of the two at the convenience store worked, but Mark just wasn't answering. Carter browsed the magazine rack to kill time. Apparently some young blonde girl was in the studio hard at work on her first album, but he wasn't sure how he was supposed to know who she was if she hadn't made the album yet.

He was thirsty so he bought a barrel-sized "Thirst Impaler" of Pepsi. While the clerk was trying to find the bar code on the cup Carter scanned the breath mints and other impulse buys on the counter, and was surprised by a box of chocolate bars. Are there really candy bars called "Doctor King"? He examined the label, and saw no references to the civil rights leader of the same name, just a cartoon face wearing a crown, a stethoscope, and sunglasses.

"I'll have this too," he said, tossing a Doctor-King bar on the counter. When the register opened Carter looked away. His face felt hot, like he was blushing.

After finishing the Pepsi he pissed in the alley. For some reason he started thinking about video games. Then he tried calling his brother again. Still no answer.

He wasn't really sure what he was going to do. It was a bummer to lose all his possessions. Most of the shit wouldn't matter. He had plenty of experience living without his books and CDs and things. The furniture would hurt considering how little money he had. But he'd probably either be staying with Mark for a while or at a hotel, so he wouldn't have to worry about it. Later on if he could find a cheap apartment, and if he was still hurting for money, he knew of a few buildings downtown where, at the right time of month, somebody usually got evicted and had to abandon half of their

14

shit at the bus stop. Sometimes there'd be a couch or a love seat, and always a mattress. It feels real morbid, because obviously that person is hurting. He'd taken a mattress like that once years ago, and he felt like a real asshole, a buzzard snacking on a corpse. But it wouldn't be left there if the owner hadn't abandoned all hope. If somebody else didn't take it, it was garbage. Might as well save some low wage city worker from having to haul it to the dump. Besides, that's where his mattress would've ended up if his brothers hadn't put it in the storage space. Hell, that might be where it ended up anyway.

No, he wasn't worried about the furniture. But the clothes? Talk about a pain in the ass, being on the outside but having only one set of clothes. He thought about checking into a hotel, but figured he should put that off until he could check his money stash tomorrow and see if there was anything left. What he had in the bank wasn't gonna last him long.

Taking fifteen quarters from his roll he caught a bus back into town and slept against the wall next to the Greyhound station.

# 2

IT WAS ABOUT a two mile walk from downtown to his old neighborhood. His underwear were still wet from washing them in the men's restroom sink, but he figured the heat from his body would mostly dry them by the time he got to the apartments. Nobody would notice.

It was a sunny afternoon, and The Dock, a small bar on First Avenue, had the door open. As Carter walked by he happened to look in all the way past the counter and through the small window into the back where the bartender was washing dishes in a sink. He did a double take. *Holy shit.* He knew that guy. They had a history, you could say. And he couldn't believe he had run into him *one day* after getting out. He could only laugh.

*Forget it Carter* he thought. *Just keep walking.*

And he did… for a few steps. But it was too much of a coincidence to just let it go. It was a sign. He had to talk to this guy. He still had a little cash and could go for some whiskey. He usually liked to smoke when he drank, though, and he didn't have any cigarettes. He bummed a lit Parliament from a young tattooed guy leaning against the wall. Carter preferred Kools, but no white people on the outside seemed to have those.

The place was empty except for the old man at the corner booth, a half empty pitcher of beer and some wadded up napkins his only company. No music was playing, leaving Carter and the old man to ponder the sounds of the sink in the back, a clunky old fan and the traffic outside. Carter pulled a stool out from the bar, scraping it loudly across the floor. He plopped down, his eyes still adjusting to the darkness.

"Can't smoke," the old man said.

"What?"

"Can't smoke!"

Carter blew out a line of smoke and stared into the kitchen. A triangle of sunlight bled in from the alley through a back door propped open with a box fan. Suddenly the sink turned off and the bartender muttered something. He came out and stared Carter down.

"What are you doing?" He was a tall guy, almost as tall as Carter. Slim, but muscular, with his sleeves pulled up to show off his arms.

Carter looked him in the eye and smiled. The guy didn't recognize him. Carter arched his eyebrows, then looked over at the old man. He realized all attention was focused on his cigarette, so he held it out in front of his face and examined it, like he was expecting to see something funny on it, maybe a fly or a picture of a naked lady.

"You're talking about *this?*" he asked, waving the cigarette, playing dumb.

"If *he* gets to smoke *I* should get to smoke!" yelled the old man.

"You gotta put it out or you gotta leave," the bartender said, annoyed.

Carter looked around, but there were no ashtrays. So he stubbed it out on the counter. "There's an indoor smoking ban now?"

The bartender sighed, seemed to calm down. "You honestly didn't know that?"

"I didn't."

"Well then I'm sorry I yelled at you, big guy. I thought you were just being a dick. Where you from?"

"Here. I've just been away for a while."

"I guess so! It's been I don't know how many years since they passed that law. It'll get changed back, all this deregulation going on. But for now we have to live with it."

"Huh." Carter was still holding the cigarette stub, looking around for somewhere to put it. He settled on laying it gently at the edge of the counter.

"What're you drinking?" the bartender asked.

"Jack Daniel's."

"On the rocks or—"

"That's fine. What kind of shoes you wearing?" The question caught the bartender off guard. He frowned like he'd asked him about his dick or something.

"What did you say?"

"I'm gonna guess some sort of Nikes?"

First a confused look, then, suddenly, a smile of recognition. "Holy shit, *Carter Chase*? I didn't even recognize you. Where you been?"

"You know where I've been."

"Yeah, I heard something about that. Well, good for you, you're out." He scooped some ice and poured the drink from a nozzle.

"You're *Jason* Fleming, right?" Carter asked. "Kerry's your brother. Or are you Kerry?"

"I'm Jason."

Carter took a drink. He leaned over the bar to look at Jason's shoes. He was right, they were Nikes, but not the same style he would've guessed. They were spotless, brand new, some sort of expensive, aerodynamic basketball shoe.

"Holy shit, what's that some kind of space slipper? They got computers in those things?"

Jason cracked a half smile. "It's not a computer, it's just a sensor that collects data. It's not the same thing."

"You know what they look like is ski bindings without the skis."

"Eh, fuck off." Jason leaned over the bar to see what type of shoes Carter was wearing. He laughed in disbelief. "What are you making fun of my Lebrons for, you're wearing old man shoes!"

"They're Bob Barkers."

"The game show host?" He couldn't stop laughing. "You're wearing shoes named after a game show host. With velcro!"

"Bob Barkers. Prison shoes. They don't have laces so you won't hang yourself. Or somebody else."

Now Jason stopped laughing. "Oh. I'm sorry."

"It's okay. I gotta admit those shoes are pretty nice. You guys were always into those Nikes. Nikes and sports. And you both used to box, right?"

"Wrestle."

"That's right. And I remember you worked at Don's at one time. Lived in those apartments in Hemdale. You were dating that girl Danni, Asian girl, waitress, studying to be a dentist or something."

Jason puffed his chest out defensively. "That's my wife."

"Oh that's great, congratulations."

"Yeah." The overabundance of personal information was getting to Jason, and he couldn't hide it. He pretended to be occupied with preparing lime slices for some upcoming rush of afternoon drinkers, but he couldn't keep it in. "You look older and more fucked up than I remember. Prison must've took a shit all over you, huh?"

"Yeah, pretty much," Carter laughed, sounding more friendly than the statement warranted. He stirred at the ice with the straw. "Yeah, you and your brother, collecting all the limited edition Nikes, hanging out with Dante when he was working at Niketown. I remember all that. You ever sell off all those Air Force Ones he hooked you up with? The Kris Krijoles?"

Jason suddenly spun toward Carter and got in his face. "What's the deal with you, Chase? You writing my biography?"

"Not today. Just reminiscing."

"Well keep it to yourself. You sound like a fuckin stalker."

"All I'm saying is you better appreciate those shoes. I did time for those shoes. Thanks to your friend Dante."

"Yeah, well, I'm not Dante. Take it up with him."

"Well if you see him, let him know I said 'howdy.'"

He stood up, stacked a five and three ones on the rubber mat on the bar, and pushed the stool in, not looking at it, but hoping his wet underwear hadn't left a mark.

20

# 3

THE NEIGHBORHOOD WAS almost unrecognizable. The record store was now a Chase bank, the book store was out of business, most of the other shops had been demolished and rebuilt with condos above them but now were empty. The outside of the apartment building was a different color than when he had lived there. The landscaping on the west side was completely different. From the glass door out front he could see the place was remodeled. Painting the halls a darker color, changing the carpet and adding some potted plants somehow made it look much more upscale. But he was sure it was the same place.

Examining the sign on the front door he noticed that the name of the company managing the building was not the one he used to write rent checks to. He couldn't remember what the name was, but it wasn't this. The place used to be Upton Arms Apartments, now it was Uptown Arms Condominiums. This company had bought it out and converted it. He didn't recognize any of the names on the directory.

Well, there goes Plan A. The apartment manager Mr. Walsh had been a nice guy, and he liked Carter. Mr. Walsh enjoyed jigsaw puzzles, and Carter had felt sorry for him one lonely Christmas and gave him one. After that they were buddies. Carter had thought he would talk to the old man, maybe he could work out a deal to do some maintenance work or something in exchange for crashing in one of the unused apartments for a month or two between tenants. But Walsh must've left when the building was sold. And Carter wasn't ready to buy a fuckin condo.

Shit.

He looked at the directory. Dialed 21 and # on the phone and stepped in close to the door so he couldn't be seen from the kitchen window of the apartments on the front left side.

"Hello?" came the voice on the tinny intercom speaker. Sounded like a young woman. Carter was envious. How could she afford to buy a condo at that age?

"UPS. I got a package for 206 down the hall but they're not answering, and the manager's not answering. Can you let me in?"

Silence.

"Hello?" He wasn't sure if she'd hung up or not.

A dial tone hummed from the speaker. But then there was a buzz and a click as the door unlocked.

His old apartment was to the right on the first floor. To his relief he saw that the old milk door had not been removed in the remodeling. It was a quirky leftover from when the apartments were first built – each one had a little cupboard in the hall at floor level where the milkman had put their milk bottles, for access from a compartment inside the hall closets. The obsolete cabinets no longer had handles, and had long since been boarded up from the inside. But he had rigged his to open and knew how to pry it with his fingers.

He reached in and felt around the top. For a moment he thought he was out of luck, but then he found it – a string of plastic film containers attached to the top by a belt of black electrical tape. Still there, still filled with the tightly wound rolls of hundreds he had stashed there for a situation like this - a situation where without this money he'd have to decide between clean underwear and burying his mom. Now, thank God, he could do both. And he thought to himself *what a wonderful world.*

Carter spent the afternoon shopping downtown, careful not to cut too far into his new stockpile of cash. He wanted something to read, so he went looking for a book store, but none of the ones he remembered were there anymore. Once he gave up on that he picked out a black suit at the Men's Wearhouse. He knew fuck-all about suits, and he knew this was kind of a chintzy place. But Nasir, the salesman, did wear suits to work every day and therefore knew more about it than him. He taught Carter that a two–button suit is more timeless than a three-button, that you never use the bottom button (why the fuck not?) and that the *only* difference between this one and one you would buy at Barney's down the street is the name on the label and about $400. When he came out of the dressing room Nasir said "Man, you look *good* in that suit!" He thought he did too, and the guy sure sounded sincere, but he couldn't help but wonder if they said that to every customer.

He had to pay extra to expedite the alterations, usually it takes a couple weeks. When Nasir said "This is Charles, he's one of the best tailors in the city," Carter thought he was making a joke and gave a courtesy laugh. Because why the fuck would one of the best tailors in the city be working at the Men's Wearhouse? But Charles didn't laugh or smile so Carter felt like an asshole. He knew he had insulted this Charles and worried that he'd fuck up the suit, like the way people say a cook might spit in your burger if you pissed them off. Who knows how these tailors operate?

He wanted to buy some jeans too, but it turned out to be too intimidating. The Levis section at Macy's was huge, divided into different numbered styles. There was a chart explaining them, but it looked like algebra to him. As far as he could tell modern jeans were worn skin tight, like wetsuits. This was especially intimidating coming out of the joint, where pants are worn hanging low. When a salesman asked him if he needed help with anything he said no and left.

Carter bought a good, strong backpack at the Army-Navy surplus store and later filled it with four pairs of boxer briefs, four pairs of black socks, some toiletries, the most comfortable pair of pants he could find – they called them khakis, but they were grey - one extra t-shirt, a small bottle of laundry detergent, a small screwdriver with a reversible bit for Phillips head or standard, a pen, a small pad of paper, and an Ontario shiv knife with a 4.5" blade and OD green paracord wrapped handle (he kind of wanted the WWII USMC fighting knife, but felt too self conscious, being a civilian). Then he checked into a hotel for the night and unplugged the TV. That way he wouldn't blow his money on pay-per-view porn.

In the morning he moved the furniture in the room so he could do his burpees. It felt weird having that much space. He'd woken up with a headache, and the exercise made it worse. When he checked out at noon he brought with him a towel and a plastic ice bucket filled with miniature shampoo bottle, two small bars of soap and a roll of toilet paper so he wouldn't have to mooch off of Mark too much.

That was if he could even get a hold of Mark, which so far he hadn't. He was a little worried about it. Mark was a responsible guy, he wouldn't just take off, especially right before Mom's funeral. He decided to call Mason from the hotel lobby.

"You heard from Mark yet?"

"No."

"Neither have I. He doesn't answer his phone."

"Maybe it's turned off."

"Yeah, it's weird."

There was a pause. Then Mason said, "Sad about that singer, huh?"

"The what?"

"That singer that died. You hear about that?"

"No, I don't know. Who died?"

"That local guy that was so popular, Creole or whatever."

"Kris Krijole died?"

"That's his name. Yeah, I guess he died yesterday. There's some kind of memorial downtown."

"Shit. That's terrible."

"Yeah, traffic's real bad."

"Huh."

Carter was genuinely surprised to hear about that. Not a fan of his music, but very familiar with his existence. It's always a shock when someone like that dies young. You feel like you know them. But he actually *did* know Mark, so he was more worried about him.

"I wonder if he went somewhere?"

"What, like... Heaven?"

"I'm sorry. Not Kris Krijole. Mark. I wonder if he went somewhere, that's why we can't get a hold of him."

"I don't know. He's a grown man, he can do what he wants."

"Well, do you think maybe he's avoiding me? Maybe he's getting cold feet about having me in his house, because of the felony and everything."

"That's what I'd do."

"Is there anyone else I should call? Does he have a girlfriend or anything?"

"You're gonna hit up his girlfriend for a place to stay?"

"No, I'm gonna ask if she's seen him."

"I don't have her number, I don't talk to them that much."

Carter fumbled in his backpack for the pen and paper.

"Here. Give me his address. I'll go try to find him."


It was a pale green duplex on a hill on the east side of town. When he knocked a young guy wearing shorts and sandals came out from next door.

"No, I'm knocking on this one."

"Right on."

There was a mail slot on the door. He kneeled down, pushed it open and yelled Mark's name into it. A few minutes later, uncomfortable with the neighbor staring at him through the window, he climbed over the fence to the backyard, a narrow strip of grass with a small square of cement in the middle. He found a fake rock with a compartment inside that held a spare key. He smiled, shook his head and unlocked the back door.

No sign of Mark inside. There was a pile of junk mail on the mat inside the door. Lots of ads for condos and politicians, books of coupons, some sort of outdoor equipment catalog, athletic wear catalog, letters from the ACLU, Red Cross, Boys and Girls Club, UNICEF, Children's International, photos of missing people, menus from local restaurants. Seemed like the databases knew more about his brother's interests than he did. That much mail is usually an indication that someone hasn't been at home, but in the kitchen a plastic recycling container was overflowing with empty glass bottles and jars, and surrounded by satellite grocery bags with more of the same. So it was clear that Mark didn't take out the recycling very often. The mail pile could theoretically be part of the same phenomenon.

There was a small garage, mostly empty, no car. There were a few tools and things scattered around on the floor, so maybe Mark didn't park there anyway.

A possibly more ominous sign was Mark's phone, which Carter found on the floor in the living room. It took him a few minutes to figure out how the menu worked, then he was able to listen to the voicemails he had left for Mark, a few from a woman named Abbey, and one from a friend of Mark's talking about getting his felon brother a job. But there was no indication that anything was wrong, other than that nobody could get a hold of Mark. Because he'd left his phone on the floor. Feeling like an intruder, Carter put it back where he found it.

The most unusual thing Carter found was the paint in the hallway. There were several buckets, all in the same mint green shade ("Spring Fresh" it was called), piled up with some newspapers, a dish and a roller. But the walls were a pale white. He wouldn't get all ready to paint the place and then just take off, would he? This was a bad sign. Something had happened to him. Or it was a good sign. He'd be back soon. Ah, who the fuck knows?

Carter thought about looking for another cheap hotel, maybe one on this side of town. But he decided that would be stupid. The one place he knew his brother would come was home, so he might as well stay here. He had the key. He had his own toilet paper. He was supposed to be staying here anyway, so he had permission.

He went out the front door and knocked for the neighbors. The young man he'd seen earlier came out.

"Can I help you?"

"Have you seen Mark?"

"Mark?"

"My brother. Your neighbor. The guy who lives there. Have you seen him today?"

"No."

"What's your name?"

"Uh, Barry. Barry Winston."

"I'm Carter Chase, Mark's brother. Mark is your neighbor. I'll be staying here for a little bit, let me know if you see him."

"Right on."

Carter noticed chips of dried paint on Barry's hands and under his fingernails. "Are you a painter?" he asked.

Barry looked at his hands, noticed the paint himself. "Oh!" he said, lighting up. "Yeah! Well, no, not exactly. I mean I've been trying to do some paintings lately, and I like it, but it's not really my strength. Most of my work is conceptual, to be honest. Temporary stuff, you know? I try to create experiences for people. What I usually say is I try to demolish the routine and ordinary and reconstruct it as something profound. Almost like sculpting reality, if that makes sense."

"I meant are you a house painter."

Barry's whole demeanor changed. "Oh. No. No, I'm not."

"Okay. Nice to meet you, Barry." He turned back toward Mark's side of the duplex, but Barry stopped him.

"Hey, uh, look, man – I don't want any trouble. Not making a judgment, I'm no choir boy myself. But if you're going to have the police coming looking for you and that sort of thing-- I mean, I got a wife and a young kid here. This is a family neighborhood."

Carter smiled an *oh for crying out loud* smile. "So you *do* know Mark. He told you about that? Look, it's fine. That was a long time ago. I've paid my debt. My brother's just helping me get back on my feet and I'll be out of your hair in a couple days. I won't scare your kids or whatever."

Barry squinted.

"It's fine. See you around, Barry. Or not. *Right on*, right?"

"Right."

Carter went out for a foot-long Subway Buffalo Chicken sandwich on Hearty Italian bread, plus a bag of pre-sliced apples for health, came back and Mark still wasn't home. He still couldn't find a book store, and no books on Mark's shelves either, so he watched TV until past 2 am. He didn't like anything he saw. It occurred to him that he could probably sleep in Mark's bed without incident, but he felt bad for even considering it and went to sleep on the couch.

At about 3 am he was laying there, awake, when he realized what he had needed: porn. He turned on the computer and after some fumbling around he figured out how to open the web browser. He wasn't sure how to find what he wanted. He started to type "fucking," but the 'f' brought up Mark's Facebook page, with the email and password saved. Curious, Carter postponed his plans to jerk off and logged in instead. He clicked on Mark's name, then found the part that said "Photos" and browsed the album. Mark smiling with friends at barbecues, handing a slice of birthday cake to Dad, posing with a woman who must've been Abbey on top of mountains, on beaches, in front of scenic viewpoints, probably wearing coats from the outdoors catalog he receives in the mail. Carter printed off one of Mark by himself wearing a puffy vest, posing in front of a weird bird-shaped rock island from some lookout point who-knows-where. He tucked the photo inside his pocket.

There were a few recent messages on Mark's wall, some with well-wishes and words of consolation from people who had heard about Mom. He clicked on "Friends." Maybe some of these people would know where Mark was. Carter recognized some of them, friends they'd shared in high school.

*Oh shit, I forgot about Gavin Clark.* A guy from his grade. Carter clicked on the name, looked at his page. Gavin had gotten fat in the face. Big belly in a tight blue shirt, red tie, works in insurance in Lake Stevens. Lots of smiles, though. Three kids. Cute wife. Looks happy. He clicked on Gavin's "Friends," and quickly sunk into a pit of nostalgia and shame looking at profiles of people he used to know. In some cases he remembered the people, other times just their names. Only a few looked young, the rest looked like their parents now – balding, thickening, ordinary. Some of the women were fighting it, their eyebrows plucked, faces caked with makeup. The men didn't give a shit, they wore sports jerseys and shorts. They all had kids, bunches of them, smiling in the sun, posing at Disneyland, building sand castles or snowmen. They had decks and ocean views, trucks, motorcycles, boats. Property.

Carter imagined their jobs, the things they had to learn about to get them, the things they had to care about to get through a shift. He'd rather kill himself than have to sit at a desk and call guys on the phone and talk about... whatever the fuck guys in blue shirts with red ties talk about at work. He'd never want to be like these people living out in the suburbs, sitting in traffic twice a day, listening to some asshole on drive time radio, spending eight hours with other people like themselves, then coming back to their huge, beautiful homes and loving families, and their weekends off, going on all these vacations they have pictures of...

How could he look down on them? What the fuck had *he* ever accomplished? He felt like he'd just left school. Time had lapped him. Thank God he didn't have a Facebook. Hopefully nobody had asked Mark about him. They didn't need to know. What would he even talk about if he ran into one of these people? "Hey, Carter, it's been forever. What have you been up to?"

Were these really Mark's friends, who might know his

whereabouts, or just old acquaintances? It didn't matter. He could never talk to these fucking people. It was a dead end. He logged out, and wasn't in the mood to look at porn anymore.

Next morning Carter got up and did burpies. Still no Mark. Carter didn't want to leave the house, in case Mark showed up, but his suit was supposed to be ready and the funeral was one day away. It seemed kind of weird to buy a suit just to wear to this one funeral, but who knows, with the whereabouts of his brother unknown maybe he'd need it again soon. As soon as he thought it he swore at himself, pictured taking a knife and cutting the thought out of his brain. Mark was a grown man. Probably went on a trip or something. Something came up. He knew Carter could manage on his own so he thought it would be okay to leave. He'd show up.

Carter tore a piece of paper off his notepad and wrote:

*Mark,*
*Got back from prison. You weren't here so I decided to move in. Take out the recycling before I get home. You're a fuckin pig.*
*Carter*

# 4

THERE WAS A SMALL GATHERING at Verizon First Methodist. The priest or whoever made the decisions there must've been too embarrassed to point out that they had no idea who this dead lady was. It was a big church, maybe she came here every now and then and they never noticed her, who knows? Mason's wife Dana brought food from some catering service, which was nice. Most of the aunts and uncles wouldn't even make eye contact with Carter. At first he thought they didn't recognize him, then he realized they probably did.

Mark hadn't shown up. Not at home, not at the church, and since nobody had actually heard from him since the funeral arrangements were made, he may not have even known where to go. No sign of the girlfriend either, not at the funeral or at the house, and no phone calls. Kind of suspicious.

Carter felt like a schmuck asking Mason and Dana if he could ride with them in the procession. But if he took the bus he would miss the burial. In the parking lot Mason turned into annoying big brother all the sudden.

"Looking for any jobs yet?"

"Nah."

"Well, you better hurry up. You don't have much money saved, do you?"

"It doesn't matter."

Distracted, Mason pointed to Carter's left side. "You got bird shit on you."

"What?"

"A bird took a shit on you."

"God damn it." It was true. White drips on the lower left side of his brand new black suit jacket. At least there was no brown stuff. But when the hell did that happen? Why didn't he notice it? Must've been at the bus stop, but he couldn't remember standing under any congregations of birds. Jesus, what a great time for this. *Sorry, mom. I tried to look nice.*

"Why'd you do that?"

"I didn't do it on purpose, Mason. As a rule I try not to let birds shit on me."

"Well, you blew it."

Dana asked what they were talking about.

"He has bird poop on him."

"Bird poop?"

Dana found a Kleenex in her purse, wetted it with spit and started violently poking at Carter's side, smearing the white streaks into the suit.

"Why'd you get bird poop on you?"

"I guess I just like birds."

Dana looked him in the eye but could not detect whether or not he was making a joke at her expense. "This is a fairly nice suit, Carter. You really should be more careful." She seemed like she knew what she was doing, but her technique didn't work.

Carter found a bathroom in the church, dampened some toilet paper in the sink and tried to get the mark off. Now he just had a big, dark, wet spot. He couldn't tell if the shit had come off or not.

The burial part was nice and reasonably quick. As they lowered the coffin Carter tried to picture what she looked like inside there, then stopped himself. These things are best left ambiguous. The fat guy at the funeral home had made a good choice with the closed casket. He really knew his job. Carter remembered his grandma's funeral when he was a teenager. They put so much makeup on her it didn't even look like her.

This was the first time he'd seen Dad's grave. It still looked shiny and new. It did not have an advertising monitor on it, despite what the guy had said about those being standard. Oh well. At least they were buried together in the family plot, that was nice.

Mom's brothers and sister were all crying. So was

Dana. Carter wondered why he and Mason weren't. They must've been more like their dad. That guy never hugged anybody in his life, and he kept his cards hidden well. The Chase men were not the type to discuss their feelings. They felt it was best to keep that stuff to yourself. Occasionally it would build up and they'd unload on somebody they didn't know very well, always a woman. But mostly they just kept it in. Ex-girlfriends had told Carter he was a robot, that he had no emotions, but this was not true. He just knew where to keep them stored. It was rare that he took them out. Yeah, he definitely got that from Dad.

It was too bad he didn't get to say goodbye to his father. Both his brothers had been there in the hospital when Dad was sick. The way Carter had heard it the old man was still talking semi-coherently with the family until close to the end. They might have even told him they loved him, appreciated all he'd sacrificed to provide for them. Dana got to be there, she probably hounded Mason into saying something. Whatever had been discussed, Carter was sure his brothers had a little more closure on the whole thing than he did. For him, life had been put on pause for those years that he was locked up, then when he unpaused it he realized he'd missed a few chapters. He could feel in his stomach that he was behind, and he was having a hard time catching up.

Dad was dead. Mom was dead. Mark was missing. The wet spot on Carter's suit had now dried, and the white streaks weren't any less visible than before. A gentle orchestral tune wafted from a small but surprisingly powerful speaker as the monitor on the grave marker came on. Tasteful white-on-black text offered the Chase family the deepest condolences of Pepsi, Diet Pepsi and new Pepsi Smooth. Carter finally started to cry.

# 5

THE SERVICE REALLY made him want to do his parents proud, stay out of trouble, be a responsible adult, all that shit. So after Mason and Dana dropped him off at the duplex he got out his notebook and wrote two lists:

> duplex rules
> 1. no fighting
> 2. no stealing
> 3. no ill-gotten gains
>
> to do
> 1. find Mark
> 2. money
> 3. revenge?

There was no way Mark would intentionally miss Mom's funeral without contacting them, so he was officially missing. Carter would have to go to the police first to report it, but he was sure they wouldn't do anything. They'd tell him Mark was a grown man, he was probably depressed over his mother's death and had wandered off for some soul searching. He would show up eventually, it happens all the time. Carter would tell them that it wasn't like Mark to do something like that. They would ask how well he knew his brother, and he'd have to explain why they hadn't seen each other much. *Oh, but you kept real good tabs on him from prison, right?*

He would take that step anyway, just to cover all the bases, but then he would start doing the detective work that the cops wouldn't, canvassing with that picture he printed off, asking around at places where Mark might've gone. He would use that cell phone, call that Abbey lady, or any other numbers that were in its memory. Find out when was the last time anybody had seen Mark, and where. Then go there and start looking for leads.

But first he would take out the recycling.

He put the note he had written to his brother in the bag with the other mixed paper. It didn't seem as funny anymore. He wasn't gonna take the paper recycling out yet, he'd have to go through that for clues later. But the bottles were out of control. Their revolution would have to be quashed.

He propped open the back door and looked out there. The backyard had a gate that opened to an alley, and he could see some garbage and recycling cans. Hopefully he could figure out which ones were Mark's.

He took off his tie and jacket, folded them over the back of a chair, then untucked his shirt and rolled up his sleeves. He picked up two of the bags of glass containers, which were heavier than he expected, and headed for the alley.

There was a black Mustang parked in the alley with its engine running. He hoped it wasn't a neighbor – he didn't want to get into some dispute over filling up the wrong bins. No fighting. And what about ill-gotten gains? Does filling up the neighbor's recycling bin count as ill-gotten? His mind wandered. He thought about putting on the suit in the morning, getting ready for the funeral, brushing his teeth. Suddenly it occurred to him – that wasn't bird shit! He must've dripped toothpaste on himself. Should've brushed his teeth *before* he got dressed.

It almost caught him completely off guard when the guy came running at him, but he managed to toss one of the bags and catch the punch in a sloppy skull and cross bones elbow block. He twisted his attacker's arm, but lost it trying to keep his grip on the remaining bag of recycling. Next thing he knew he was on the ground, bottles and jars bouncing, rolling and exploding all around him, launching tiny crystal-like shards that cut into his arms and stuck all over his nice suit pants. He was glad he had taken the jacket off, but regretted rolling up his sleeves. He was being kicked by two brand new

36

pairs of Nikes. *No fighting, huh? Great idea.*

He struggled to his feet holding the top half of a 33.8 oz. iced tea bottle for protection. *Self defense shouldn't count as fighting,* he thought. *This shouldn't count.*

He recognized three of the four attackers: his old friend Dante, and Jason and Kerry Fleming (the Nike Brothers). The fourth was some dipshit musclehead kid who probably idolized Dante. His intern.

"Missed you guys at the funeral," Carter said. The musclehead flinched as Carter lunged toward him with the bottle. In the back window of the duplex the blinds flipped open and Barry looked out, clutching his young daughter in his arms. Carter mouthed "sorry" and held up his index finger. When Dante and friends looked over to see who he was gesturing to, Carter took off down the alley, leading them away from the house.

He only made it maybe twenty feet down the alley before he felt something hit the backs of his knees and buckle his legs beneath him. His head hit the pavement. He was so tired. He closed his eyes and for just a second he was at peace, then he opened them again just as a fist hit the back of his head, knocking his forehead back to the cement and making him see stars. His mouth tasted like blood and electricity. Little pieces of rock stuck to his bloody palms and elbows, giving company to the splinters of glass. He wasn't sure where his glass shank had gone.

One of the Flemings rolled him over with a foot. "Get up!" Dante yelled.

"You guys look cool from this angle, real tough guys," Carter said. He groaned as the guy whose name he didn't know yanked him to his feet. He felt dizzy and weak. There was no fight in him. He thought about the shiv knife inside, in his backpack, but knew it was for the best that it wasn't on him. Better to get beaten up than be a murderer. Plus, there were the rules. No fighting.

Dante stood above him and got a good look at his face. "It *is* you," he said. "How'd you get out early?"

"Not for good behavior," he said.

"I heard you wanted to say 'hi'."

"I believe it was 'howdy,' actually."

"Anything else you want to say?"

"No, 'howdy' is enough, I guess." He tried to wipe the blood from his lip onto the back of his hand, ended up getting glass in his mouth.

"Well there's something I want to say to *you*, Carter. Niketown was a long time ago, dude. We *all* got fucked on that deal. Man, we knew you'd come after us when you got out. You're so fucking stupid. We're not giving you anything. Mark my words - you go around threatening my friends, you'll regret it."

"Especially not my brother," Kerry said.

"And don't you fucking come into The Dock anymore," Jason added. "You got that?"

Carter's eyelids felt heavy, in fact his whole head did – he was wobbly like he'd had a couple too many drinks.

"Answer him!" Kerry yelled.

Carter smiled like a drunk, looking down at the shoes on the Nike Brothers. Jason's were a shiny black hard plastic, Kerry's were white. So he spit the blood on Kerry's.

"*Fucking* cocksucker!" Kerry yelled, jumping back way too late to save his shoes and pants. He tried to wipe the blood off with his hand while the others leapt on Carter and continued his beating.

# 6

EVERYBODY THOUGHT OF Carter as a troublemaker, not a career criminal. He thought he'd grow up and find some job that made him happy, he just didn't know what it would be. While his brothers were knee-deep in collegiate academics he was working shitty service jobs and getting into a lot more fights than anyone could consider reasonable. He was an intelligent young man in virtually all respects except for that one that keeps you from doing stupid shit that you're gonna regret. He hated working paycheck to paycheck, late shift to early shift. He wanted more money so he could have more time and then maybe he could figure out what he should be doing with his life.

Whatever it was, it wasn't work. Sometimes he thought about what it would be like to live in caveman times, or to be a wild animal, like a pigeon or a seagull or something. You'd have to find food and fight off attackers. You could go wherever you wanted. Hang out on a cliff somewhere to enjoy a nice day. You could sleep when you felt like it. You didn't have to worry about showing up to work on time, or making it to the weekend, or getting the days off you need. He was so tired of it. Tired of going to bed thinking about work, waking up thinking about work, and then going to work.

That was his rationalization for why he started stealing money sometimes. Just every once in a while. Petty asshole things like pocketing till money at a grocery store he worked at or swiping cash boxes from people selling necklaces or sunglasses on the streets. One time he managed to pry open the pay box at a parking lot, a surprisingly good and completely satisfying score. Some asshole renting out little squares of concrete? I think he can go without one day's pay from one of his lots. But for Carter that money went a long way.

On two occasions Carter had held up convenience stores using a toy gun. The first time his heart beat so fast he thought it might kill him, the second time he was eerily relaxed. But he still felt sick afterwards. It seemed so pathetic. He wasn't a crackhead, why was he doing this shit? It was stupid.

He'd known Dante for a few years, since they were both fry cooks at a shitty little Westside diner called Don's. Dante had been the one who trained him in the kitchen. They worked together for less than three weeks before Dante got fired for skimming the till. Carter didn't stay there much longer. But they seemed to run into each other a lot, just walking down sidewalks, riding the bus or sometimes going to see some rapper at one of the clubs downtown.

Dante was a dick, but he was a funny guy. Everybody liked being around him, including Carter. Sometimes they'd end up hanging out and having a couple drinks. This happened four times before Dante finally remembered that Carter had quit Don's and could not update him on who still worked there. After they'd passed that roadblock their conversations went a little deeper, until one day they started bragging about their criminal activities.

Dante had done a lot of shoplifting and figured he was on his way to being Scarface. Carter told him more than once about the parking lot score, but it was a while before he admitted the convenience store stickups. As soon as the words were out of his mouth he knew it was a mistake, and he tried to avoid the topic of crime from that point on.

Carter could never figure out how Dante went through so many jobs. He seemed to get fired all the time, but could still find someone else to hire him. Apparently he'd even put the jobs he was fired from on his resume, knowing from experience that many employers wouldn't bother to call for confirmation. When he heard Dante was working at the Niketown store downtown Carter figured good, at least that till money will be skimmed from a major international corporation, not a local small business owner like Don.

40

Somehow Dante kept that job for over a year. That's a fucking career by Dante standards. He should be eligible for retirement by now. Get him a gold watch.

The shittiest thing Carter ever did was Dante's idea. Once he was firmly ensconced in the athletic shoe industry, Dante was three jobs removed from a small independent bookstore over by the college campus. He only lasted two months, that time because he was bad at the job and not because he had been stealing. But that was more than long enough to notice the store's process for depositing money. They would let their cash and credit slips pile up in the safe all week. David, the owner, came to pick them up on Monday and sometimes Thursday afternoons and walk them over to the bank, then he would bring back small bills and rolls of change for their tills. It was completely casual, he did not bring backup. There were no security measures and they'd never had any trouble. Because they usually didn't hire assholes like Dante.

Carter and Dante staked out the block on a Monday in the second week of December, betting on a big deposit after a weekend of Christmas shopping. Dante sat on a bus stop bench with small binoculars. Carter looked at magazines in a newsstand café around the corner from the bookstore, carrying a cell phone they had borrowed from Dante's sister. It felt like some spy shit.

A little after one the borrowed cell phone rang.

"It's not David, it's his wife Cindy," Dante said. "Straight hair, glasses, wearing a blue long-sleeved t-shirt. Black bag in her hand, that should be our money. Coming around the corner right now."

Carter had psyched himself into a nihilistic just-don't-give-a-fuck type of mentality. He had to. It wasn't that a part of him knew it was wrong - his whole mind and body knew it was wrong. But he still wanted the money. He was ready to be stone-hearted and cruel with this David, a bearded hippie type according to Dante. But somehow the sudden realization that

41

he had to rob a woman gave him pause.

He spotted her right away. The shirt was faded navy blue with a cartoon of a cat on it. She had the bag over her shoulder and didn't act like it was precious cargo. Maybe it wasn't the deposit? Or maybe she was stupid for not being more careful. For a second he considered saying *fuck it*, going home without the money but with a small amount of personal dignity still intact. But before he even knew he'd made a decision he found himself running toward her, poking her side with the same toy gun he'd used in the convenience store robberies. He was too embarrassed to say anything, instead he just grabbed the strap on the bag and tried to unhook it from her shoulder. She yelled "Hey!" angrily. No way she believed it was a real gun. But she was caught off guard and it was easy to tug-of-war the bag from her.

He ran down two blocks, around the corner, through a small city park and out the other side where Dante picked him up in his Mazda. It was no problem losing her. As they drove off he opened the bag. It *was* the deposit.

Well, the cops weren't about to put together a task force or anything, but compared to their previous crimes this was a good score. This was back when the economy was better, and when people still bought books, and the store had had a big weekend. More than half was on debit cards, so David and Cindy would be able to keep that much. But there was still a whole hell of a lot of cash for young thieves, and for just a couple hours of work.

They did a 50-50 split. Carter had taken the physical risk, but because Dante knew the victims he was more likely to be connected to the crime. So it evened out. Carter hid his share in his closet for a week, then he went to the bank with the bundles of twenties, tens and fives, along with some cash he'd saved up from years of Christmas bonuses. He traded for stacks of hundred dollar bills.

Carrying home that much cash made him nervous, but he figured if he got robbed it would serve him right. At his apartment he rolled the hundreds tightly, stuffed the rolls into

42

some old plastic film containers, taped the containers inside the vintage milk delivery compartment outside his place, and vowed to himself and to God, the universe and the collective unconscious that it was his last god damn strong arm robbery.

When the idea for the Niketown grab came up Carter knew he should say no. The original plan was to storm in and steal the till money at gunpoint after hours. But not just any night. Dante had a certain one in mind. Several times a year Nike would release a limited edition shoe. Usually sales were limited to "Nike Urban Indie Elite stores" in three to four American cities. Each store would get one shipment (usually 250 pairs, but it would depend on the size of the edition) and they would sell them off in a few hours, limit two pairs per customer. They were so in-demand and instantly valuable on the collector's market that lines of at least 50-100 weirdos would line up two or three days in advance to buy theirs. And there were serious collectors like the Nike Brothers, Jason and Kerry Fleming, who would actually drive across the country to go to these stores. But sometimes, like this time, they didn't have to, because the Niketown that Dante worked at downtown was one of the chosen stores.

Dante told Carter that he grew up with Jason Fleming, but it wasn't quite true. They did know each other as kids – they were in the same grade and had gone to the same schools since third grade. But they'd never really been friends until he and Jason worked together in the kitchen at Don's. They lost touch for a few years until Dante started at Niketown. One day he went for a smoke break and saw Jason and Kerry sitting on lawn chairs playing cards on the sidewalk. It was Tuesday and they were first in line for a shoe that went on sale Friday at noon.

That weekend they started drinking together and shooting the shit about old times - who from their high school was married, who had gotten fat. Dante was even willing to use his employee discount to buy shoes for Jason and his brother. They were obsessed with those fucking things. Carter never knew them well, but sometimes Dante would bring him to parties at Jason's apartment, or he'd run into them at bars, and he'd always quiz them about shoes. Their endless knowledge of Nike history amused him, and their enthusiasm was strangely contagious. Next thing you know he'd be rambling excitedly about the gorgeous simplicity of the swoosh. Their girlfriends would roll their eyes and try to change the subject.

Dante's plan wasn't bad. It was timed to the release of the Nike Air Force One Limited Edition Kris Krijole Redesign Low Cut. Kris Krijole was some god awful rock singer that the high school kids liked, a local boy made good. His success brought everyone in town a sort of pride, if you could call it that. But it was just good marketing to give his hometown store 250 pairs of this shoe with its gaudy black and metallic silver splatter design personally approved by Kris himself. The most unusual feature was a picture of Kris's face embroidered into the tongue along with a lightning bolt KK logo. Most of the redesigns didn't get something like that.

For the last limited edition sale Dante had had to work a double shift, which gave him the idea for this caper. If he was there from the beginning of the sale to the end he'd be a perfect inside man. The store's credit card machines were clunky, they still worked on phone lines at the time and they were known to break down at inconvenient moments. In the morning he would put a cut in the phone line – just the wire, not the rubber casing, so nobody would see it. That would force them to do all credit and debit card transactions manually, taking imprints of the cards and calling the numbers in to the bank individually. It wouldn't seem suspicious because isn't that the way things are, you got a line literally around the block you know your credit card machine is gonna break.

Selling the shoes this way would take for-fucking-ever, and if no other employee had the presence of mind to do it, Dante himself would go out to the line and apologetically explain the reason for the delay. He would encourage

44

everyone who planned to pay with a card to consider going to the ATM machine across the street and getting cash. But it was up to them.

There were only three tills, and with that much cash in them no doubt the managers would unload it to the safe throughout the day. But at the end they'd count it all together to get the day's totals. Dante would make a "dumb mistake" like taking the garbage out to the dumpsters and leaving the door unlatched, allowing an unknown assailant in a ski mask to run in and bag up the cash at gunpoint. Dante would probably be fired for his mistake, but everyone would feel bad about it. *Sorry kid, it's just the policy, somebody has to take responsibility.*

Carter was impressed by Dante's uncharacteristically well thought out plan, but he didn't like it, because he had promised himself to quit the armed (or seemingly armed) robbery. Unfortunately he was the only one Dante knew who had experience in that sort of thing, and the kid had some kind of whiny form of charisma that was somehow very persuasive. Carter tentatively agreed to the job, but in the back of his mind he figured he would back out at the last minute. He was just humoring Dante.

Then, four days before the Kris Krijoles went on sale, there were Jason and Kerry already first in line. And there were a good twenty-five or thirty people behind them. Carter joked that it was too bad they couldn't just steal the shoes and sell them on the black market, then it would be worth two or three times as much as the retail cash. And Dante started thinking.

Over the next two days Dante had lunch with the two Fleming brothers – each separately of course so the other brother could hold their place in line. Somehow he was able to goad them into taking part in a new plan. They were not criminals, but when faced with the mental image of 250 pairs of Black/Metal colorway Air Force One limited editions stacked in their living room they would've signed on in baby's blood if Dante had asked them to.

Carter was pretty sure the new plan wouldn't work, but it was still a better deal for him. He had to go in a day earlier than in the original plan, and he was gonna have to find a costume. Instead of threatening Dante's co-workers he'd be going in after they left for the night. The Flemings would later be selling the shoes on eBay and to collectors they knew, and that was the part that seemed doomed to failure. How would they sell that many shoes? Especially a shoe where it's known that only 1,000 pairs exist and one fourth of those were stolen? It would be like trying to sell the Mona Lisa, except some rich asshole would be willing to buy a stolen Mona Lisa just to give himself a boner. That same guy would not want 250 pairs of rare Nikes. These boys were collectors, they must've known what they were doing, but to Carter it seemed certain they weren't thinking things through properly. They were blinded by all those swooshes.

But Dante had promised $2,500 up front to hire him, another $2,500 in a month and then 1/4 of any profit they made higher than that. The Nike Brothers estimated that they could sell each pair for "at least 300." So $300 x 250 pairs = $75,000 (!), divided by Carter, Dante, Jason and Kerry equals $18,750. That was a liberal estimate to be sure, but shit, cut it in half - $9,375 is a real good night, especially if you don't have to point a weapon at anybody. That would pay his rent for most of a year, and he'd use that time to find a legit job that made him happy. This would be his last robbery for sure.

Now that they were going to be partners in crime Carter made a point of avoiding the Flemings. He said they shouldn't be seen together, which was true, but he was thinking more along the lines of not getting to know them well enough that they'd come crying to him for help when they realized they could never sell off all those stupid shoes.

On the big night Carter only felt a little nervous. The one part he was worried about was getting into the store. Dante knew the alarm code – all the closers did. Closing shift assistant manager Ed Janssens was lazy and would tell people the code if he was locking up and they needed to run back inside because they forgot their coat or that sort of thing. So the alarm was no problem, but the door was since he didn't have a key. His solution, which Carter wouldn't have believed would work if he hadn't seen it with his own eyes, was to tape a thin square of plastic over the latch on the door and pull it shut. What he didn't realize was that the alarm would sense that it was not latched, so the display screen said "AREA 4 NOT READY." Luckily Ed was closing manager and didn't bother to check. He glanced at the doors, saw that they *appeared* closed, and force armed the alarm.

Just before midnight Carter and Dante arrived in the back alley dressed as janitors. Conspicuous hats and shades hid some of their identifiable facial characteristics, and Dante swore that the security cameras were "blurry as shit." Dante, Jason and Kerry all believed the real night crew never came earlier than 1 or 1:30, so they had a good-sized window. Dante drove a borrowed pickup truck on which they had loaded two stolen carts, one equipped with brooms, dustpans, mops and spray bottles (for looks), the other with two empty garbage cans with clean liners (for transporting shoes). Steam poured out of a manhole at the end of the alley, partially obstructing their view of the street. At least it made it harder for someone to see what they were doing.

With his gloves on Carter couldn't dig his fingernails into the unlatched back door, but he found a screwdriver in the glove compartment and used that to pry it open. Dante stayed in the truck so his face wouldn't be caught on the security tape.

As he walked in there was a repeating, high-pitched beep, the sounds getting closer together each time like a ticking time bomb in a movie. Carter typed in the alarm code Dante had given him. It worked just like the door did. No problem.

The design of the store was nearly perfect for their purposes. Most of these downtown establishments had windows all along the street, but at Niketown only the front doors gave a view inside. The main display floor was a rounded area in the center, an arena of shoe displays, and it was mostly obscured from the front. The Nike Brothers had their lawn chairs set strategically in front of the doors, and were awake for lookout duty or creating a distraction. But the hope was that if anyone did look inside they'd see the cleaning supplies and assume everything was on the up-and-up.

The Kris Krijole boxes were stacked in a perfect pyramid next to a life-sized cardboard standee of Krijole and his guitar, which had silver and black splatters matching the ones on his shoes. Looking at them, Carter was a little disappointed. He wasn't sure what he thought they would look like, but he definitely pictured something sleeker, more elegant. He thought they were tacky. Too busy. He would never wear them.

Carter re-positioned the standee to further block any potential view of his activities. Then he started loading the shoe boxes into the garbage cans.

The garbage thing, it turned out, was an unnecessary flourish. He couldn't fit more than about twenty boxes per can without crushing them, and nobody was watching anyway. After his dissatisfaction with the first load he left the cans in the back of the truck, doubled up two of the black garbage bags they'd brought and carried a load over his shoulder like Santa Claus. Or the Grinch, I guess.

Between loads Dante complained that they would have to organize all of them by shoe size before they could sell them. Carter ignored him.

Within fifteen minutes the pickup was overflowing with equipment and lumpy garbage bags, and Carter had loaded up all 250 pairs. He should've left, but it all felt so easy that he started to get greedy. What about the back room? There had to be other shoes back there that were worth something.

"How many more are left?" Dante asked impatiently as Carter headed back in for one last sweep.

The door to the back was closed. He tried it, but of

48

course it was locked. It was a heavy door. Even if it wasn't, it wouldn't be worth spending the time to bust it open. Oh well. He had what he'd came for, better make off with it.

As he came back out to the display floor there was a loud "TOK TOK TOK" at the front door, and his stomach dropped. Kerry was banging his keys against the glass as a warning. Spinning red and blue lights hit the floor and danced along the shoe racks like reflections off a disco ball.

Carter sprinted to the back door and slowly opened it, peering out half expecting to see more cops. But Dante and the truck were still alone in the alley. Carter jumped in. "Cops up front! Go!"

Dante flipped the ignition and hit the gas before Carter realized they were headed toward a one-way street aimed straight at the cops. "Wait—back up. We gotta back up and go *that* way."

Dante did as commanded, heading down the alley faster than anybody ought to drive a truck in reverse. He looped around the corner, hit the brakes and peeled out. The bags slid across the truckbed and slammed against the gate, but nothing fell out. Dante took an indirect route to his house in case anyone was following, but no one was. They never saw the cops. The officers the Flemings had warned them about had no idea that anything was going on inside. They were busy shining flashlights at a confused elderly black man on the sidewalk, asking him if he'd been drinking.

The Nike job came very close to success. It was not the robbery itself that undid them, it was the double shift Dante had to work the next day, having requested it as part of the original plan. He was not good under pressure, and there was no way he was getting through a sixteen-hour shift without acting weird. Maybe if it had been an ordinary day at Niketown he could've put it out of his mind. But they had to begin the morning shift by discovering there were no Air Force One Limited Edition Kris Krijole Redesigns to sell to the 75+ crazy shoe collectors and music fans lined up around the

49

block. So it was a weird shift. He tried to play act, imagining what a normal person who had not stayed up all night breaking in and stealing 250 pairs of shoes might have said in this situation. "Are you sure they were delivered yesterday?" (Even though he was there when the display was set up.) "Could they have been recalled for some reason?" "No one could've broken in, there were people lined up out front, they would've seen it." "Where was the last place you saw them?"

When it was time for his first lunch break the day manager and assistant manager asked him to come into the back, the same room where they detained kids when they caught them shoplifting. They told him straight up that they thought he was acting bizarrely and they knew he had something to do with the robbery. He only denied it twice.

Dante, it turned out, was not the master criminal he'd always assumed he was. And he would've been the first to admit that he was lucky not to have himself as a partner. There was no torture involved. They didn't even have to yell at him. He just spilled it.

He explained everything - how Ed Janssens had given him the alarm code, how he had had it written down in case he needed it, and this guy he used to work with named Carter Chase had taken it from his wallet and said he was gonna go get himself some free shoes, ha ha ha, but Dante didn't know if he was really kidding or not. And how Dante had tried to get this guy to give back the code, but he refused, and he should've told his boss about it but he was afraid he'd get fired and maybe get Ed in trouble. And he thought Carter would never really use it but now that the shoes were missing he knew it must've been him that did it, Carter Chase. Poor Dante had been afraid to say anything because he didn't want to get his friend in trouble.

It was a ridiculous story, but maybe they would buy it. After all, he never went inside, he wouldn't be on the security tape, only Carter would be. It was his word against Carter's.

Carter was making a burrito when his phone rang. The caller ID said "UPTON ARMS APT," which meant somebody was at the front door. He looked out the kitchen window and made eye contact with one of the two cops there to arrest him. He couldn't hide his "oh shit" expression.

Not about to give up he sprinted down the hall, down the stairs and out the back door by the dumpsters, where he met the two other cops blocking his escape. *Then* he was about to give up. What was he gonna do, anyway, head for Mexico?

Carter had never been in an interrogation room before, so that was exciting. It kind of reminded him of having a doctor's appointment. Detective Wood, who was in charge of the case, seemed very polite and non-threatening as he asked Carter about what happened and quietly took notes about his denials.

Another officer came in. He opened up an old laptop as he sat down at the table next to Detective Wood. He introduced himself as Detective Harris.

"Oh, here we go," Carter said. "This is the bad cop?"

"No," said Wood. "This is the guy who has the security camera footage of you breaking into the Nike store."

Detective Harris squinted at his screen. He was having trouble opening the file. "Hold on," he said, the chance for any sort of dramatic timing going out the door. Then he said "There," and turned the computer around to face Carter. "Push the space bar," he said.

Carter' hopes sunk as he watched the video clip. "I was told it would be blurry," he said.

It didn't take long for them to turn him. Since he was the only one on camera they didn't know for sure who he was working with. He knew he was roasted, so he took full responsibility. What they couldn't get him to do was rat out his "accomplices." He didn't have any deep thoughts about honor among thieves or any shit like that, but he knew what things he could live with, and narcing on his old friend wasn't one of them. He probably could've done less time if he'd worked with the police and just told them the truth. But he was stubborn and refused to implicate anybody but himself. He didn't realize at first that Dante had a different understanding of friendship protocol. When he did figure it out his pride wouldn't allow him to turn back.

He was able to piece together from their questions that Dante had claimed not to be there, that he'd just made a mistake letting Carter find out the alarm code, so he played along with that. His story made no sense, and did not account for the whereabouts of the shoes.

Detective Harris didn't stick around long. Detective Wood got bored quick. At one point he went for dinner, left Carter alone for more than an hour. Eventually he brought in Mark Cobbs, one of the officers who had been outside Niketown that night, to take a look at Carter. The guy didn't recognize him, had never seen him.

"You really carried off all those shoes by yourself?" Cobbs asked.

"Yeah. Just took a lot of trips back and forth."

"To your car?"

"No, I piled them up in the alley."

"They told me you don't have a car."

"Yeah."

"So you... carried the shoes home?"

"I would've, but I got scared when I saw you guys so I left 'em in the alley."

"Left 'em in the alley."

"Uh huh."

"See, it's been this since four in the afternoon," Wood complained.

Cobb was amused. "Where are they really, though?"

"Still in the alley, far as I know."

The two cops looked at each other and laughed. Carter got impatient. "Look, I *told* you I broke in. Fucking charge me, I'll plead guilty. But I only moved them to the alley, then I bailed. If somebody else took 'em after I did... well, I'm not surprised. It's a bad neighborhood. You guys need to stop

52

fucking around and clean that place up."

No officer he talked to appeared to believe his story. But it was some missing shoes, not a homicide. Charging only Carter and using Dante as a witness meant less work for them. From what he heard from the public defender the Nike Corporation wasn't exerting any pressure either. They seemed content with the promotional value of the incident, showing their products as desirable loot, like diamonds or gold bullion. Nevertheless, prosecutors piled on charges of criminal mischief (they claimed that the door had to be repaired after Dante rigged it) and resisting arrest (for running out the back door) along with second degree burglary and first degree larceny, all of which Carter was ready to plead guilty to.

So, case closed. Maybe this kid really *did* act alone. Why would he lie about that? You gotta be able to trust *somebody* these days.

*   *   *

After the beating in the alley Carter was sore all over and looked like shit, but the emergency room experience wasn't that bad. He only needed two stitches on his bottom lip. The nurse cleaned him up, pulled out the remaining glass shards, disinfected all the scrapes on his face and arms, taped him up a little. They had a lot of questions about what it said on his medical record, but he wouldn't talk about it. He didn't have insurance but they let him pay in hundreds, and he insisted that they keep the change.

Afterwards he went back to the front desk and asked them to see if Mark had been checked in there, which he hadn't. He showed the photo around, but no luck.

As he walked gingerly down the stairs in front of the hospital, his knee and hip killing him with each step, he started thinking about the joint. He hadn't felt this defeated since he first went in. Didn't take long to start second-guessing his "just take the fall" legal strategy. There was a lot of fantasizing about how to avenge Dante. Complex schemes, setups, playing one guy against the other, all that mastermind shit. For most of his sentence he'd fully intended to go after his money as soon as he got out. Track down Dante and the Nike brothers, ascertain the status of the loot, force them to give him his share, make them regret selling him out. He would crawl out from beneath the bus they threw him under, tire marks on his face, and take a bite out of them. Then get back on the bus.

And that idea was starting to seem appealing again, but he didn't want to disrespect Mark's wishes, at least not until he found him and until he moved out of his house. So he better hurry up and do that.

How was he going to find him, though? Realistically he was gonna need to make some compromises. He took out his notebook.

duplex rules
1.   ~~no fighting~~
2.   no stealing
3.   no ill-gotten gains

As he came through the back door at the duplex, exhausted, he heard a sound coming from inside. Music of some kind. Tinny, annoying music. "Mark?" he called. But there was no answer. He put the house key between his middle finger and his ring finger and formed a fist.

Then he realized it was Mark's phone ringing from the floor. It took him a few seconds to figure out where to touch on the screen to answer it.

"Hello?"

"Mark?"

"Mark's not here. Is this Abbey?"

"Who's this?

# 7

AT 12:10 THE NEXT DAY Carter found nomi (all lower case), the restaurant where he'd agreed to meet Abbey at noon. He spotted her looking at her phone, sitting at a tiny metal table in the slim outdoor eating area. She wore large sunglasses that hid half of her face, but he still recognized her from the photos.

"Abbey? Carter."

"Oh my God, are you okay?"

"Little fight. Don't worry about it."

She didn't seem to believe him. She couldn't look at him without wincing. "You look terrible. But it's nice to finally meet you."

"What about you?" he asked. "You hiding a shiner behind those things?"

She lowered her sunglasses for a second – her eyes were fine. They both laughed, then caught themselves.

"Where the hell is he?" she asked.

"I wish I knew."

Once they were both sitting down they acted like everything was normal. They found shelter in the menu. Carter was shocked at the prices and descriptions.

"Raw salad with fennel. Ten dollars. And that's an appetizer."

"Well, this isn't prison. You have to pay for it."

"Yeah, well, you got fifty bucks and you want goat meat you're fine. Ten bucks and a cheeseburger you're out of luck."

She laughed. "I'm sorry. I didn't really think about it. Mark and I have lunch here a lot. But, you know, we're foodies, so..."

"Foodies? They got a name now for people who eat food?"

"It means, like… enthusiasts. We're food enthusiasts."

"Huh."

"Don't worry about the prices, it's my treat. And seriously, this is one of the best chefs in the city. You'll be amazed."

"Okay. But later I'm gonna shit it out."

On principle he chose the cheapest item on the menu, a bowl of carrot soup, and then quizzed her on Mark. It turned out the two of them weren't as close as he'd assumed. They'd only been together for about four months, and Abbey had been on a business trip in San Diego for the past two weeks. She hadn't heard from Mark in one week, which she didn't like, but sometimes he got busy at work and was hard to get a hold of. When Carter brought up the funeral she was aghast. She had no idea that their mother had died. After some thought she decided that Mark had kept it from her so she wouldn't cut off her trip to come home. Which did sound like Mark.

Carter took out his pen and notepad. "I gotta do some detective shit now. What type of drugs is Mark on?"

"No type."

"Are you sure?"

"Yes."

"Does he have a drinking problem?"

"Not at all."

"Had he been acting differently? Depressed or anything?"

"No, not before I left."

"Any enemies?"

"No, of course not. He's Mark. Everybody likes Mark."

"What about you? Do you have any enemies?"

"No. We're not that type of people."

"Any mean ex-boyfriends, anything like that?"

"Well, yeah. I guess kind of."

"*How* kind of?"

"My last boyfriend… I actually ran into him, like, a week before I left for San Diego I think it was? We don't get along, we got into kind of a yelling match. He *is* kind of stalkery. But I don't think he'd ever—"

"Prob'ly not, but it's worth checking out. Do you know his address?"

"No. We lived together and then I made him move out."

"Write down his name and phone number for me, I'll look into it. Worst case scenario I cross him off the list and give him a few pointers about how to move on after a failed relationship."

She smiled. "I'd like to see *that*."

"I don't use guns, and I probably wouldn't beat him up, if that's what you're thinking. I'm trying a whole going straight thing. There was a no fighting rule--"

"No fighting rule? Is that how you got that?" she said, pointing at his bruised face.

"Actually, yeah." He didn't want to go into it. "Therefore I'm suspending the no fighting rule until we find Mark. But I am a positive individual. I'd like to keep any violence to a minimum, out of respect for my brother and his household."

"Seems reasonable."

"There's no car in the garage, and I didn't notice one parked out front..."

"Oh, he's trying to be more conscious about the environment, so he sold his car. Kind of ridiculous though because I still drive him around a lot."

"Do you know the address of the place he works? The name of his boss, anything like that? Write that down on the top there."

"Okay."

"You said you guys liked to come here. I want you to write down for me every other place he liked to go. Restaurants, bars, stores. Whatever you can think of." She thought about it, and started to write down the places that came to mind. Watching her, Carter smiled and shook his head.

"What?" she asked.

"I'm sorry. It's just—those glasses."

"My sunglasses?"

"I can't see your eyes when I'm talking to you. You might as well be wearing a motorcycle helmet."

"I'm sorry," she said, taking them off.

"They're fucking huge. They're like novelty sunglasses. That's what people wear now?"

She frowned. "That's the style now. That's a pretty normal pair of sunglasses for a woman. Small, even."

"I don't mean to make fun of you," Carter said. "It's just—I want to buy you a rainbow afro wig."

He finished his soup quickly. He was still hungry, so he dug around in his backpack and found the Doctor-King bar he had bought his first day out. Abbey's jaw dropped as he took a big bite out of it.

"I know, isn't this crazy? 'Doctor-King.' That's why I bought it. I couldn't believe it."

"What are you talking about?"

"Doctor-King. The name. It's like Dr. King. MLK. It's just so weird that they would try to change the meaning of the words 'Dr. King.'"

"Okay, but I was thinking it was weird you were bringing your own candy into a restaurant."

"We're outside. It's legit."

She asked the waiter for the check, trying to hurry out of there now.

"Maybe that's what I should read about, I should find a book about Martin Luther King. Do you know where there's a book store around here?"

"A book store? No, I don't know where there would be one."

"Well, where am I supposed to buy a book?"

"Just get a tablet."

"Get a what?"

"I have to get out of here. Let me get your number," she said, flipping through the menus on her phone.

58

"I don't have a phone."

"What do you mean?"

"I mean I don't have a phone."

"I don't—I mean, how do you—" She was having trouble wrapping her head around it.

"Just call Mark's phone. It's still on the floor. I'll answer it if I'm home."

"I'd feel better if you carried it with you, so I know I can get you."

"I don't know."

"Mark's not using it."

"Fine." He didn't feel good about it, but it couldn't hurt. "Did he ever do this before?" Carter asked. "Just leave and not tell anyone?"

"No, never. Not since I've known him. I'm worried about him."

"I am too."

She put her phone back in her purse. "I still can't believe you don't have a phone! What do you do when you're going to the bathroom?"

"What do you mean?"

"I just don't know what I'd do without a phone!"

She paid with her Mastercard. She insisted it was her treat, but he made her take forty bucks and left the tip.

"Could this be related to you getting out? Maybe those guys had something to do with it. Those guys who did that to you."

"Nah."

Back at the duplex he turned on Mark's computer and, although he wasn't good with technology, he figured out how to open the web browser. He'd seen on an old *CSI* or something how you could look up information on these things. He could tell from the ads that kept popping up what Mark had last shopped for online: Adidas running gear, protein shakes, paint rollers. He typed in "Josh Steed," the name of Abbey's ex, and the phone number she had written down. After clicking through some of the pages that came up he found that a few matched a local musician who had been advertising for a new lead guitarist in his band.

Carter called the number from Mark's phone and talked to Josh. They hadn't found a replacement yet. Carter made up some names of bands he'd played in, said he thought he'd be a good fit and they made arrangements to meet at the band's rehearsal space the next day. They could jam and see where it went from there.

Next Carter called Mason.

"I met Mark's girlfriend just now. Seems nice. She was out of town, didn't even know Mom died."

"She doesn't know where he is?"

"No idea."

"That's weird that he wouldn't tell her if he was going somewhere. Maybe he's leaving her."

"She seems nice."

"I stopped by the duplex last night, you weren't there," Mason said. "Did you find a job?"

"No, I got beat up. Dante and the Fleming brothers and some other guy jumped me in the alley when I was taking the recycling out."

"Oh man."

"Yeah, well, I'm used to close quarters fights, where you mostly use your elbows. A regular street fight is pretty different, you know. Also I was trying not to fight at that point, out of respect for Mark."

"That's charming, Jimmy."

"But yeah, they kicked me up pretty good and some of the glass broke on me so I was probably getting some stitches when you came by."

"You should sue the shit out of them," Mason said.

"Oh, for fuck's sake."

"That's what *I'd* do."

"I know it is."

Carter cleared his throat. "She wanted to know if maybe Dante and them had something to do with Mark disappearing."

"And what did you say?"

"I said no. It's weird though, man. Those guys really thought I was coming after them. They fucked up the whole Niketown deal, blamed me, I took the fall and they got to keep the shoes." He smiled. "So now that I'm out, they thought I would come for the money or something. Funny thing is, I wasn't necessarily planning to, originally."

"Don't talk to me about crimes, Carter."

"Oh, don't be so judgmental. Do you know what they call a gang in England?"

"What?"

"A firm. You can't tell me you're not breaking any laws at that place you work at."

"We *don't* break the law! We're very careful about that."

"Never mind. I'm just saying, you better watch your back, Mason. It's not a good month to be a Chase. Mom dies, Mark disappears, I get the shit kicked out of me. You're next, Mason."

"Oh, that's great. Thanks."

Through the window Carter noticed a black car in the alley with the engine running. He craned his neck to figure out if it was the same one he'd seen there before he got jumped. But that one was a Mustang, this looked like a Camaro. Whoever it was, they didn't like him noticing them, so they sped off.

"Was she happy before she died?"

"Mom? I don't know. She was lonely. She could've used more company."

"I don't know if she would've wanted to see *me*."

"Of course she would. You're her son."

"She was still mad at me, though."

"Yeah, but she was excited to see you. Actually, did I tell you she had a basketball in the car?"

"No. What does that mean?"

"I don't know, you used to play basketball."

"When I was a little kid."

"Well, they found a basketball in her car, and *she* didn't play. Obviously she got it as a gift to give to you."

"Well, that's weird. But it's sweet."

"Yeah."

"Well, anyway, I've got a few things I'm gonna look into, hopefully we'll clear all this up soon."

Carter knocked on Barry's door. "Hi Barry."

"Hi Carter."

"Just wanted to apologize about the other day. Those guys thought I wanted their money. It was all a misunderstanding."

"Okay."

"If it was up to me it would've went down somewhere else, but they jumped me in the alley. I know how you feel about that kind of thing, with your kid here and all, so I led them away from the house."

"Okay, thanks."

"Also the language, there was a lot of profanity, so I knew you wouldn't want that around, this being an area for families and all that."

"Thanks."

"Hey, your kid—does your kid play baseball?"

"She's three years old."

"Well, do *you* play? I'm trying to borrow a bat."

"No."

"Okay, just checking. Well, anyway, just wanted to apologize. Won't happen again."

"Right on."

"Thanks Barry."

# 8

THE BUS TO DOWNTOWN was running late. Since Carter didn't have a book to read he brought an REI catalog Mark got in the mail. He wasn't learning much. While he waited a small crowd formed at the stop. First an elderly man, then a man in his early twenties, then a teenage girl, who stood behind them all. When the bus finally showed up it stopped with its door exactly halfway between Carter and the old man. Carter looked to the man and gestured for him to go first. He didn't bite. The bus driver and his passengers stared impatiently. Carter gave up waiting and rushed for the door, the younger man following him.

"Ah ah ah!" bleated the old man. Carter stopped mid-step. *"Ladies..."* said the old man, gesturing to the teenage girl.

Carter and the younger man turned to look at the girl. She looked at them, then at the old man, then at them again, then at the door to the bus. She shrugged, worked her way around the men and onto the bus.

"And... *gentlemen*," said the old man, smiling proudly. Carter and the other guy looked at him for a clue as to whether this meant to get on now or wait for him. He didn't budge, so they got on first.

On the bus Carter fumed. Motherfucker using a loophole to cast aspersions on his etiquette. He wasn't some punk kid with no manners. He was trying to be polite by allowing the oldest person at the stop to go first. He tries to be nice and the old fuck still has to show him up, make him look bad by pulling out some conflicting protocol. What is this shit about "ladies first" taking precedence over actual courtesy? That girl's not feeble. If somebody's old and has a hard time walking they have a legitimate reason to get the first choice of seats. Plus, as the person who had been waiting the longest it was *Carter's* choice if he let someone else go first.

He turned and glared at the old man. Wanted to fucking punch him. But that would be rude. Oh well, at least there was somebody more obsolete than he was.

After Carter calmed down he went through the numbers in the memory of Mark's phone. He felt self-conscious making calls on the bus, but he'd heard plenty of assholes doing it, it seemed to be accepted by modern society. And old Mr. Manners there would probably tell him if it was a no-no.

Mark had a lot of friends. Carter got off the bus and stood in a park by the waterfront while he finished making the calls. Nobody who answered had seen Mark in the last two weeks. Most did not know he had a death in the family. Either he was a very private person or he wasn't very close with the people in his phone. They weren't any help.

Carter was sick of holding the phone to his head. He had another headache, his lip still stung like hell, his ribs were sore and his legs ached whenever he bent his knees. It was a reminder of what he had to do, who he had to talk to. But he didn't even know where Dante lived.

The building where Mark worked was tucked away under the freeway, kind of a sketchy part of town, but new and modern on the inside. Pop art murals and colorful furniture everywhere to make up for the lack of sunlight. The secretary seemed to be afraid of Carter, but offered him bottled water, a Clif Bar or coffee. He chose the coffee.

The supervisor's name was April. She hadn't seen Mark, but hadn't expected to, because he'd scheduled two weeks off. He'd had a lot of vacation hours piled up and she thought he was just burnt out. She had the idea something was going on, because he was less talkative than usual. He hadn't told her about Mom, and now that she knew she thought that explained it.

"I think if I was in mourning like that, I might go rent a cabin somewhere and not tell anyone. Just to be myself and think about things."

Maybe. And he had the presence of mind to get the time off from work. He might not bother with that if it was some depressed suicide trip. But missing the funeral was still weird.

She showed him Mark's desk. There was an old framed photo of the family next to the computer. No pictures of Abbey. "That's me," he said, pointing to the little doofus on the left. Didn't look like him at all. The sides of the cubicle were covered in posters – pictures of musicians and paintings and National Parks, things to stare at to escape staring at the computer.

There was one thing that was odd: a Post-It note hanging off the bottom corner of Mark's monitor:

*Jimmy – Sat. 5<sup>th</sup>/~~Sun. 3<sup>rd</sup>~~/Sun. 1st*
*4<sup>th</sup> + Jackson – noon*

Carter pulled the note off, held it up for April to read. "Any idea?"

"No."

"This Saturday is the 5$^{th}$, right?"

"Yes."

"Weird."

Maybe Mark just had the wrong date written down, and that's why he wasn't around to pick him up when he got out. It's a theory. But what would the other dates be? And what about this 4$^{th}$ & Jackson business? That's not the cross street to the bus station. It had to be something else. Maybe one of those job hook-ups he'd been working on. Hard to say. Carter put the note in his pocket.

He stood in the middle of an aisle between rows of cubicles and blurted out "Anybody seen Mark Chase since he went on vacation?" They were jolted out of their private worlds where they tapped away at their keyboards and let their minds wander. Some of them removed one earbud as a sign of respect. They shook their head 'no.' None of them spoke. He decided to leave it at that and let the awkwardness pass.

As he left he felt like he towered over them. Their heads quickly ducked down and feigned hard concentration on their work. Only one man looked up and made eye contact, but he quickly looked away. It made Carter proud. The guy was younger than him and better looking and better dressed, but intimidated. Because Carter had something he never could. He knew he didn't belong there, with his weather-worn clothes and callused hands, and he didn't want to belong there. He'd rather jump off a bridge than live this life. He knew he was a scumbag, but was *this* any better? Was this really working for a living? If he knew what they did here maybe he could be sure. What is a "systems analyst" exactly? Wasn't that what Mark was? Something like that. He felt sure that these people weren't better than him. They wished they could walk out that door too, into the sunlight, the air, the freedom. But they'd never leave, not truly.

As the warm sun hit his face he took a deep breath of exhaust and before the door latched behind him he realized he had to shit real bad, had to go back inside and ask the secretary where the can was. Should never have taken the coffee. He heard strange bleeping and animal noises from the stall next to him. Some guy playing games on his phone. *That's* what Abbey was talking about, why she couldn't imagine not having a phone.

He stopped by the police station downtown to take care of that missing persons report. Abbey had already filed one. Otherwise the conversation went down pretty much as pictured. A Detective Rogers was in charge of the case. He told Carter exactly what he thought he would: that Mark was an adult and could do what he wanted and chances were he'd show up sooner or later. If not that was his prerogative, maybe he wanted to start a new life somewhere else.

"So what happened? Your brother beat you up before he left?"

66

"Nah, I fell. Taking out the recycling."

He gave them his name and number (actually, Mark's number) to add to the report. On the way out he passed a cop he thought he recognized, so he put his head down and didn't make eye contact.

He was a little late getting to the rehearsal space, which was in a rented warehouse next to the train tracks. He had to talk into an intercom and get buzzed in.

As soon as Carter saw Josh's pretty haircut and skinny jeans he felt sure he was not a killer or a kidnapper. But the rhythm section - two burly guys with shaved heads and tattoos - stood there like bouncers, puffing their chests out and giving Carter the stink eye. He wanted to see how far they would take it. And tell this dipshit to leave Abbey alone.

"Oh shit," Josh said. "That's not him."

"Not who?" Carter asked.

"Well, the name on the Caller ID, I could've sworn... what's your name again?"

"Carter Chase."

"The Caller ID said *Mark* Chase."

"That's me. I go by my middle name, Carter. What's up, did I come at a bad time?"

Josh relaxed. "I'm sorry dude. I've had some problems with a guy named Mark Chase, I thought you were him coming here to mess with me."

"Yeah, there's a couple of Mark Chases. I prob'ly have some of that guy's mail."

The drummer shook his head at his stupid friend. "Weed makes him paranoid," he laughed. He and the bass player loosened up, and walked across to where the equipment was set up: a drum kit, microphone stand, guitar and bass guitar on stands.

"Well, since I'm not here to mess with you, do I get the audition?" Carter asked.

"Yeah, cool man," Josh said. "But it's for a lead guitar player."

"Oh, I thought it was for a human beatbox."

"You're a human beatbox?"

"No, but I'm eager to learn. Just show me the ropes, man."

An awkward silence. The air was tense again.

"I'm just fuckin with you, man. My guitar's in the shop. The guitar shop, or guitar repair shop, you know. Music shop. Whatever."

"Well, maybe some other time then."

"Is that a Gibson?" Carter asked, rushing excitedly toward Josh's guitar, which said "Gibson" on it. Josh winced and reached for it as Carter picked it up and put the shoulder strap over his head. It looked like a nice guitar, although it had some ugly stickers on it for bands with names like "The Dangers" and "The Windows," and a weathered one with a solemn profile he was pretty sure was the late Kris Krijole.

"Too bad about Kris, huh?" Carter said.

"Yeah," Josh said suspiciously. "You're a fan?"

"Oh yeah."

"Since how long?" the bass player interjected. Putting him on trial.

"I'm a real fan, if that's what you're asking. I even have his Nikes."

"No shit?" the trio said in unison. "I've seen guys in bands wearing those. I always wanted a pair," Josh said, letting his guard down again. "But they're super-rare."

Carter walked over to a metal chair and sat down with the guitar balanced on his calf. He made a big show of stretching his fingers and getting comfortable. He strummed a few chords he'd learned from stoner friends in high school, and was surprised he still remembered. Then he reached down and pulled up his pantleg. The shiv knife was wrapped in cloth and tied to his leg.

He jumped dramatically to his feet and held the guitar up by the end of the neck, like dangling a dead cat by its tail. The blade was underneath the guitar strings, and he jerked it out, successfully slicing five of the six. Then he dropped the guitar head first on the cold cement floor. The loud crunching sound made everyone in the band wince.

"What the fuck!?" Josh yelled.

"I'm sorry fellas, I misled you. I'm not a guitarist, or a beatboxer. I *am* here to mess with you. I have a few questions to ask."

The bassist was furious. He had his fists up and was moving toward Carter.

"I *knew* you looked like Mark," Josh whined. "You must be his brother. His crazy brother that was in prison."

Hearing that, the bassist spun around and rejoined the drummer in the "not involved in this dispute" area. But Josh ran at him. Carter turned sideways to dodge him, caught his right arm and twisted it behind his back until he cried out. He respected him for facing off with the knife so he kept it away from him.

That over with, Carter went straight into his questions. "You said you had problems with Mark Chase. What did that mean?"

"He stole my girlfriend!" Josh sounded like a whiny bitch. The drummer snorted, unintentionally, almost caught himself, but didn't. Carter pointed the knife in his direction.

"What is it, Drums?"

The drummer didn't want to say anything. He looked at Josh, and back at Carter. "It's none of my business."

"Come on, spill it."

He looked at Josh again. "Sorry, I love ya Josh, but he didn't steal her from you. You were already broken up."

"We were fighting! That's normal! We would've straightened it out, but that fuckin guy comes along--"

"All right, all right," Carter interjected. "So you were mad at Mark Chase. What did you do to get back at him?"

"Nothing. I barely even know him."

"Do you know where he is?"

"No. What do you mean?"

"No idea at all?"

"No! I've only met him a couple of times. He's just the

guy that goes out with Abbey."

Carter nodded. "I believe you. Sorry about the guitar." As he was walking out, he remembered: "Oh yeah, and leave Abbey alone. If you go anywhere near her I'll take back my apology."

suspects
1. Dante
2. ~~Josh Steed (Abbey's ex)~~

*Well that was a waste of time* he thought as he left the warehouse. *But fun.* In fact he had really enjoyed it. Better than cigarettes, better than porn, better than sleep, the best time he'd had since messing with Jason Fleming at The Dock. He'd been having so much fun he'd almost forgotten why he was there. And it worried him.

At least he'd eliminated a suspect, leaving only one on the list. But Dante didn't feel right. The way he talked, it seemed like he hadn't known Carter got out early. So why would he have already done something to Mark at that point? And he couldn't have Mark as a hostage, or that's the threat he would've used against Carter.

Or did he? Maybe he was trying to imply something about Mark without incriminating himself? Didn't he say something about "Mark my words"? What kind of a thing is that for a real person to say? That would be just like Dante to try to be a big shot by speaking in code, and then fail to get the message across.

How would the timeline have worked? It could've happened the day after Carter got out. Mark misses picking him up at the bus station for some unrelated reason, he's not missing at that point. But Carter threatens the Fleming brother at the bar, Fleming calls the other guys pissed off, they look up Mark's address thinking Carter is gonna be there, end up attacking Mark in his place... hopefully they took him, didn't accidentally kill him. Then that would explain why they thought Carter would come back after them. Could that be

70

what happened?

Well, only one way to find out: ask.

There was one person he could think of that could tell him where Dante lived. But there was something he had to get first, and he was hungry too. There was a hot dog stand on the wide sidewalk next to a tall office building with a small line of white collar workers waiting. When it was his turn he ordered a jumbo dog with grilled onions and melted cheddar. The old man made small talk while he cooked the onions.

"You do good today, my friend?"

"I'm good, how 'bout you?" asked Carter.

"Very good, very good. You- you don't look so good."

"Yeah, well, the body heals."

"This is true," the old man laughed. "Are you a fighter? You do the UFC?"

"No. Not a fighter."

The hot dog stand was covered in photos, stickers, newspaper clippings. There was a flyer about a missing parrot.

"Hey, if I came back with a flyer for a missing person, would you hang it up here?"

"Of course. Who are you missing?"

"My brother Mark."

"Your brother? You really *aren't* doing good. I'm sorry for you, my friend."

"Oh, it gets worse. My mom just died too, in a car accident. Just a couple blocks that way, actually. On 5th Avenue."

"The one recently? I think I was here that day."

"It happened at night, actually. They all said she shouldn't've been driving after dark. She wasn't that old, but..."

"I'm the same. My night vision gets worse every year. I'm sorry to hear that, my friend. That's terrible."

"Yeah, it is."

As the old man handed the finished hot dog to Carter

he made eye contact and gave him a very serious look, the familiar *I'm trying to do something supportive for you but all I have is this look* type of look. So Carter changed the subject. "Hey, uh, do you know if there's a sporting goods store downtown anywhere?"

"No, I don't think."

"I need a baseball bat."

"Baseball bat? You go to KFC. Nice gift shop at KFC."

"That sells baseball bats? At Kentucky Fried Chicken?"

"No no no. KFC is the field. KFC-Taco Bell Field. They have gift shop. Team store, I mean. They have jerseys, bats, everything."

"Oh, the stadium. Or the ballpark, whatever. Good idea. Thanks."

# 9

JASON FLEMING HATED working days at The Dock. It was more peaceful than nights, obviously, but an eight hour shift felt more like 48, and the tips were almost non-existent. He just sat staring off into nothingness, the yellow shine of the Corona light on the window becoming a blur against the gloomy darkness of the dimly lit room.

Two middle-aged tourist ladies had just left and he was wiping off the spillage from their Long Island Ice Teas. As often is the case this time on a weekday, the only customer was Vic Clements, sitting at his usual booth staring off into space. Jason's co-worker Brad was in the back frying up some onion rings for the lonely old drunk.

Figuring he had a window, Jason put an unlit cigarette in his mouth. Just then his rag dripped several drops of brown liquid onto the pristine white full-grain leather upper of his left Nike Jumpman Team Elite.

"God damn it," he muttered. He dampened a clean white cloth and gently dabbed, then dried the toe. It would probably be okay. Close call though.

When you wear white shoes you make sacrifices. But maybe it was time to wear darker shoes to work. He preferred white but he always dreamed of imaginary colorways. What if everything was black, maybe a flint grey for the outsoles. The only splash of color would be in the forefoot, or maybe the midsole accent. Like a pine green or a varsity red. Or maybe not even that. All black but then the sole is blaze orange. So it looks dark until you lift your foot up, then it's like turning on a light. Shoes that tell a story. It would be great.

"Hey Brad, I'm takin' a smoke break," he yelled into the back.

"That's cool."

The door to the alley was already propped open. He

opened it more and stepped around the box fan. His eyes struggled to adjust. Looking at his feet he started to think maybe all black or grey would be too obvious for the Team Elites. It should be more subtle. What about a really dark brick red, almost brown, with a charcoal grey for the midfoot, collar and laces?

He looked over to his Mustang parked on the corner, chalk marks on the back tires – he still had about 20 minutes before he had to move it across the street. As he lit his cigarette he heard the door shutting, saw it out of the corner of his eye. Shit. Now he'd have to go around to the front just t--

He shuddered as he realized that it had not shut itself. Carter Chase lunged toward Jason with a baseball bat, holding it at both ends like a handlebar, hitting him right in the mouth with it. Holy fuck, it hurt like hell, and his whole jaw was vibrating. He spit out a mouthful of blood.

"You asshole!"

"What did you to do my brother?"

"Wh-what? I don't even know your brother!"

"Where does Dante live?" Carter asked.

"Fuck you!" Jason said. Carter started poking at him with the end of the bat. Not real hard, but enough that it hurt. Jason hid his face behind his upraised arms. He was backed against the wall.

"Where does Dante live?"

"Quit fuckin hitting me with that thing!" Carter gave the bat a light swing right into Jason's knee.

"Oh, fuck! What are you doing, man? That hurts!"

"Where?"

"You think you're a man, coming after me with a fucking bat?"

"You brought three friends to get me. I don't have three friends, so I brought a bat. Where does he live?" Carter held the bat up over his head, like an ax he's about to chop wood with.

"Okay man, stop! I'll tell you the apartment number, the phone number. Whatever you want, just fucking stop!"

Carter made him write it on his notepad, then turned to walk away. He stopped and looked at the spot of blood Jason had spit up. "Did she make it?" he asked. "Your wife, I mean. Did she become a dentist?"

Jason didn't answer, but Carter crouched down, picked up a little piece of tooth off the ground and handed it to him. "Sorry about that man. I didn't mean to hit you that hard."

The address was an apartment building across the street from a grocery store. Carter bought a cheese sandwich at the deli. There was a small seating area at a window with a view of the front entrance to the apartment. Earlier he'd tried calling up to Dante on the intercom. There was no answer, but he was able to snoop around and thought he'd figured out the layout of the building. Judging by its number Dante's apartment should be on the east side of the building, opposite of the side entrance, so it seemed logical for him to use the front entrance. But there was no way to be sure. At least he had a good idea this was the right place, since Dante's name was in fact in the directory under the correct apartment number.

But Carter knew it was a foolish stakeout. He had no idea when or if Dante would be coming home. When he did, Jason Fleming would definitely have tipped him off about who was after him. So he'd probably be with friends, with weapons, and looking specifically for Carter to be there. To make matters worse Carter had dropped the bat back off at the duplex. He felt weird carrying it around in public. You don't sit in a grocery store eating a cheese sandwich if you're carrying a blood stained bat. He did have his knife, but he'd already broken the "no fighting" rule and although he hadn't made a specific "no stabbing" rule he felt it was at least implied and he'd feel bad breaking that one too. He kept the knife tucked away, and the screwdriver he had was small and not very good for stabbing.

Half an hour after he finished the sandwich he decided to take a few walks around the block. On the second lap as he was passing the side entrance he heard the door opening. He fumbled in his pockets as if looking for his keys. The young woman who was coming out smiled and held the door for him.

His hunch about the building's layout was right. #108 was on the first floor, far end, on the corner of the building. He knocked on the door. No one answered and there was no sound from inside. The door was old and beat up, and he thought he might actually be able to kick it open, to see if Mark was inside. But he didn't believe anybody could keep a hostage in this one-bedroom apartment without the neighbors finding out. It would be better to wait for Dante to show up.

He went back out to the street. There was a basement floor, so the first floor was a little higher than street level, but low enough that he could climb in if it wasn't for the bars on the window. He found the screwdriver in his backpack and, with some effort, unscrewed the 9 bolts that were holding it into the brick façade of the building. He pulled slightly; whatever was holding it didn't feel strong, and he was confident that he could break it off. The screws were pretty heavy duty, so he thought about saving them to put between his knuckles during a fight, but then he decided that was a stupid idea and dropped them on the sidewalk.

He sat on a bus stop bench for a while. He loitered by a liquor store. Eventually he went back to the grocery store and drank a large Pepsi at the same table he'd been at earlier. If he saw Dante coming he would run out there, but if he missed him it might even be better. As soon as he sees movement through the window he could pry the bars off, throw a rock through, climb in and knock over some furniture or something. Storm in like a berserker and make him shit his pants.

"Hi Carter," came Dante's voice from just behind him. He was carrying a half full bag of groceries he had just bought. Carter leapt to his feet. He looked over at the old security guard sitting at his stool by the entrance.

"Outside." Dante agreed, didn't put up a fight at all.

He was disarmingly calm. "Don't tell me you're mad that we jumped you," he said when they were out on the sidewalk. "You know you started it coming after Jason at his place of employment, trying to act tough with your little Wild Wild West routine."

"My 'Wild Wild West routine'?"

"Coming in threatening him. And now you break his tooth with a baseball bat? What more do you want?"

"*Wild Wild West* was an old TV show, kind of a comedy. I think you mean to say '*Wild* West routine,' but that means somebody comes in and shoots up a place, which is not what I did. You're an idiot."

"Shut up, Carter. You know what I mean."

"Let's cut the shit," Carter said. "You know what I want."

"Of course I know what you want, but they're not here, they're at a storage space."

"They?"

"They're at a storage space."

"Who are you talking about?"

"Who are *you* talking about?"

The confusion enraged him. "Who the fuck do you *think* I'm talking about? My brother. Where is he?"

Dante's cool started to visibly fade. He put his hands up in surrender. "Swear to God, Carter, I don't even know what you're talking about."

"You didn't *kill* him, did you?"

Dante laughed incredulously. "Are you serious?"

They locked eyes. Carter didn't have to say anything, his face did the work. Yes, he's fucking serious.

"Here," Carter said, pulling out his wallet. He produced the business card he got from the man at the funeral home. "Put this in your pocket. This guy knows his shit, I think your family will be very happy with his work." He had a hand inside his backpack, holding the shiv knife.

"Jesus, Carter. What are you doing? You're gonna stab me?"

"Ah, you know. We'll see where the day takes us."

"Man, if I knew anything I would tell you. I haven't seen either of your brothers in years. Which one is it that's missing?"

"Mark."

"I don't know anything about Mark being missing."

"I'm not stupid, Dante. I got your hint. And I've seen you and your buddies spying on me. If it was just me that's one thing, but going after my family to get to me--"

"That's not true, man! I seriously don't know what the fuck you're talking about. What's going on here?"

"Just fucking tell me what you know. My mom just died, I don't need *this* shit to deal with too."

"Oh fuck, is that the funeral you were-- I'm sorry, dude. I swear I don't know anything about it. That sucks, man. Your mom was always nice. I liked your mom."

Carter's shoulders loosened. His whole posture changed. He wasn't sure how he'd expected this conversation to go, but this was one outcome that had not occurred to him: Dante was saying he had nothing to do with any of this, *and Carter believed him.* He zipped his backpack closed.

"It's cool, man. We can work something out. I should at least get you—what size of shoes do you wear?"

"What size of shoes?"

"The Nikes. You should at least get a pair, all you've been through."

"You still have the Nikes?"

"Yeah, most of them. I thought that was what you were after."

"I don't need any Nikes. They let me keep my Bob Barkers."

Dante didn't push it. "Well, I'm sorry about all—all this," he said, gesturing at Carter's wounded face. "I don't know, I just thought—"

"Forget it."

"Swear to God I'm not usually like that anymore, dog. I don't get in beefs or nothin. I'm a grown ass man, I'm tryin to

78

be positive."

"You can't imagine how proud that makes me."

"Seriously. You'd be surprised. I used to clown a lot when you knew me. But now, like if you saw me somewhere with some friends, and you came over, I'd prob'ly be talking about... *intelligent* things, you know? Just, like – knowledge, positivity. My friend would be like, he'd say something real philosophical or political or whatever. And I'm just like *yeah, it's an interesting point, but I disagree, because blah blah blah* and I'm just schooling him, just dropping science, talking about all these deep things... That's what I'm interested in now, things like that. You'd be surprised."

"Okay," Carter said.

"Man, you must've been into that stuff in prison, right? Reading books and everything, educating yourself, like that one guy. What's the guy's name?"

"The guy?"

"Remember, the black guy who read books in prison?"

"Malcolm X?"

"Yeah, like Malcolm. I bet you were like him, just... getting knowledge and everything."

"Well, you're actually right. There was a prison library, and also they let my brother bring me books sometimes."

"What kinda books? Deep stuff, like the Koran or whatever?"

"Like, books about the civil war, stuff like that."

"That sounds dope."

"Yeah, you shoulda been there."

"No, you're right. You're right. You're a good man for what you did. You gave me the chance to get to where I am. I never thanked you for the whole thing. For not turning me in."

"Yeah."

"That's fucked up what you did to Jason, though! What the fuck was that?"

Carter shrugged.

"Weird couple o' days."

"Yeah."

"You just got out too, didn't you?"

"Yeah, about... five days ago? Then it was a funeral, a hospital..."

"You got out early, didn't you?"

"Yeah, a little bit."

"You didn't... say anything about—"

"Fuck no!" Carter objected. "I wouldn't rat somebody out. I don't believe in it. That's some other asshole."

"You're right, I know. I deserve that. What can I say? I'm sorry I did it. I was young and stupid. I fucked up."

"Well... okay."

Neither knew what to say after that. They stood awkwardly, looked around at the cars and shoppers passing them by. A petition gatherer on the corner was looking their way, had probably heard most of their argument. He turned the other way when they made eye contact.

Dante was the one to break the silence. "Well, I got ice cream in here. I don't want it to melt. Can I go home now?"

"Okay."

"Man, this sucks," Dante said. "We used to be friends. All this over money. And by the way, I didn't even get that much. Kerry and Jason are still sitting on most of those shoes, those and some other ones they collected, we got a storage space full of the fucking things. They couldn't figure out a good way to sell them."

"You're breakin' my heart, Dante. That sounds like a real god damn tragedy there. The suffering, man. Almost inconceivable." They both laughed.

"Well, now that Kris Krijole is dead maybe we'll be able to sell them. If Jason and Kerry will let me."

"What do you mean, they don't want to sell them?"

"Yeah, they got a fetish, it seems like they'd rather just keep 'em all. Don't even get me started. But I love 'em. They're like my brothers."

"Well, so was I."

"Yeah. Well if I do sell 'em maybe we can work

80

something out, give you a cut. Hey, believe me man, I hope you figure out about – Mark is missing?"

"Yeah."

"And you talked to his girlfriends and work and everything?"

Carter nodded.

"Pigs wouldn't do anything?"

A head shake.

"Well, I wish I could help."

"Yeah."

They both looked at the ground.

"You need some weed or anything?" Dante asked.

"No thanks."

"Okay, cool."

"Hey, thanks for offering the shoes. I appreciate it. But I got a rule against… 'ill-gotten gains' is what I've been calling it. Trying to follow the straight path."

"Okay man," Dante laughed.

"Could I—you mind if I get that business card back? I don't know if my brother is gonna—well, I should hold onto it."

Dante handed it back. "It's all good. Do you still think I did it, or can we declare peace now? Can we stop all this shit? This indigenous cycle of violence?"

Carter laughed and decided not to correct him. "We're cool. I'll cross you off the list." Carter walked away, and Dante went back to his apartment.

Ten minutes later Dante was on the phone talking to Kerry Fleming, telling him what had happened. Glancing out the window at the sidewalk across the street where it all went down he saw Carter outside his window, putting the screws back into the security bars.

"What the fuck are you doing?!"

"It's fine," said Carter. "Don't worry about it."

"You motherfucker, I thought we were cool!"

"We are, I'm just, I had to fix what I--"

"I thought we were cool! You're on my shit list now!"

"Fine, Dante, then you're on my give-me-my-fuckin-money list!"

# 10

AT QUARTER TO NOON on Saturday the 5$^{th}$ Carter went and stood at 4$^{th}$ and Jackson, the corner Mark had written on that Post-It note at work. Loitering made him nervous about cop harassment, so he found himself pacing back and forth. When he almost stepped in dog shit left in the middle of the sidewalk – who *does* that? - he decided to stop moving and lean up against the brick wall between two businesses.

His wildest hope was that Mark, wherever he was, would keep this appointment, whatever it was. That would be the ideal anticlimactic ending to the case of the missing brother. But he wasn't holding his breath. It did seem possible that whoever Mark was supposed to bring him to meet would show up, and he could quiz them about what was going on. But they might not know anything, so even that wasn't necessarily gonna help him much, other than to maybe put a face to one of Mark's friends he talked to on the phone.

This didn't seem like that kind of meetup spot, though. There were a few small restaurants on the block, but not the type that Mark and Abbey liked to go to. Just little shops with burritos or bagels or cupcakes to sell to the people who work in the office buildings downtown, and they were closed for the weekend. So if it was a lunch meeting it was poorly planned.

Across the street was a small public skate park. A handful of kids, maybe 15 and younger, took turns careening back and forth across the smooth cement curves. He had no idea how they stayed balanced on those things. He watched them for a couple minutes, but when it occurred to him somebody could think he was a pedophile he turned to watch the cars coming up the street.

There was a decent amount of foot traffic, the occasional jogger or dogwalker. But nobody stopped like they were looking for Mark. The only person to acknowledge

Carter was a jittery guy with a lazy eye who tried to sell him batteries.

On the other side of the street, just past the skate park, a woman in those big sunglasses stopped and sipped from her paper coffee cup, her back turned to her little greyhound as he took a shit. She fuckin knew what was going on, but averted her eyes. Plausible deniability. And she was out of there.

When Carter realized she wasn't gonna clean it up he yelled, "Hey!" She ignored him, and he let it go.

One of the skateboard kids, maybe 12 years old, looked over at him. The kid launched off the curb, his wheels rumbling, then squealing as he rolled in a U in front of Carter.

The kid turned back around, raised the nose of his board and spun on his rear set of wheels, skidding to a halt. He stepped off his board, stomped on the tail so it popped into his hand, parted his long bangs and stared blankly at Carter. There was a large, scraped-up sticker of Minnie Mouse covering the bottom of his board.

"Can I help you?" Carter asked rudely.

"No," the kid said, turning around and hopping back on his board. He looked over his shoulder at Carter timidly before two big pushes sent him back across to the park.

Carter felt like his forehead was getting sunburned, so he stepped over into the shadow made by a small tree in the sidewalk. He heard a voice down the block – another dogwalker in shades, this one a man having a loud phone conversation. The man stopped right in front of Carter as his pug sniffed around at the tree.

"I told her I'm in negotiations for an associate position at my firm, so we should put the brakes on moving in. That's what I came up with."

Carter took a step backward to get out of his way. The guy looked at him, not smiling, as if it was Carter that was intruding on *his* space.

"How's it goin?" Carter said to him. The guy just stared, listening to his phone. He glanced down as the dog squeezed out a long piece of shit, then yanked on the leash and continued down the sidewalk.

"I know, can you believe it?" he said. "I'm totally gay for that show. What episode are you on?"

"Hey!" Carter yelled at the guy's back. "Come pick this shit up."

No response. He kept yammering.

"Hey, I'm talking to you, asshole. Come pick your shit up!"

The guy looked back at him and started to walk faster, so Carter ran after him.

"Hold on a second," the man said bitchily into his phone. "Some guy's yelling at me." He finally took the phone away from his face. "Excuse me, is there a problem?"

"Yeah there's a problem. Some piece of human garbage just let his asshole dog take a shit on the street where humans walk."

He scoffed. "What are you, the sidewalk patrol or something?"

"Yeah, something like that."

The asshole snorted. "Somebody's got too much time on their hands." He turned and started to walk away again. "Sorry about that," he said into the phone. "What was I saying before I got so rudely—" but he dropped the phone when Carter put him in a choke hold and dragged him back to the scene of the crime. His forearm tight around the man's neck, Carter pulled him toward the ground, grabbed his wrist and forced his hand over the offending dog waste.

"I'm not gonna let you breathe until you pick it up," he grunted, pulling the hold tighter. The man's face was turning red and puffy. He closed his eyes as he gave in and closed his hand around the shit. Carter pulled him back up, let go of him, and shoved him from behind, causing him to stumble forward. When the man caught his balance he let the shit drop to the ground. He crouched for a second, wiping his hand on the sidewalk. Standing up, he looked at the mess on his hand and held it out to his side as if the limb didn't work anymore. With the other arm he reached beneath the pug, scooped him up and held him close to his body. Then he began to flee.

Before he made it two steps he leaned forward and his cheeks puffed out. He started to raise the shit-hand to his mouth but caught himself, and vomited all over the front of his shirt and the top of his dog. Then he ran.

When he reached the end of the block he turned around, his eyes surrounded by tears that could be from terror or from puking, and yelled "Asshole!"

"Don't fuck with the Sidewalk Patrol!" Carter yelled back.

The skateboard kids saw the whole thing, and they were laughing. The kid with the bangs rolled over to him again. "That was awesome," he said.

"Thanks."

The kid skidded on his tail, did a wobbly 360 degree spin.

"Hey, why Minnie Mouse?" Carter asked.

"Fuck you, I like Minnie Mouse," the kid said. He ollied onto the sidewalk, then off again. *Sh-clank.* "Got a smoke?" he asked Carter.

"No!" Carter laughed.

By now it was past 12:30, and he didn't know if the dogwalker might come back with the cops, so he left.

Back at the duplex he decided it was time to go through the mail and the papers in the recycling to see if there were any clues. There weren't. Just a lot of advertisements, coupons, catalogs, magazines, bank statements, credit card offers, grocery store circulars. 0% fixed APR came up a few times. No annual fee, pre-approved, platinum benefits, your last issue unless you act now, see terms and conditions inside. Packed in the middle of a tabloid sized collection of mail-away offers and manufacturer's coupons was a shrink-wrapped CD titled *Dr. Pepper's Lonely Hearts Club Band*, an abridged, promo-only version of the classic Beatles album. So they *do* still make CDs. He set it aside in case he needed something to listen to.

He dumped the pile of junkmail into the recycling bin and searched his pockets for receipts or scraps of paper he didn't need anymore. Then he remembered his notebook. Abbey had given him that list of places she and Mark liked to go. God damn it. No suspects. Carter really had no idea what was going on. Now he had some fuckin work to do.

# 11

ON THE BUS Carter caught a glimpse of his reflection in a window, and for a second he thought he was looking at a woman. *Jesus* he thought, and got off to find a barber shop and get his head shaved. When he finally got back to the duplex he felt similar about Mark's half of the yard, overgrown as it was with weeds. Barry Winston's side was perfect.

Carter felt like an asshole. In the garage he found a lawnmower and started hacking away at the front lawn, but it was electric and he kept almost running over the extension cord. He had the height adjusted too low, the thing started choking on all the grass until a puff of smoke came out where the cord attached to the mower. He had to find the fuse box and reset one of the switches. He didn't think it was safe to use the cord, and just as he was contemplating leaving the yard looking even worse, with sort of a reverse mohawk, he spotted an old hand push reel mower in the back with some other garden tools.

As he was finishing Barry came out and gave him a thumbs up. "Lookin' good, man."

"The hair or the lawn?"

"Both."

"Yeah, I figured maybe Mark would show up if I mowed his lawn. Soon as I finished. That's how my luck works."

In a way it felt like a weight off his shoulders, a fresh new start, cutting away all that hair and grass. The act of mowing cleared his mind, and as he put the mower away and wiped the sweat from his brow he realized it was time to get a job. Not only had he been paying Mark's rent and utilities, but he found out about this data storage thing. He'd had to have Abbey explain it to him, how instead of owning movies and albums and stuff Mark paid monthly for access to some of them on "The Cloud." And Carter would be damned if he was gonna let all his brother's... cloud or whatever get hauled off to the Goodwill. But after two months of paying all those bills Carter was concerned about the size of his roll. Clearly it wasn't enough to coast off of for the rest of his life. If Mark showed up Carter would have to move out, and he'd need to have enough for a deposit and first and last month's rent and all that. And anyway it would be good to count on money that wasn't dirty. There had been that whole idea about cleaning up his act and what not.

He went through Mark's old voicemails and found the one from his friend Jake Duley:

"Hey what's up Mark, Jake Duley. Uh, listen, I got your email about your brother. Yeah, that's no problem. I can help you out. You say he's a smart guy, I believe you. Absolutely. So I talked to my guys, they said we can move some things around, call it a paid internship. And don't worry about his record, that's nothing new. We have a lot of guys in defense that we have to fudge some details on their files. Just, when he's ready, have him give me a call here, I'll fill him in on the details. And if you need anything just reach out, shoot me an email, shoot me a text... you know the drill. Thanks buddy. Peace."

The caller ID was his work number and it said "JML CONSULTING." Typing that into Google Carter found the address in the top floor of the Rossi Building downtown, and a website that did very little to answer his question about what the fuck "consulting" was.

He decided if he showed up in person instead of calling it would make a strong impression, show that he's one of those "go-getters" people talk about. But the receptionist seemed scared of him. That surprised him because he felt so clean-cut with the short hair and the funeral suit. The tie covered up the bloodstains on the shirt, so it wasn't that. Maybe he accidentally gave her that prison stare.

Jake Duley seemed flustered too, unprepared to meet

him without an appointment. He looked Carter up and down and forced an unconvincing smile. Carter shook his hand hard.

"Hey, what's up, man? You're Carter? You're Mark's brother? I've heard so much about you. I should say, I got a conference call in two minutes, but it's great to meet you, man. Great to meet you. How you doing?"

"Fine." The speed of the conversation made Carter uncomfortable.

"Your brother. Did he—tell you to come here?"

"Yeah, he said you were looking into finding me a position here."

"Okay. Okay. Hmmm..."

"Is there a problem?"

"No, no problem, Carter. Listen, uh..." he exhaled nervously. "I feel terrible about this, but we can't hire felons here, because of security clearances and all that. Personally I think it's bullshit, but it's just a blanket policy for the firm. I tried pulling some strings but my hands are tied on this one, I'm sorry. It's just something we've never been allowed to do."

"Huh. I heard differently."

"Yeah, no. Sorry. Sucks, man. But if you need anything just reach out. Shoot me a text." He tilted his head slightly and smiled condescendingly, to show he was one of the good guys, with nothing but compassion for upstanding ex-cons looking for legitimate work to turn their lives around. "Anyway, gotta make this call now, sorry to cut you off."

They shook hands again, to signal the end of the conversation. "Your hands are very soft," Carter said. "What kind of lotion is that?"

"It's... I think it's just Nivea or something. But, uh, good to meet you, Carter."

"Yeah, I'll tell Mark you said 'what's up.'"

The job search over the next several days didn't go much better. More awkward conversations with people he could tell didn't like him. "We're not hiring right now, but we're always accepting resumes." The worst were the uncomfortable talks with old acquaintances who weren't quite in a position to vouch for a felon. "I gotta get back to work. Good to see you, Carter!" He hated to put people on the spot like that, but he didn't have much of a choice.

Walking downtown he saw a small restaurant called Bubble Lounge and recognized it as one of the names on the list of places Mark liked to go. Carter went in and showed the head waiter Mark's picture. He did recognize Mark as a regular diner but said he hadn't seen him in a while. When Carter explained the situation the waiter seemed really sympathetic and upset. "I like that guy. He seems really nice."

"Yeah. Well, thanks for your help."

"No problem. I hope he's okay."

"Yeah. By the way, do you have any applications?"

"What do you mean?"

"For jobs?"

"Oh—well, I don't think we need anybody on the wait staff right now."

"What about kitchen?"

"You have sous chef experience?"

"I don't know, but I used to work in the kitchen at Don's. You know, it's like a diner or a café?"

"I don't know the place."

"It might not still be there. I've been – it's embarrassing – I've been in prison for a while. I mean don't worry, not for a violent crime or sex crime or anything. And I don't have a drug addiction. It's a long story."

"Well anyway, I don't think we're hiring."

Even if he didn't have to worry about his record he would've had a hard time with this. He didn't even know what to look for or what he was capable of. He was hoping not to have to be tempted by a till full of money, but he'd take what he could get.

When he gave in and went to a temp agency it was pretty discouraging. He liked to think he didn't want to work

92

in some office building downtown like Mark did, with all those yuppies he saw on the bus in the morning. But then he felt kind of hurt when they didn't ask him to. *What, I'm not good enough to bring you fuckers bottled water and Clif bars?*

Instead of the penthouse he ended up on the sidewalk. Four-hour shifts, alone or with one other guy, holding a GOING OUT OF BUSINESS SALE sign for a mattress store. He figured the sign could do the job just as well without his help, but oh well. He added that human touch. When the gig ended in a week and a half there would be an opportunity with American Tax Services, but for that one he'd have to wear an Uncle Sam costume. There was also one for selling condos wearing a Pink Panther costume, as if somebody might be driving by looking for a condo and say, "That seems like a good one, the Pink Panther is pointing to it." For the mattress store there was no required uniform. He liked to wear his suit from the funeral and pretend he was a professional, but maybe he looked sleazy, like a guy passing out flyers for a strip club. He wasn't sure.

Four hours is a short time to work, but it's a long time to stand on the side of a road doing tricks with a sign. At the end of a shift his wrists and fingers were sore. He could smell the sweat and dirt on himself and taste the car exhaust in the back of his throat. Still, it was a good job for him right at this moment because it gave him time to think. Standing there waving at cars, looking through them, meditating on the state of his life's journey. After a few days of that it really sunk in how important it was for him to straighten out his life at this juncture. A lot of people his age still struggled with figuring out what to do with their lives, but he felt several steps behind those people. Some people waste years getting a degree they don't know what to do with. But they didn't have to check off that felony box when filling out job applications. They had it easy.

Somehow he had to find something he was good at, something he enjoyed, that also happened to pay enough, and at a place that either hires ex-felons or doesn't ask about it. But how could he concentrate on that when he still didn't know what happened to his brother? He had to get that out of the way first. Either find his brother, or if that's not possible, find the person responsible and return the favor. He just had to cross that off his list in time to become a productive member of society afterwards.

So the short shifts were good for that. Before and after work he'd spend an hour or two canvassing, showing Mark's photo around, hanging up flyers, staking out the fancy restaurants that Abbey had told him about. There were a few nice people along his route - like Tony, the old man at the hot dog stand downtown - who kept his flyers up, and he would check in with them occasionally to see if anyone had said anything. But no luck. Mark was officially a missing persons case now, but the police still weren't doing much investigating, and were still feeding Carter that line that his brother could do what he wanted.

He seemed to always wake up with headaches now. He knew they'd go away in the afternoon, but that didn't make them any more pleasant, especially when the neighbors were mowing their lawns or drilling or something. One morning it was somebody banging around on *his* roof. He went out front and yelled up to the two workers who were building a huge structure on top of the duplex. "What the fuck are you doing!?"

"Are you talking to us?" one of them asked.

"Yeah, what the fuck is that?"

"The billboard." They worked for a company that installs advertising space for home owners to rent out. Barry came out when he heard the commotion, he didn't like the idea either so he called the landlord, who said he'd be right over.

Carter wanted to make a good impression, so he put on the black suit. Bill, a balding computer programmer who rented the house out almost as a hobby, showed up wearing shorts. To him the issue of the billboard was not as pressing as

94

the issue of why this guy he'd never seen before was staying in his house. Carter explained who he was and the situation with Mark. Barry backed him up and that seemed to give him some legitimacy, he wasn't just some random squatter. Bill insisted as the property owner it was his right to lease the roof out to advertisers. He also said he'd been meaning to come by to ask why the rent had been paid in cash. He leashed his golden retriever on the porch and came inside.

It turned out Mark's lease was over at the end of the month. If he wanted to stay he'd have to sign a new one and be willing to pay $90 more rent per month. Bill was sympathetic about the missing persons case so he offered to work up a provisional contract for Carter – he would pay month-to-month at the new rate until Mark showed up again to sign a new 12 month lease. He said he'd bring the contract in a week or so, but he'd have to do a credit check also.

"That might be a problem. I don't got a lot of credit. I have some cash and an empty checking account. I just started a new job, though. I get my first paycheck tomorrow."

"Where do you work?"

"I work for Mattress Warehouse."

"I thought they went out of business?"

"Yeah, they're working on it. I hold the 'going out of business sale' signs. It's a two week job."

"What will you do after that?"

"Well, I might do this tax service thing, they said it might be available."

"Tax service?"

"Not as an accountant or anything. Another holding a sign gig. Seasonal work."

"But you don't have a full time job?"

"Look, I'm gonna be straight with you, Bill. I'm a felon. I just recently got out, my brother Mark was gonna help me get a job, but now he's missing. I'm trying to be a good guy here, believe me. I'm looking for work, I'm looking for my brother. When I find him I want him to still have this place to live in. Then I'll get the fuck-- excuse me, I'll get the *heck* out,

95

and you won't see me again."

"Well, I don't know what to tell you. I might be willing to skip the credit check because of your situation, but you have to have a regular paycheck. Otherwise I can't risk you."

"I got money saved up, I can pay you a couple months in advance." He pulled out his roll.

"In cash?"

"Yeah, cash."

"No, I don't think I feel comfortable with that. Just get that bank account, get a full time job…"

"If I can do it that's what I want to do. I'm trying."

"Okay, I'll call you next week. If you have a job then I'll bring over the contract. Otherwise--"

"Fair enough."

When they shook on it Carter tried to slip Bill a twenty. Neither knew what to say as Bill awkwardly handed it back.

# 12

ON SATURDAY CARTER was supposed to meet Abbey at Aerohead for lunch. He beat her there, and he was antsy. On a whim he decided to call Dante.

"Hello?"

"Hello sir, this is a courtesy call from Carter Chase, I am calling regarding the Niketown incident. According to our records you have an outstanding balance on our give-me-my-fuckin-money-list. When can we expect your fuckin money?"

"Fuck you, Carter."

"Okay. Later bud."

When Abbey arrived she seemed way more manic than before. Pessimism was seeping in.

When the waiter took their orders he asked Carter if he wanted the usual, and he said yes.

"The usual?" Abbey asked, surprised.

"Yeah, I've been in here a lot."

"I thought you hated this kind of food?"

"The food's okay, it's the price I don't like. I could go get a burrito for cheaper and be just as happy."

"Well, some day you'll have to come with us to some of the other ones. This place is good, nomi is good but..." she leaned in and lowered her voice, "there are better."

"Oh, I've tried all your favorite places. Remember the list?"

"The list?"

"I had you write down the places you and Mark like to go. That's what I've been doing the last couple weeks, looking into those. No luck yet, nobody's seen him. But I've been rotating through them all, eating my meals there every day, keeping lookout."

"Every day?"

"Just about. I got a temp job now. I'm saving up to buy a Greek salad."

"You've really gone to all of them?"

"Yeah, you can quiz me. I could tell you the cheapest thing on the menu. At nomi you get a spread for $5.50, that comes with one pita. Breakfast menu you can get a scone for $5. They seriously got a $12 bowl of oatmeal though. Fucking ridiculous. The Castle is hard, the closest things to affordable are appetizers, the organic deviled eggs with bacon or the olive poppers with sour cream, $9. They have a burger at that place but it's $15 and doesn't even come with fries. You gotta get those on the side and they call them 'frites' to justify charging $6.50. I'd usually go for a soup or salad, which is $10."

"That's not that bad."

"Yes it is. But Ella's is worse, a salad is 11 bucks on the lunch menu. If you want dinner you're fucked. Cheapest is the salmon belly tartare, fourteen bucks. I'm not sure what tartare is."

"Did I put Shear Elegance on the list?"

"Actually I couldn't find that place. I thought I had the address but it turned out to be a hair salon."

"Oh no, that's just the theme. It looks like a hair salon in the front lobby but you go through into the dining area."

"But they had, like, hair dryers, and racks of shampoo and stuff. Hair clippings on the floor."

"I know, it's great! I think you would like it there, real down to earth kind of food. How 'bout the Bubble Lounge? Did you go there?"

"Lunch menu, creamy tomato soup with brown butter croutons, $8.50. Dinner menu I avoid because either you only get an appetizer or you pay $24 for lentil cakes. When I realized that the first time I pretended I already had dinner and ordered from the dessert menu. But it's $10 for apple sorbet and it's the size of a ping pong ball. Maybe smaller."

"The wait staff must love you."

"Not at first, but they recognize me now and

remember I tip well. It's not the money, it's the principle. It's not right to charge an extra fifteen bucks for little designs squirted around the plate."

"You and Mark are very different."

He laughed. "Can't deny that. I still don't get why you'd want all that specialized knowledge about nothing. I mean who gives a shit? It's food. Some is better than others, but you don't need to fucking dissect it and draw a diagram. It doesn't make any sense. What good is it?"

"Well, what good is specialized knowledge about robbing a Nike store? Or *trying* to, I should say. At least he was doing something he loved."

He watched her hand. She tried to stay cool, but by the violent way she gestured as she talked he could tell she was pissed, offended by what he said. "Well, shit. I'm sorry. I didn't mean it as an insult."

"I know."

"By the way, thanks for not wearing sunglasses."

This time she smiled. "I knew you'd bring that up again."

"You know they got one now, it's just one glass the size of a dinner plate with a little hole in the middle you stick your nose through."

"Yeah, I have one of those."

"I wouldn't be surprised. Anyway here's the deal. Dante doesn't know anything. But somebody does. Is there anyone else, anyone at all, who had a problem with Mark?"

"I already told you about my ex, Josh Steed."

"Oh, I talked to Josh Steed. Now he knows to leave you the fuck alone. Other than that he knows nothing."

"Are you serious?" she laughed. "I thought you were a positive individual now!"

"I didn't hurt him. Just his guitar. Anybody else?"

"Not at all. We don't have a huge amount of friends, but no enemies."

"That's too bad."

"What about you, Carter? I don't want to—I mean let's

99

be honest. You *are* a guy with enemies. Maybe it wasn't this Dante but maybe someone else who has it in for you, somebody you stole from or something."

"Nah. I mean-- we're talking about petty crimes. You steal money from somebody's register they're gonna be upset, but they're not gonna track you down years later and kidnap your brother."

"What about people you knew in prison? Were there, like, gangs that had a grudge against you or whatever?"

"You know, that's actually a myth. Most cons get along really well in prison. I mean you have your egos and everything, guys'll turn into drama queens every once in a while but in the end they're brothers. It's more like a sports team than anything, guys kinda look out for each other and work together. They're really cool in there."

"Are... are you serious?"

"No. But nobody really had it in for me that bad that they'd come after my family."

She didn't give him the courtesy of smiling at his joke. "No other enemies?"

"No, not really. Maybe one other guy from a long time ago. If it's somebody's enemy it's not one of mine. We'll just have to keep canvassing I guess."

When they were done Carter said he needed a ride somewhere. He kept referring to a folded up computer printout from Google Maps. He had Abbey slow down as they passed a small house with very young kids playing in the front yard. A shirtless guy with a huge beer belly was waxing a yellow Corvette in the driveway. Carter reached over and honked the horn. The guy squinted at him, showed no sign of recognition as he walked toward them.

"Okay, keep driving."

Carter had her turn around and drop him off downtown. "Who was the guy with the car?" she asked.

"Some dude I knew after high school. Guy I firebombed."

"Wow," she said. "*Wow.*"

100

He'd been maybe 20 or 21 at the time. Carter's friend had had a girlfriend who'd cheated with that guy. They'd felt his actions required a response, and blew up his car. These days he didn't look like a guy who would hold a grudge, and if he'd had a kidnapping plot against Carter he'd probably know what he looked like. Not surprising that it was a dead end, but Carter knew he should follow any lead he could think of.

"Well, I'll keep snoopin. Call me if you think of anything."

He had her drop him off at Tony's hot dog stand so he could get something to eat.

"Any news on your brother?" Tony asked as he grilled the onions for Carter's usual Jumbo with cheddar.

"Nothing," Carter said, looking at Tony's collection of photos taped up around Mark's missing flyer. They showed Tony and his wife in front of waterfalls, his son at the Grand Canyon, some minor celebrities posing in front of his stand. A skinny kid was squinting, staring at the menu board, but didn't look like he was really reading it.

"You know what you order?" Tony asked.

"Still deciding," the kid mumbled, his voice cracking.

When the kid finally grabbed the tip jar he got maybe six feet down the sidewalk before Carter got a grip on his basketball jersey. He yanked him by the shirt, pried the jar from his grip and pinned him to the ground with one hand. He looked at Tony and shrugged. Almost as an afterthought he elbowed the kid on the back of the skull. Completely unnecessary, but he didn't put much weight into it. Just hard enough to rattle the brain a little.

Carter watched the kid shake the cobwebs off, get up, yell "Fucker!" and run away. He felt like an asshole for doing that, since he had been that kid before. But Tony was a good guy, he didn't deserve to be robbed. And anyway, getting caught had been a good thing for Carter - it made him go completely straight, or plan to at least. On second thought maybe he should've dragged that little shit by the ear to a cop. Maybe next time.

Carter had already paid for his hot dog, and Tony tried to give him the money back. "No Tony, come on. It's no big deal."

But Tony wanted to reward him. He offered cash. He offered a check. He offered free hot dogs for life. He offered free hot dogs for life *and* a check.

"You know what – I don't need money. The whole point is that kid was trying to take your money. *Your* money. You keep it, not him, and not me. But if you want to write me a check this is what would help me. You make up a check, like a paycheck. Just make it look like I'm your employee. I won't deposit the check. I just need it to show to my brother's landlord, because I have to have a regular job or he's gonna kick me out. I don't need a reward but if you want to reward me that's what I could use."

Tony didn't like it. "No, I don't think so Carter. No faking. I can't reward honesty with lies."

"Okay man, no problem."

"How 'bout I give you job for real?"

"No no no, I'm not trying to guilt you into a job."

"No guilt. No guilt. I work too much. Have to stay in business. But I'm an old man. My wife wants me home more. I need someone I trust to fill in some days."

Carter laughed. "Somebody trusts me, that's a new one. Yeah Tony, I might do that."

# 13

ON SUNDAY THE 1<sup>st</sup>, two months after Carter had waited on the corner for clues and instead found a new calling as a dog poop vigilante, he went back to 4<sup>th</sup> & Jackson. The Post-It note had had "Sun. 3<sup>rd</sup>" crossed out with "Sun. 1<sup>st</sup>" written next to it. At first he thought it was a correction, but looking at the calendar he realized it was three different dates and the second one must've been cancelled.

Surprise surprise - he wasn't having any more luck. If Mark had really meant to meet somebody here on those dates then that somebody forgot, or never confirmed, or knew Mark wouldn't be there, or was invisible.

Carter was glad the dogwalker he'd assaulted didn't come by. That was probably a mistake what he did. He'd rather not get into it again.

The only thing going on was the kids in the skate park. When one kid rolled across to his side of the street he recognized him as the one with the Minnie Mouse board.

"Got a smoke?" the kid asked.

"No."

"Hey, you're the dog shit guy, aren't you?"

"No. I get that a lot, though."

A silver Mercedes was coming around the corner onto 4<sup>th</sup>. It wasn't going fast and had no problem stopping for the kid, but the driver laid into the horn like it was life or death.

"Eat a dick!" the kid yelled, holding up his middle finger and rolling very slowly into and then out of the way of the car. The driver honked again. As he passed the kid lifted his board above his head and brought it down hard against the trunk of the car. It made a small scratch at most, but also a loud sound.

The car's tires squealed as it skidded to a halt. The

driver left the engine running, put the emergency brake on and got out. He was somewhere in his 40s, receding hairline, well-dressed, trying to look younger.

"You want to damage my car, huh? You want to damage my car? Why don't you do it again, huh? I dare you to fucking do it again."

"You don't want me to do that," the kid said.

The passenger door opened. A good looking young blond in a shiny dress popped her head out. "Paul, come on!"

"What's the matter? You're afraid now? You seemed pretty fucking tough before. Do it! Hit the car again."

"Okay, man," the kid said. "If that's what you want." He lifted the board up, swung it down again, but this time hit one of the metal trucks square on the edge of the trunk, then slowly swiped it across, making a nasty foot long scrape in the paint.

That might not have been what the driver was expecting. He put his hands on his head and looked like he was gonna cry before he lunged at the kid. Carter made a move to intercept, but was beaten to the punch by the blond, who had gotten out of the car and thrown herself in the middle of it like Pocahontas. Or like a girlfriend who has to do this a lot.

"Paul! Come on! It's a kid! We're leaving!"

"Is that your wife or your daughter?" the kid asked.

The driver screamed like the Incredible Hulk, paced around in a circle a few times, then got in the car. It took a couple tries to turn over the engine, but when the Mercedes started to move forward again the kid hit the trunk a third time.

The car jerked to a stop. They could hear muffled screaming inside, but the doors didn't open. When another car pulled up behind and honked, the Mercedes peeled out and took off like it was a drag race.

The kid only half smiled with pride as he pushed off and dropped into the cement ramp. The other skaters were all laughing in disbelief, and Carter was too. That kid needed adult supervision.

*Oh, shit!*

"Hey Minnie Mouse," Carter shouted down into the cement bowl. "Come here."

The kid skidded out. "What? You saw what happened. He started it."

"It's not that. I want to ask you something."

The kid didn't seem interested, but he wasn't intimidated either, so he rolled over to Carter.

"I already told you, I just *like* Minnie Mouse."

"It's not about that either. Your name is Jimmy, isn't it?"

"Y-- Oh shit, are *you* Mark?"

"No, I'm Carter, I'm Mark's big brother." Jimmy stared blankly. "I mean, he's my younger brother. He was supposed to come meet you here last month, wasn't he? And then today. The Big Brother program or something?"

"Boys and Girls Club."

"Well, I'm sorry he didn't show up. He's missing. I knew he was supposed to meet someone here so I tried to come tell them, but I didn't realize it was you."

"That's okay, I didn't really want to do it anyway."

"Well, he's a real good guy. When I find him you should meet him, he would be a good influence."

"Fine."

"But, you know, until then if you need somebody for, somebody to spend time with, an adult... but somebody that's cool, you know, that understands—"

"No offense, but I don't think my mom would want me spending time with you, man."

"Yeah, you're right."

# 14

THE NEW JOB seemed to pacify Bill the landlord, at least for the time being. Carter felt comfortable enough to ask if he'd sent people to check on the place, people that might park their cars in the alley and spy on him, and Bill clearly had no idea what he was talking about. Carter also asked about the paint cans. Bill confirmed that he'd given Mark permission to paint some of the walls. The billboard didn't come up.

Carter got to like staying in Mark's neighborhood. It had good bus access, it was walking distance from downtown, but it was quieter than downtown. You still heard drunks out after the bars closed at two, but mostly the young women screaming and crying at their boyfriends instead of the older, angrier men. In the mornings there were women jogging everywhere, usually pushing a baby cart, walking a dog, or both. There weren't any obvious junkies hanging around, and only one homeless guy who would come through sometimes with an old beat up radio and a comb sticking out of his afro. There was a café on the corner but it was usually too crowded for Carter, especially on Sundays when families would be lined up outside waiting for brunch. These weren't his type of people, but it was probably best for him to stay away from his type of people for now on. This would have to be his home.

At first they did shifts together so Tony could show him the ropes. It didn't take long for Carter to pick it up. Selling hot dogs was surprisingly fulfilling for him. A good hot dog he could understand more than a raw fennel salad. And compared to most of the jobs he'd taken before it was almost artistic. He got pretty good at making the dogs and took pride in his craftsmanship. Within two weeks he had developed what he considered the perfect hot dog which had sauerkraut, pickle relish, hot mustard, a little bit of garlic aoli, some horseradish, topped with melted sharp cheddar cheese and caramelized onions. The masterstroke was when he started marinating the dogs in apple juice and a little apple cider vinegar with some chopped sage leaves mixed in. He called it the Mark Chase and tried to push it on all his regulars – the guys from the bank, the bike messengers that hang out on the benches by the espresso stand, the skateboard kids, the guys from the advertising firms in the Rossi Building, the war protesters, the war protester-protester who stood across the street from the war protest every day holding different flags and playing with his radio-controlled tank.

One day when he came to work there was a giant Mountain Dew advertisement behind the cart.

"What the fuck is that?" Carter asked.

"I don't know," Tony said. "It's just here in the morning." Someone or something had scrubbed the wall of all remnants of its usual wheat-pasted mini-posters and replaced it with a street-side billboard. It was so huge and gaudy it was hard to ignore. But life would go on. And Tony would start stocking cans of Mountain Dew.

Every once in a while Carter had a customer who actually knew his brother. They always seemed worried when they brought it up. It made no sense that he hadn't come home yet. They all pretended to be optimistic but probably agreed it looked grim. And they all gave Carter that look.

Tony let him eat hot dogs on his lunch break, but he tried not to fill up at the stand because he still had his patrol to do. Every day that he could he visited a different food enthusiast joint. Every couple weeks he would try the hospitals and a homeless shelter or two. He still couldn't figure out how to use the internet on Mark's phone, so he'd go back to the duplex to use the computer, occasionally finding a new missing persons site to post the picture on. A lot of them required subscriptions, though, and he didn't like to shell out.

Abbey had tried going to the media, but since they weren't married and didn't have any kids it wasn't all that compelling. A few bites with neighborhood news blogs, not much.

Visiting the restaurants was hard on this new schedule. It varied, but a lot of times Tony liked him to work late afternoon and early evening. Most of those places weren't open for breakfast. Sometimes if there was a concert or a nighttime baseball game Tony would have him come late and keep the stand open at night, so those nights he could have an early dinner.

But the more he worked for Tony the less he started to make the rounds. Before long it was mostly just on his days off that he would go to the restaurants. When he did it made him feel closer to Mark, made him feel like he was at least trying, but he had a hard time even remembering why he was doing it. What did he think might happen? He'd overhear some yuppie talking about Mark and mentioning where he was? Or Mark would come into nomi for dinner, Carter would be sitting there eating a slow poached hen egg and say "Hey, it's me, your brother, why don't you come home?" and everything would be all right? If Mark was still alive he'd probably snapped and started a new life in another state, or he'd come down with amnesia. He'd be on the streets somewhere, you think he'd come into one of those places? You'd have a better chance of running into him at the Jack in the Box or the homeless shelter.

That's what Carter was thinking one night when he got off work. So instead of going to The Castle for some deviled eggs he went to Jack in the Box for a Double Bacon and Cheese Ciabatta Burger. It tasted like shit, and he started to wonder if eating all those expensive appetizers and side dishes had ruined his life.

Back at the duplex he wanted to put on the Dr. Pepper's Lonely Hearts Club Band promo CD, but couldn't figure out where a CD would go into the computer. Luckily it turned out not to be a CD at all. It was made to look like one, for nostalgia's sake, but it was printed with a password and instructions which he followed to download the album onto

Mark's iTunes. He realized he hadn't listened to the Beatles in years, but it seemed like all the songs were fading out early. He remembered them being short songs but not one, one and-a-half minutes.

He took the mail out of the box. A bunch of junkmail postcards inside a circular. As he was about to dump it all in the recycling an envelope, like a bill, fell out. He was surprised to see his own name peering from the transparent window. *What would they be sending me?*

He tore it open. Some kind of credit card deal or something? It was one of those mock checks they use for special offers, made out in his name for the amount of $26,586.22.

But *wait a minute*. It looked awfully—*no, that's impossible. Isn't it?* He stared at it, turned it over, stared at it again. But he was sure it wasn't a mock check – it was real. It was a quarterly commission check from the Pepsi Affiliate Program.

"God damn, Mom," he said.

On the iTunes, "A Day in the Life" faded into background music for four cheesy voice actors who discussed cool, refreshing Dr. Pepper in mock Liverpool accents.

# TWO

# 1

THE MONEY WOULD change everything, he figured. It would give him more time to investigate. It would light a fire of guilt under his ass, making him think more about his parents and what they would've wanted him to do about Mark, and about his life.

He felt loyal to Tony, didn't want to leave him high and dry, and he felt like having a regular job was what his parents would've wanted, and the discipline he needed. So he kept working part time at the hot dog stand, mostly early shifts now. In his spare time he knew he would have to step up his game.

to do
1.  find Mark
2.  ~~money~~
3.  revenge?

The day he cashed the first Pepsi check he decided he owed Mom and Dad's graves some new flowers. A long row of cars was parked along the road to the north section of the cemetery where the family plot was located. It looked like Mom wasn't so lonely anymore. There was a crowd there – centered down the row from the Chase family plot, spilling over to all the graves in the area. Busy day at the cemetery, but it wasn't Memorial Day, was it?

He had a hard time finding the marker under these young people, mostly teenagers, sitting Indian style. The odor of incense and clove cigarettes barely covered the stench of their unwashed clothes, which smelled worse than a bunch of convicts in the summer.

Some of the kids were crying, a few of them were singing. A pouty girl with facial piercings and candy-colored hair was using mom's grave as a stool.

"Excuse me," Carter said, showing her the flowers. She managed to work even more disgust into her frown as she moved out of his way.

Carter looked at the other deadbeats sitting on his family plot. "You guys gypsies or something?"

Nobody answered. He figured he should ignore them anyway and get to the mourning, but he was inexperienced and wasn't really sure what he was supposed to do. He tried nodding his head and closing his eyes, but he felt self conscious with all these kids around. When he looked up another dozen or so were filing in from the parking area, heading straight for him. Three teenage girls approached, clutching some kind of collage tributes they had made.

"Here it is," one of the girls sobbed.

"No, this is mine," Carter said.

"Could you sit down? You're blocking everybody's view," said another girl. When he turned to answer he noticed what had attracted the new girls: the screen on his mother's grave was showing a slow motion clip of Kris Krijole playing an acoustic guitar, part of a stirring memorial montage ending with the hashtag "#PepsiRemembersKris." And suddenly it all made sense – Krijole was buried here. Mom shared a neighborhood with a celebrity, and her sensors were registering all his visitors.

*Well how about that*, Carter thought. There was money in the Kris Krijole business after all. Just not in the shoes. For such an unlucky bastard, Carter had really lucked out on this one.

As he left the cemetery he happened to glance into one of the parked cars and as he made eye contact with a middle aged man wearing a suit and tie Carter realized he had a big grin on his face that might not be appropriate to share with other people visiting the deceased. They quickly looked away from each other and Carter felt like an asshole.

The thought of coming home to the duplex and its

114

giant rooftop billboard of creepy local newscasters depressed him. As he was trying to decide where to go for dinner it occurred to him that having money in the bank might be a good enough reason to start eating entrees. He could go to one of Mark's hangouts and have some kind of goat meat or something like that. Foam all over it, things frozen with liquid nitrogen for some reason, crazy food enthusiast shit. He could find out what the hell fennel was, maybe.

When he walked into Shear Elegance he understood what Abbey had been talking about. What he'd mistaken for a chintzy hair salon before was really a high class restaurant made to *look* like a chintzy hair salon. The illusion was very detailed, right down to the beat-up *People* magazines in the waiting area and the Nagel-esque glamour woman line drawings on the window decals.

He had something called the red wattle pork chop. It sounded like a dish that fancy people have while pretending to be regular, so it would be a good beginner dish for a regular person pretending to be fancy. He sat facing the door – not because he really had to watch his back like that, but because he read about it in *The Autobiography of Malcolm X*. As he nibbled on sauerkraut he watched a soccer mom type in sweats come in and try to get a manicure. The woman at the front desk – authentically dressed like a hair stylist, not a maitre d', he felt - snottily dismissed her. The poor mom never got the message that this was a restaurant, just that they didn't do nails.

The pork chop was okay; the feeling of not having to worry about the price was fantastic. To compound the point he ordered a chocolate ganache from the dessert menu (he was even less sure what "ganache" meant after it arrived) and then walked over to Mobb for drinks.

A great way to celebrate a windfall – sitting alone at a bar wondering how to find out if your brother is alive. The tables were crowded with groups of people young enough to make him feel old. Most of them sat scrolling through things on their phones, not talking to each other.

He chose his drink by looking for the most expensive special on the cocktail menu, which was called a Double Penetration (pineapple infused vodka, white rum, Midori, Triple Sec, cranberry liqueur, organic blood orange peel). He should've guessed from the description that it would come in a silly looking hurricane glass with a fat red straw, a sugared rim and a cucumber slice cut into the shape of a flower. As he took a sip through the straw a woman who was buying a pint of Guinness down the bar looked at him and smiled. She held up her phone and took a picture of him. His expression didn't change because he was already frowning.

"I'm sorry," she said, picking up her glass and moving to sit next to him. "It just made me laugh - a guy that looks like you with a drink that looks like that. I'll erase it if you want. It's cute though, look."

He looked and still didn't smile. "It's fine," he grunted. He pulled the straw and cucumber off and started drinking straight from the glass.

"I'm Margaret, by the way."

"Carter."

"Nice to meet you."

"Yep."

It was no act. Carter wasn't in the mood, which amused Margaret even more. "What do you do?" she asked.

"Besides drink? I'm in advertising."

"Oh really? So am I. Which firm?"

"Well I—I'm not—it's not what it sounds like. It's hard to explain."

"Oh yeah?"

He finished the froofy drink and waved down the bartender. "Can I just get some Jack Daniel's?" The bartender nodded.

"You got me," he said. "I'm full of shit. I just got my first royalty check from an advertising thing. I'm not really in that industry, per se."

"Okay."

"In fact I don't really drink that much either, I'm not

sure why I said that."

"Well, I don't know if you want to be in advertising anyway. It's a ridiculous industry. I'm pretty good at it, though."

"Where do you work?"

"Here, I'll give you my card." She pulled a business card from a pocket inside her purse.

He read it out loud. "Mind Bandit?"

"So embarrassing. It's a stupid name."

"You do ads on TV and stuff?"

"Sometimes. And posters, web campaigns, different things."

"Well, like, what was your most recent one?"

"We've been doing prescription drugs..."

He finally smiled. "That looks like a great drug, I gotta get my doctor to prescribe that shit to me!"

"I know, it is pretty weird. We do other stuff too, though. We did all the bumpers for the film festival this year."

"Okay. Culture. That's good."

"And today we got this healthy candy bar thing, I don't know. It's not a very exciting job I realize now that I'm talking about it out loud to a stranger."

"I'm not big on commercialism and name brands and all this."

"Oh yeah? Didn't I hear you order Jack Daniel's by name?"

"He's different."

Another young woman approached, giddy from the drinks. "Let's go get dessert, bitch!"

Margaret looked over to her group of friends, then back at Carter.

"You want to go with us?" she purred, her voice suddenly higher in pitch, like a little girl asking Dad for a Barbie.

"No, I don't."

She wasn't used to rejection. She laughed. "Well, it was nice meeting you, Carter."

# 2

WHEN HE GOT BACK to the duplex around 2:30 am, something was on the porch: a basketball, with a piece of paper taped to it. "Carter - I thought you would want this. – Mason." The ball that Mom had had for him in the car when she died. It was in good shape considering what it had been through, and it seemed like a pretty good one. Not that he would know. He probably hadn't touched a basketball since high school gym class.

Carter turned the back porch light on and carried the ball to the small square of pavement. He stood in place and just dribbled. It felt good. He wasn't about to start busting out the Harlem Globetrotters routines, but he could control it okay. When he played as a kid he was decent at maneuvering, he just didn't have the confidence or the skills to get the ball in the basket. He would usually pass to someone else, and they made him feel he'd contributed by saying he was good at assists.

The team was great – in fact, undefeated in the four years he played – but he knew it was more despite him than because of him. He was the second worst player on the team. He comforted himself with the knowledge that he wasn't as bad as this kid Nate Cobrin, who was taller than him but clumsier. They would all laugh about the time the ball rolled right to Nate's feet and he just stood there and stared down at it. It never occurred to Carter until now that when he wasn't around they probably said similar things about him.

As he bounced the ball these memories came flooding back. He thought about Mack McGinnis, a notorious opposing-team coach who was more than once ejected from a game for throwing shit fits at the referees; about the end-of-season parties in the back of the pizza parlor, where everybody got trophies and played video games; about waiting outside the gym during a thunder storm because practice was cancelled due to a power outage and he had no way of calling Dad to pick him up early.

Why did he play, anyway? Was it only to be with his friends, or did he really enjoy it? Maybe he would've liked it better if he was on a weaker team, where he didn't feel as much pressure and shame. Maybe if he'd kept playing he would've gotten good. He had flashes of what the world looked like from the height he was then, of the feeling in his stomach during a game. He thought about standing on the sidelines, kind of wanting to be put in, kind of hoping he wouldn't be.

So young then. He could've done anything with his life, he just would've had to figure out what. As he dribbled faster he felt his cheeks burn and his eyes fill with tears. He didn't even know what specifically was upsetting him. He was just overwhelmed by emotions he could never explain.

What did it mean that Mom wanted to give him a basketball now? He could never know what she would've said to him about it, but he could still find meaning in this gift. It was her last message to him. By leaving the ball in the car she was saying *remember this? You used to enjoy this. You weren't the best at it, but you weren't the worst. You just need to keep practicing. You just can't give up. You have to set your mind to it, and not worry about what other people think about you, and you'll do fine.*

And also *keep your eye on the road in case of sudden stops.*

He woke up feeling glum, stumbled out to the backyard to dribble his basketball, got more depressed. Next thing he knew he was on a bus coming back from Target lugging a Spalding portable hoop that weighed about 85 pounds.

Back at the duplex he realized his brother didn't own a toolbox, or if he did he couldn't find it, and he needed a hammer, some wrenches and a metal file. So he had to get back on the bus and find a hardware store.

120

Five hours and some mild aggravation later he had assembled a ten foot regulation-ish hoop that he was worried would tip over, but it seemed to be doing okay so far. He stood back and looked at it, exhaled, and felt better. He missed his first three layup attempts, but he'd always been better at assists anyway.

He had planned to do some canvassing, but it was getting pretty late now, and shooting free throws was addictive. But he was missing more than seemed reasonable. Something just felt... wrong. How could he concentrate on the search for Mark when the vibe at his house was so off? *Vibe*, he thought. *Who am I, Barry?*

That wasn't fair. Barry wasn't burning incense or playing didjeridoo right now, he was in the front pulling weeds like a responsible citizen. He saw Carter and he said "hello" like a normal person, and "Nice hoop."

"Yeah, thanks," Carter said, distracted. Standing on the sidewalk looking at the house, he figured out exactly what the problem was. He stood with his arms folded staring at it until Barry came over and joined him.

"Atrocious, isn't it?" Barry said.

"Yep."

They must've changed the billboard while he was at work yesterday. The newscasters were gone, now it was a dramatic shot of a sweaty runner wearing Nikes.

"I talked to Bill about it again," Barry said. "He won't budge. Says we should be thankful, that it keeps the rent down."

"Yeah. This one's killin me, though," Carter said. "I got personal issues with Nike."

"Well, you should. They're not exactly kosher when it comes to worker's rights and all that."

"Don't worry," Carter grunted. "I'll take care of it."

A few minutes later Barry interupted his yardwork again to look up at Carter paint-rollering over the billboard.

When he was done there were no Nikes, only a perfect rectangle of Spring Fresh green.

"It actually looks kind of nice," Barry yelled up to him.

When Carter was back down on the ground Barry ran up to him laughing, happy to be sharing in the mischief. "I don't know how I'm gonna lie to Bill about this one, but I'm sure gonna try."

Carter made his next five free throws, all net.

# 3

IT KEPT NAGGING AT HIM that the canvassing wasn't really doing anything. He enjoyed touring the different restaraunts every day, and got more and more opinionated about their menus. But none of the waiters had seen anything, he wasn't getting any new leads, nothing. Enough time had passed that there was some turnaround, and some of the staff at these places had never even served Mark. Carter was afraid it would seem like he just liked going to these places to eat food.

One Thursday he was doing an early shift for Tony, and right in the middle of the lunch rush there was Margaret from the bar. He didn't recognize her in her business clothes and sunglasses, but she was laughing in a way that made it clear she knew him. "So you *are* in advertising," she said, nodding to the wall of Mountain Dew logo at his back. Flirtatious, he thought. Not mean.

"It's Margaret, right?" he said.

"That's right. Good memory."

He talked her into a Mark Chase dog, and briefly explained the backstory behind the name. "Oh, I'm sorry to hear that," she said. He thought her sympathy sounded more sincere than most. He kind of liked her. He even made small talk while he grilled the onions.

"What's the name of your company again?"

"Mind Bandit. Right down the block, in the Rossi Building. Top floor."

"No shit? I've been up there. There's a consulting firm up there, right?"

"Yeah, JML. Our neighbors. There's a bunch of us crammed up there."

"I get a lot of my customers from that building."

"Yeah, I think you've sold me a hot dog before, now

that I think about it."

"Well, I do what I can."

The eye contact she made as she left made him feel something he hadn't in a hell of a long time. File that away for next time he jerks off. Jesus, why hadn't he gone with her that night? Something was wrong with him.

Next in line was a kid with a baseball hat pulled down low over his eyes. He was shaking one leg like he was really impatient or had to piss real bad. As he stepped up to the cart Carter grabbed his hand, bent his wrist back and held the hot metal spatula to his forearm like he was branding him.

"Aaaah, fuck!" the kid screamed.

"Next time I see you it's palm down on the grill, you piece of shit. Get the fuck out of here."

"What did I do?"

"You grabbed the tip jar. But I grabbed it back. Remember?" He held up an elbow and patted it with his other hand.

"That wasn't me."

"Don't lie to me."

"Come on man, I'm not gonna steal from you. I just wanna sell you some change."

"I'm not making change for you."

The kid held up a plastic bag full of coins. "I don't need you to make change, I already got it. I just want to trade it for bills. The other guy does it for me sometimes. Please, man?"

"Look at the menu board. All the prices end with two zeros or a fifty. What would we do with your bag of nickels and dimes? Get the fuck out of here, junkie."

"Fuuuuck, man," the kid whined, holding his burnt arm as he limped away.

After work Carter met Abbey at Bubble Lounge. Neither had much new to say about the search for Mark. Carter mentioned that he was thinking of hiring a private investigator now that he had money. Not much else to report, but dinner was nice.

"So you're full time looking for him now?" she asked.

"I still work a few shifts at the hot dog stand."

"And between that and the Pepsi money..."

"I don't really need to work, I just like it. I don't know why. It's the only time I like talking to people."

"Well, that's good. We can't just stew about this thing 24-7. Sometimes you need that sense of community to help you through it."

"Yeah, you know, I think I get the food thing now. Why food is so sacred to you and Mark."

"Yeah?"

"It's the last independent expression in this culture. The last neighborhood business. We don't have the corner store anymore, or the hardware store with, like, old Pete or whoever that knows what you're working on and what type of nails you need. There's no bookstore, record store, video store. Nothing local, or individual. But what Tony has there, or a little diner or café somewhere, that's the only place you can come in anymore, everybody knows your name."

"Yeah, like Cheers," she said. They laughed.

The waiter refilled their water glasses. "Thanks, Tim," Carter said.

"You're welcome, Carter."

"But that's why it's important. Restaurants are the last business that can be just some guy opens up one place, wants to make food the way he wants to make it, the way the people there want it, not answering to some corporate headquarters somewhere. It's a little bite of freedom."

"And later you shit it out. That's what you said before."

"Yeah, I stand by that. You still shit it out. But it's freedom."

She'd never heard him talk so much, or seen him order a full dinner. They enjoyed the black cod and muscovy duck breast with preserve and forgot about the private investigator.

125

# 4

CARTER PRETENDED not to know anything about the damage to the billboard. When Landlord Bill pointed out the coincidence of the paint matching the color that Mark had purchased for the walls, Carter just acted confused. It was a ridiculous defense, but it worked, because Bill was too timid to press him on it, and was happy to at least have the rent paid on time.

It helped Carter's case a little when some of the other billboards on the street started to get painted over in different colors. He wondered if that was Barry's handiwork, but Barry denied it. "People like to borrow a good idea," he said.

And he might've been right. Carter started to notice it here and there around town – various posters and billboards neatly painted over, just like his billboard. It looked very pleasant, just simple squares and rectangles of various hues and shades, gently replacing what was once visual clutter. The best one he came across was a rotating billboard – someone had managed to paint over all three sides of every piece so that every 30 seconds or so it would change from turquoise to salmon, salmon to yellow, yellow back to turquoise. And there was that little moment as the pieces were mid-turn when it would create the illusion of the colors dissolving into each other. Beautiful.

Funny to think they might've gotten the idea from him, but it was probably a coincidence. Either way, it was becoming a concern for advertisers. One day Carter had to open the hot dog stand an hour late because the Mountain Dew billboard had been painted over during the night and workmen were already replacing it with a glossier, more paint-resistant version.

That day, during the lull between lunch hour and dinner time, the kid with the bags of change hassled him again.

"Hey look man, can I buy some bills from you, please? No nickels or dimes this time. It's all quarters."

"I told you we don't use change."

"It's just quarters though. You use quarters, right?"

"I have enough."

"Come on, bro. It would really help me out."

"Yeah, it would help you out 'cause your dealer won't let you pay in quarters."

"No, man. It's for food. They get mad when you pay in change."

"I'll sell you a hot dog for change, I won't sell you bills. You're telling me I burned your arm last time, you came back again, and it's not for drugs?"

"Come on, man."

"Quarters are legal tender. If it's a legitimate business they have to accept them. If it's not a legitimate business, I don't know - find a dealer that plays a lot of Ms. Pac-Man."

"Shit," the kid whined. He turned his back and exhaled dejectedly, his two worn plastic bags of dirty coins slung low, weighing him down, his cross to bear.

Carter was heating up a dog, to be ready for the next customer, or maybe just to keep himself occupied. It was a slower day than usual. The sky was grey and the tourists were staying in. Not many actual customers wandering the streets right now, mostly low lifes and on-duty city employees. There weren't even any skateboard kids in the park around the corner from the Subway across the street. A middle aged man in a baseball hat who had been milling for quite some time suddenly got upset and ran across traffic to a car on the corner being examined by a Parking Enforcement Officer on a Segway. Carter watched the man's animated movements as he argued with the officer and tried to take his stylus away from him. When the man angrily took off his hat and spiked it on the sidewalk Carter laughed, then thought maybe he recognized him. And his black Camaro. Where did he--

Oh, that's weird – he'd seen this guy in the cemetery.

The guy he'd made eye contact with. Was he in a black Camaro then? It was a black Camaro that Carter had seen in the alley behind the duplex, that drove away quickly when spotted. And now one parked by where he's working.

This motherfucker was following him!

Carter threw down the tongs and sprinted down the block. The stranger saw movement in his peripheral vision, turned to see Carter and panicked. He grabbed the ticket from the officer, hopped in the Camaro and scrambled for his keys. Carter pounded on the trunk of the car as it pulled out, almost sideswiping another car and causing a flurry of angry honks. Carter hesitated on the side of the road, not wanting to get hit by the other cars. The light was green and the Camaro took off.

"Whoah whoah whoah," the officer said, holding his hands out in front of Carter to block him. "What's this about?"

"That motherfucker's been following me!"

"Okay now, watch the profanity please, sir."

"That *gentleman*'s been following me. What's the license plate number?"

"I… I didn't get a chance to get it down. He just ran up and started yelling at me."

When Carter returned to the hot dog stand the dog on the grill was blackened and smoking. He picked it up with the tongs and dropped it in the trash. The kid with all the quarters was still standing there. "Everything okay, man?" the kid asked.

"It's fine."

"Okay," the kid said, and walked away.

With a sudden jump, Carter checked the till – still there, and the tip jar too. He glanced around at his backstock and his tools. Nothing out of place, nothing stolen at all, from the looks of it. He couldn't believe it.

"Hey, hold on," he called after the kid, but the kid didn't hear him, just kept going.

# 5

DETECTIVE ROGERS WAS in the middle of getting his ass chewed out by Sergeant Cobbs when he got the call. He probably wouldn't have taken it otherwise.

It was Carter Chase, the pain-in-the-ass brother of one of his missing persons cases. Chase was rambling about being followed around, kept saying the name of a witness.

Rogers made Chase repeat the story a few times, both to humor him and to delay returning to the Sergeant's lecture. On his tablet he jotted down the highlights: black Camaro, the name of the witness, apparently a PPE.

"Okay, thank you sir. Give me a call if anything else comes up," he said.

Much to the detective's dismay, Cobbs listened to the whole thing, and asked him about the case. More of his infamous micromanaging. The Sergeant was a nice guy, really, just difficult to work with if he thought you were taking short cuts. He was very opinionated about how things should be done, and Rogers always dreaded him sticking his nose in like this.

"Are you going to talk to the PPE?" the Sergeant asked.

"Probably not. Would you?"

"Probably not."

"There's not really any meat here, sir. We get a couple of these a month. He's an adult. He's allowed to take off for a while. There's nothing that suggests foul play."

"You checked cell phone records, bank transactions?"

"No."

"Why not?"

"Didn't need to. I talked to the guy's employer, and he had put in for a vacation. Turns out his mother had just died, traffic accident. So the guy's in mourning. The girlfriend who filed the report hasn't even known him for very long, and was out of town when this all happened. The guy I was just talking to, the brother, is a felon, recently released. Very paranoid. I figure the guy just wants to be left alone."

"You still need to check the records. Don't be lazy."

"You're saying I'm wrong?"

"No. You're probably right. But you need to confirm that. Check those records."

# 6

CARTER HAD THE weekend off. He thought about checking out a new Greek place up north that was supposed to be pretty good, but paranoia about being followed made him want to get out of town for the day.

He got up early and caught a bus to downtown, waited to transfer on 3rd Ave and journeyed down the freeway. Saturday traffic was maddening, and when he got to the Park & Ride he'd missed his transfer. He had to wait 45 minutes for the next minibus, which crawled slowly through town before getting on the interstate and heading east. By the time he reached his destination, a stop at a freeway interchange, he felt like he'd just gotten off a long day of work.

At least it was good weather for the hike. Sunny but with a breeze, not too hot. The trail went through woods, over a small creek, around a hill with a nice view of the water. In some spots the trees above were so thick it started to look like night had come already, but then he'd come to an opening, sun beams shining down and lighting up dust and spiderwebs.

The quiet was a shock to the system. No cars, no radios, no people, not even airplanes flying over. He could hear birds, a little wind, an occasional twig breaking on its own, or a leaf falling. He could hear the creek running! He couldn't remember the last time the world around him was so peaceful. If ever.

There was a spot along the cliff where the trees had been cleared and a wooden structure like a porch was built so hikers could safely stop and enjoy a view of the coast. He rested for a few minutes, trying to let his mind be empty, looking out on the glimmering surface of the water and the big rock out there. It was shaped sort of like a bird. He reached for his wallet, pulled out the tattered photo he'd printed of Mark and held it up. This was the same view, the same place. He was on the right track. He could almost feel his brother's presence.

On the other side of the hill the trail did meet up with a winding road. There was no sidewalk but he didn't hear any traffic coming and thought it would be safe to walk along the edge.

He followed the road about a mile and a half before he came to a small beach community. There was a little café with a weather worn, hand painted sign. Shops selling wind chimes, paintings of seagulls, things like that. Mom would've loved it. Dad would've tolerated it. He felt like a tourist at best, an intruder at worst. The locals would know he didn't belong here. As he was wondering what people around here were like he caught himself and remembered that he was just outside of town. It just *felt* like a thousand miles away because this was not the type of place he usually sought out.

He continued down the street, paying attention to the numbers on the houses. The address he was looking for he'd found in an email from a few years back. Mark had reserved a cabin here, and the message from the owners made it sound like it wasn't his first time. This would've been before he met Abbey, so their photo on the trail seemed to indicate this was a place he came to a lot. Or at least a few times.

It was a pretty big cabin with two garage doors on the front, and a wooden stairway that went up the side. The driveway led to an open space that went right up to the beach. Carter walked around to the back to get a look at the place.

What was he looking for? He didn't even know. Maybe just a sense of the places Mark liked to go, other than the damn restaurants. The restaurants were getting to be too much. They weren't getting him anywhere. Sometimes he thought they put him in a mind state where he could understand Mark better. Other times he thought they just kept him distracted, in denial about the dead end he'd come to in his search, and in his life. Maybe he had to get the fuck out of the city, go walk in dirt, touch a tree, talk to a bird.

He took his shoes and socks off, felt the dirt and grass on his bare feet. He knew it was weird, but fuck it. It felt good.

He pictured Mark standing on the porch, drinking a cup of tea, looking out at the morning fog, peaceful shit like that. He wanted to stand where Mark would stand, so he walked up the stairs onto the back porch.

Well, there wasn't fog, but the view was nice. It was kind of a big place for just one or two people. He stepped up and looked through the sliding glass door. There was a small table there, a nice place for breakfast with a view. A little kitchen with a counter. To the right was an opening into a living room with a fire place, a pile of wood, a bunch of chairs. He saw the back of a head peeking up over one of them.

"Mark!" Carter yelled, knocking on the glass. Inside a dog growled, ran to the door barking angrily.

The chair spun around, but it was not Mark. A short haired woman, older than Carter, jumped to her feet and ran out of the room. She looked terrified.

Mark was down the side stairs and running down the middle of the road by the time she came outside. He knew as soon as he saw her eyes that she was going for a gun. She held him in her sights as she stood in the driveway watching her big brown Labrador chase Carter, clutching his Bob Barkers, trying not to step on anything sharp.

Actually, maybe he should keep going to the restaurants. The sun was still up when the cab arrived at the duplex, but he wanted a drink. He took a shower, realized he was starving, got right on a bus and headed to that Greek place.

He justified it to himself as more canvassing. It was the same owners as Ella's, if Mark was just in hiding he'd still be a food enthusiast, maybe he'd come here. He'd want to check out the promising new restaurants too, right?

On the way downtown, when his bus was stopped at a light, Carter saw an inspirational sight out the window. Dante was on the sidewalk, walking with some dude Carter had never seen before. The guy must've been in his mid-twenties, but he dressed like a 1980s elementary school super-nerd – a playground bully's wet dream. He sported a bowl cut, thick, round glasses, a puffy red coat and sky blue highwater corduroys. *Holy shit*, Carter thought. *Dante's a big brother too. Taking care of retards.*

He thought about what he knew of Dante's family. He couldn't remember hearing anything about any developmentally disabled relatives. Even if this was a cousin or something it was a surprise to see them out and about together. Dante was laughing and talking with the poor guy, having a good time. He didn't look uncomfortable or embarrassed at all, just hanging out with his buddy.

A wave of emotion washed over Carter. He got goosebumps. He could feel his eyes on the verge of misting up. To see a person like Dante, who had never been anything but a selfish prick for as long as he'd known him, doing something to help a disabled kid – it was a real shot in the arm, like seeing Israelis and Palestinians jump-roping together. If *this* could happen then *anything* could happen. If this could happen, there was no excuse for the world not to become a better place, for him not to become a better person. If Dante could be a nice guy then Carter could be too. Niketown was a long time ago. It was time to move on. There was no reason to let his situation hold him back. He could get a real job like his brother had, make his parents proud, wherever they were.

He laughed when he realized what Dante's friend was wearing on his feet: brand new Kris Krijoles. Gotta find *someone* to wear those ugly fuckin things.

Leto, the Greek place, was crowded and noisy. Just as Carter was silently grumbling that he couldn't get a table against the back wall, he sensed someone approaching behind him without a plate or a pitcher of water. Reflexively, he reached back and grabbed a wrist – thin, feminine.

"Hi Carter," she said, surprised but not threatened by

his grip.

"Margaret," he said, turning and looking her in the eye unreasonably long before letting go. She placed her hand gently on his back.

"This place is great! You haven't ordered yet?"

"No," he said, setting down the menu. "Recommend anything?"

"Yes, I recommend you come sit with me and my friends. We ordered family style, they keep bringing out more pitas, Berkshire pork kebabs, leg of lamb, squid..." He looked over at the long table she was gesturing toward. Her friends looked back, smiling, some waving hello.

As he turned to tell her "No" his head was near the low neckline on her blouse and he accidentally said "Yeah, sure."

Without exception, Margaret's friends were friendly and welcoming as she introduced them: Dawn, Danielle and Thom from Mind Bandit, Polly who she'd known since college, Craig and Pete from JML Consulting.

"How do you know our girl here?" Craig asked.

"I rejected her at a bar," Carter said. They all laughed.

"That's true!" Margaret said. "He's not lying!"

"Oh yeah, at Mobb, right?" Danielle asked. "When we were celebrating getting the Doctor-King account."

"Yeah, this is the guy, right?" Dawn asked.

"Dr. King?" Carter tried to interject.

"Yeah, this is the guy from the picture!" Thom said. "The guy with the cocktail!"

"Wait," said Carter. "You showed them that picture?"

"I'm sorry," Margaret said. "I used it in a presentation, as inspiration for a proposed campaign. We would've restaged it with a model, but the client chose to go in a different direction anyway."

"That was *such* a cute picture!" Dawn said.

Margaret stopped a waitress passing their table. "Excuse me, we added another member to our party, could you put that on our bill?"

"Of course. Thank you for telling me."

"And could you get him some Jack Daniel's?"

Thom saw that Carter was surprised. "Don't worry, it's on the expense account," he said.

"Best boss ever!" Margaret, Dawn and Danielle said in unison.

"Best *neighbor* ever," Pete said.

Carter liked the spreads, the squid kebabs with the crushed chili, the chicken dipped in yogurt dill sauce. When the conversation turned to his occupation he did okay explaining the Pepsi situation. They even seemed impressed by his need for honest work at the hot dog stand.  "Holy shit, I knew I recognized you!" Pete said. "The Mark Chase Dog! The Mark Chase Dog is the shit!"

The young woman who was refilling Pete's water glass had a look of recognition at the mention of the Mark Chase Dog. She caught herself, not wanting to eavesdrop, but Pete noticed. "You know the Mark Chase Dog?" he asked her.

"What's that?"

"Oh man, you gotta try it! It has, what? Sharp cheddar, garlic, horseradish, sauerkraut... what else, Carter?"

"Caramelized onions, pickle relish, hot mustard. And a special marinade for the dogs. That's the secret."

"It's the perfect combination of flavors. We all work in the Rossi Building, and they sell it at the hot dog stand near there. This guy invented it."

"He named it after his brother, who's missing," Margaret added.

The server stopped where she was. "I know a Mark Chase. He was a regular at Ella's when I used to work there part time."

"Yeah, that's him," Carter said. "That's my brother. Have you seen him?"

"No, not since I left there. But I remember-- I'm trying to think if this was the last time I saw him..."

"How long ago?"

138

"I want to say it was my last week working there. So, around the end of May."

"Okay, and what happened?"

"Well, he was really upset because he said some guy was following him. He saw the car parked out front, cancelled his order and left. I remember it because he was in there all the time and he'd always been so nice and laid back, I never saw him worked up like that."

"What kind of car was it?"

"I don't know, a black sports car? I don't know the brand."

"Camaro?"

"Maybe. It sounds right. I don't know cars."

"You never saw him again?"

"No, but like I said I stopped working there."

He drank the Jack Daniel's fast, gave the waitress and Margaret his phone number, and got the fuck out of there.

# 7

ABBEY AND MASON both knew that being summoned to the duplex meant something serious. Carter had even neatened up the place and vacuumed. Mason still brought snacks - a platter of vegetables with Dana's home made dip, and a chilled six-pack of new Pepsi Smooth – as if it was a casual get-together. Mason and Abbey did the whole "nice to finally meet you" thing and they all discussed their opinions of the new soft drink. Eventually they gave up beating around the bush, and the guests sat solemnly on the living room couch for Carter's presentation.

"So this is what we know," Carter said. "Shortly before Mark disappeared, he complained of being followed by a man in a black sports car. Since then, I've also been followed by a man in a black sports car. He was watching me right here at the duplex, parked in that alley out there. He was watching me at the cemetery visiting Mom and Dad. He was watching me while I was at work. At least three incidents."

"So call the cops," Mason said.

"I did. They had nothing."

"So you think this is the guy that did something to Mark?" Abbey asked.

"Well, it's possible that he thinks he's still following Mark. I've been staying in Mark's house. Sleeping in his bed. Going to all his favorite restaurants. Having lunch with his girlfriend. Even using his cell phone."

"Yeah, but you don't look much like Mark," Abbey said.

"And I'm sorry but Mark would *never* work at a hot dog stand," added Mason.

"Okay, I agree, so yes. I think this guy did something to Mark, and I think he wants me next."

"So what do we do?" Abbey asked.

"I have some thoughts. But that's not why I wanted to talk to you two. I just want to make sure you guys know what to do if you don't hear from me for a while. Mason, I want you to take this number. That's Detective Rogers. If you don't hear from me for a week or more, call him and tell him everything you know. And tell him to go fuck himself. Or that you're gonna sue the whole department, something like that.

"Okay, I guess I can do that."

"Abbey, if *you* don't hear from me for a week or more, I want you to come here to the duplex. There's a shovel leaning up against the house in the backyard. Stand with your back touching the back side of the basketball hoop, take five steps – *big* steps I guess, since you're shorter than me - and start digging until you hit a paint bucket. Take the money inside the bucket, put it in the bank, and write a check to Bill for Mark's rent, and pay for his… clouds or whatever. If you ever find Mark, he'll still have a place to stay, and if there's any money left over you guys can keep it for letting me stay here and use his bed and everything."

After he got them to leave he went out back and shot free throws for about half an hour to get his mind straight. Then he called Margaret at her work and asked her out for drinks. That was the real reason he'd cleaned up the house – just in case. He'd also bought a bottle of Moet, ready to put in a bucket of ice, the expensive cubes by Evian. He bought candles (the scent he chose was "Tear Drops on a Love Letter") but felt embarrassed about it and left them in the bag on the counter. Margaret seemed surprised and happy to hear from him, and suggested a place and a time (around nine).

Next, because it was the best idea he had, Carter called Dante. It wasn't easy convincing him to meet, but he let Dante choose the spot and said to bring the same guys that beat him up before, or whoever he wanted. "Don't worry, I still don't have any friends," Carter said. "I'll come alone."

Dante chose The Dock. Carter was very respectful and didn't bring cigarettes or a bat this time. Dante brought both

Nike brothers, the young musclehead guy he recognized from the beating (turned out his name was Russ), and another one just like him named Ivan. They all sat behind Dante at a separate table facing Carter, and behind them was Jason Fleming, working the bar. He had no distractions, because the only customer was the old man Vic Clements, at his usual booth.

"Thanks for meeting me," Carter said. "I think we started off on the wrong foot last time."

"No, we started off okay," Dante said. "Then you fuckin'... were doing something to my window. And then started calling me and threatening me all the time."

"Well I'm sorry. I had you figured wrong."

"No shit you did."

"I really didn't trust you, but then I saw something that made me realize you've changed since I knew you. Maybe you've grown up more than I have."

"What are you talking about?"

"Well—" He looked at the guys at the muscle table. "Can we—look, you *know* I'm not gonna get the jump on you. Can we have a little privacy here? This is kinda personal."

Dante thought about it. He turned to his friends. "Why don't you guys wait for me outside. Jason'll get you if there's any trouble."

"Thanks," Carter said. He leaned in and lowered his voice, embarrassed to be talking about something that legitimately moved him. "I saw you from my bus the other day, over in Belltown. You know, with your friend."

"You did?"

"Yeah, I did. And... good for you, man!"

"Oh, you recognized him?"

"Recognized?"

Dante seemed confused. "Why do you say 'good for you?'"

"I just never seen you hanging out with somebody like that before. That's cool that you do that now. My brother was gonna start doing that actually, right before he disappeared.

143

But just with a younger, troubled kid, you know. Not disabled."

"I don't think I-- *who* did you see me with? I thought you were talking about Ian Blair."

"Is that his name?"

"Yeah, you know, the drummer for the Dangers?"

"I don't know what that is."

"The Dangers. It's a band. They're getting really huge, actually. They just got their song on a Visa commercial, it's a big deal."

"Wait, are we-- this is the retarded guy you're talking about?"

"Retarded guy?"

"I'm sorry. Not retarded. Mentally, uh--"

"What are you talking about?"

"I saw you taking care of him. In Belltown."

"You must've-- I don't know about any retarded guy."

"The guy with the bowl cut, highwater pants, puffy red jacket?"

"That *is* Ian. He's not a retard! Oh shit, I'm gonna give him some shit about this!"

"The guy with the bright blue pants? And the glasses? You're telling me that guy's not retarded?"

"That's Ian, that's the drummer for the Dangers!"

"I don't know what that is, I just thought you were volunteering or something."

"Why the fuck would I be volunteering for a retarded guy?"

Carter got angry. "You're telling me a guy dresses like that on purpose?"

"That's-- they dress like that. Some of those indie rock guys."

Carter was incredulous. "Why would they do that? Do they ride around in wheelchairs too? Is that fashionable?"

"I don't know, man. All I know is--" Dante stopped, looked up at Jason. He hunched over and started talking much quieter. "All I know is he paid me $1,000 for those Kris

144

Krijoles he was wearing."

"You're shitting me. You can't take advantage of a retarded guy like that. It's unethical."

Dante laughed. "No, some of these rock guys, they collect kicks, and they love Kris Krijole because he's dead and everything. Do you know how rare those shoes are?"

"Of course they're rare. We stole most of them."

"Yeah, and these bands have all kinds of money from advances and touring and shit. And of course as soon as Ian starts wearing 'em everybody else wants 'em and the price goes even higher. So I've been meeting some of these guys... I used to sell them pills and shit, but I get so much more selling them shoes."

"Financially, or spiritually?"

"I gotta say both."

"Well, at least you're finally getting some use out of those fuckin things."

"The Kris Krijoles, yeah. I might start selling other ones too. The Fleming brothers have been collecting for years, you know about that. You should see this storage space. We got the Krijoles there plus the overflow from their collection. It's fucking incredible."

"That's cool."

"Ian's a size 11, same size as Kerry, you should've seen him eyeing those fuckin things when I took him there!"

"Size 11? Seemed bigger when he was kicking me."

"Yeah." There was an awkward pause, as both realized it was time to cut to the chase. Dante did the cutting: "So, uh, what's up, Carter? What's this about?"

"Look, I know we're not exactly in good standing. But I'm coming to you as a man and telling you that I need your help."

"Help with what?"

"There's a guy that's been following me. Guy in a black Camaro. Remember, I thought it was you?"

"It *wasn't* me."

"Right, it was this other guy. I think he knows what

happened to my brother."

"Okay."

"So basically you and your guys, I just want you to follow me around until you see a black Camaro, and then help me grab the guy."

"And what do *we* get out of it?"

"Well, what your buddies get out of it, they get to beat the shit out of a guy, maybe trash a nice car if they're interested. They enjoy that type of activity, right?"

"Sure."

"And what *you* get out of it... if you do this then we're even for Niketown. You won't owe me money, you won't owe me shoes, I won't guilt you for, you know, what you did."

"Wow."

"It'll be easy, man. I'll be going around town, tonight, he'll probably show up. Maybe as soon as we leave. I wouldn't be surprised if he's snooping around out there right now."

"I know, it sounds like a good deal, I wish I could do it. But those guys," he tipped his head in the direction of his muscle out front, "those guys would never go for it."

"How do you know until you've asked them?"

"I know," Dante said. He leaned back in his chair, looked up to the bar and nodded. "I'm sorry buddy. As far as I'm concerned me and you are good. I wish it was up to me. But I can't speak for everybody. You're on your own on this one."

As he got up, Carter didn't have to ask him what he meant. He knew it before he turned around and saw that Jason had put in a mouthguard to protect his precious teeth.

"I really am sorry," Dante said. He left out the front door as the others filed back in. Jason came around, flipped the sign to "closed" and locked the front door. Russ and Ivan ran at Carter and grabbed him by the arms, pinning him back down in his chair, turning it around perpendicular to the table so the Nike brothers could get in his face.

The brothers stood in front of him, laughing, tssking, drawing the foreplay out sadistically. Finally Kerry said, "This is for my brother's tooth!" and punched Carter in the mouth. His lip bled, but he'd had worse. Recently. From the same guys.

"Thish ish for—" Jason slobbered through the mouthguard, before pulling it out and starting over. "This is for my brother's Lebron PS Elites!" He put the mouthguard back in and hit Carter on the top of the skull with a pint glass. It didn't break as he probably intended – on impact it slipped from his hand and rolled across the table - but it hurt like a motherfucker.

Another trip to the emergency room would interfere with Carter' plans for the evening, so he decided not to just sit there and take it. He brought his knees up to his chest and kicked Kerry with both feet. Kerry grabbed his legs, absorbing the impact, but Carter pushed off of his rib cage, leaning the chair backward until it fell to the floor. In the scramble Kerry and Russ both lost their grip, Carter rolled backward and got control of Ivan's arm. He twisted it, kicked him in the back and let go.

But he wasn't about to stand there and take on all four guys, and they were blocking his path to the exit. He ran back into the room, behind the bar, started taking bottles off the shelf and tossing them.

Jason was the only one to followed him. Even in the heat of battle the other three didn't feel comfortable entering an employees only area. Carter knew better than to just shoot in on a wrestler, so he kicked him hard in the side of the leg first. As Jason winced and turned, Carter deftly lunged the other way and got an arm around his neck. He elbowed him on the top of his head and could've kept doing that, but when he looked down at the bar equipment he couldn't resist wrapping the hose from the bar gun around Jason's neck and spraying Coca-Cola in his eyes. As Jason clutched at his face Carter fish-hooked him, then pulled his bottom jaw down, spraying into the space between his upper teeth and the mouth guard, causing him to gurgle and choke.

When Carter ran out from behind the bar Russ and

Kerry were dancing around, fists up. Ivan was closest to him, holding up a bar stool, ready to toss it. Carter bum rushed Ivan, reached up over the stool and pushed a hand in his face. Nobody saw the knife at his side – he'd pulled it from behind the bar because it was quicker than getting his own from the leg-holster. With a half dozen quick slashes he butchered the faux-leather seat of the stool and shoved Ivan about a foot backwards by the cheek.

"Let it go," Carter said, switching to a triangle stance and a show-offy fencer's grip. Ivan grimaced, spit, then gently set the stool down and adjusted it until it was about where he'd found it. He backed away with his hands up in surrender, and the other two did the same.

"Geeeeeeez!" old Vic said from his booth, then took another drink from his glass.

Carter didn't want to steal, so he tossed the knife behind the counter. He flipped the sign back to "open" on his way out.

148

# 8

MARGARET LEANED AGAINST the railing, looking out at the city lights reflected on the water. She'd made extra effort to look good, wearing her favorite blue dress, adjusting it for the highest quality booty presentation. It amused and embarrassed her to think how attracted she was to Carter. With her friends she pretended there was some kind of irony involved – *can you believe I'm going out with a guy like this?* – but really the attraction was deep. It wasn't like she'd ever had a thing for bad boys. But he was just so different from the men she knew from college and from the firm, and it made her crazy.

It was kind of weird that he didn't have a car, and that he wouldn't let her pick him up. But he was almost exactly on time, according to her phone. So he was responsible.

His lip was scabbed over, his face kind of puffy, but he smelled freshly showered. She decided not to ask. More mystery.

She'd chosen Surface, a 21-and-over aquarium on the waterfront. It was a popular club, pretty crowded wherever there were tables, but large enough that you could wander down long hallways to look at tropical fish and the bottoms of sea lions in relative privacy. Depending on how the night went she could get closer to him or have some distance.

There were three bars and the same amount of DJs playing different styles of music, all of them kind of obnoxious. She always wondered how the fish felt about the thunderous bass rumbling through their miniature eco-systems. A huge octopus, crammed lifelessly inside an arch-shaped tank, didn't seem to give a fuck. Carter went up close and stared into its eye, nodding as if in solidarity. She thought it was adorable.

She didn't mind how bad Carter was at small talk. It was part of the mystique. She could tell he was pained asking "How's the ad biz treating you?," so it was sweet that he made the effort. She complained about her data plan – *when the hell are they gonna upgrade that network, am I right?* – and he grimaced like she was farting at him. He was more responsive when she asked about his brother. There were new developments, he said, but he wouldn't elaborate.

He had a strange look to him. A little weathered for his age. Mean looking brow, but with gentle eyes. She noticed one pupil looked bigger than other, but he didn't seem high.

A lot of the guys here dressed kind of the same. Shiny button-up shirts with pointy collars, expensive jeans designed to look like regular jeans, carefully groomed hair, lots of product. Some had a way of dressing up to look dressed down. White undershirts and slicked-back hair, but had they ever entered a garage in their lives? So much thought and resources put into looking tough, and Carter couldn't be bothered. He was effortless. He was just… Carter.

Was it some primal thing? A big, strong man to protect her? She'd never had this before. And she never knew how to do this girl stuff. Always felt like such a clumsy spaz. But tonight she could tell she looked good because she could see them looking at her, eyeing her round ass through their thick-framed non-prescription glasses. But not one of them tried to talk to her. Carter scared the shit out of them. They backed off when he walked toward them. She made him order the drinks. People would get out of his way.

He seemed distracted, always looking around at the other people. She asked why. He said there was someone he was worried he might run into.

"The guy that did that?" she asked, pointing to his lip.

"No," he laughed. "Nothing like that. Don't worry about it." She didn't, and eventually he didn't seem to either.

He knew weird things about the fish – names, habits. He said that the bigger clownfish were the females, that they were the dominant sex. In fact the most dominant male in a

150

group would *become* female. Like, *okay, if you're going to be in charge we better promote you to a lady.*

"Are you making that up? How do you know that?"

"I used to read a lot when I was, uh-- when I was younger."

They talked about where they grew up, where they lived now. About their families – he just had two brothers, no parents left – and how he ended up getting his bills paid by Pepsico. They bonded over their favorite places to eat. He knew a lot about food. And Abraham Lincoln. And prison.

She always gravitated toward talking about work. It seemed like he was interested, so she kept going. It was easy when she was working on a campaign like this, one that genuinely excited her. The client was a new phone OS that could browse with limited advertisements, and her spots took inspiration from the Rectanglers, the local street art movement that painted over billboards and other advertising. A lot of her co-workers worried about Rectangling, because it was an entire art movement based around opposition to what they did for a living. But she thought it was beautiful. She thought they could use it.

"That's funny," Carter laughed. "I did that too. Didn't want a Nike billboard on top of my house so I painted over it."

"That's actually how it started. Somebody painted over a Nike billboard, and the other artists followed his lead. They wanted to basically censor consumerism, and the visual clutter of urban space. Make everything more simple and pure." She'd done a lot of research.

"Well, I didn't know that was a thing, I just did it."

They went around in circles for a while before it sunk in that Carter was the unknown vandal who had sparked an important artistic movement. His story fit with everything she'd learned about the time frame and specifics of what inspired the Rectanglers, but he didn't seem interested in taking credit. It didn't even seem to occur to him.

She knew it was true. It just felt right. Her date was an artistic pioneer. No wonder she'd gravitated toward him, against all natural inclinations. This was meant to be. This was perfect.

She had to drive herself home, and she had to work in the morning, so after two drinks she just had ginger ale. But she was doing things she wouldn't usually do with a guy she was just getting to know. Putting her hand on him more than necessary – his back, his arm, his neck. Leaning into him, pretty blatant with the cleavage. Prolonged eye contact. Was she a slut, she wondered? It didn't matter.

She told him it was getting late, that she had to go home and get to bed. A pause. A chance to back out. But she dove head first: "You want to come with?" The little girl voice. A pained look, ready for rejection, for embarrassment.

He smiled and went with her to the car.

She tried to play it cool. It was hard to drive, she wanted him so bad. She put her hand on his thigh. Started creeping down. He was hard. She wanted to punch it, just tear ass through town. Or skid to a stop on the side of the road and unzip him. What do they say? Think of baseball. Season opener at KFC-Taco Bell. Nice, sunny afternoon. Sitting in the foul ball seats, mitt at the ready.

She wasn't supposed to do this. This was bad. She had to slow down a little. She wasn't going to stop herself. But geez, Margaret. Have some dignity.

At the traffic light on 1st, before passing under the viaduct, she figured out what to do. Talk to him about business, about art. About the relationship they could have. Show him that they weren't just animals fucking. They shared a future. They were *collaborators* fucking.

"Before we go to my house, can I show you something?"

"Sure," he said. Very polite.

Luckily there wasn't a game that night, so she found a parking space under the freeway. She grabbed him, kissed him deeply, clung to him. He was into it, but when she pulled away he let her go.

152

"Don't worry Carter, I'm not leading you on," she said. "You're going to get laid tonight if you want to. But I need to show you this first." When she turned from him to open the car door she winced, horrified at the words that had come out of her mouth. But they were honest.

It was a pedestrian overpass that went to the ferry terminal, but you could stop and get a good view of the water. That wasn't what she was interested in. Her spot overlooked a warehouse and some other old buildings – an art supply store, some kind of factory, some rundown offices for non-profits or something. She had discovered it during her morning jog last weekend. Her mind was percolating ideas for the campaign, she stopped to tie her shoe, looked up and saw this.

The side of the warehouse facing the bridge was used for wheatpasting blocks of posters. The technique had been invented by small-timers, independent record labels and concert promoters, but had since been co-opted by corporations to promote new movies, major albums, energy drinks, anti-perspirants, whatever. Margaret herself had had a hand in campaigns like that. On their website Mind Bandit boasted about their "grassroots-style street promotions."

But at this particular time, on this particular wall, there was no promotion going on. Someone had carefully painted over all of the posters – not just with one color, but with an array of them, carefully covering each individual poster like tiles in a mosaic or patches on a quilt. It looked gorgeous in the dark, light bleeding onto it from a billboard on the roof, which itself was painted over. Beyond it, each of the well-lit billboards down the block was Rectangled in a different shade: pearl azure, burnt sienna, lemon, moss.    "Look at this," she said.

He seemed to like it. "Have you taken a picture of this?" he asked. "I gotta show my neighbor."

She held up her phone and took one.

"Now turn around," she said. On the other side of the bridge were buildings that the Rectanglers had not gotten to yet. A Maker's Mark billboard. A Gatorade. A local news team. A new coffee drink at McDonalds. Lights and clutter and crap everywhere.

"Imagine this, but worse," Margaret said. "A dystopia, like *Blade Runner*. Corporate logos on everything. Not real ones, but believable. Billboards, posters, buses and taxis driving by with ads on them, giant pictures on the sides of buildings in lights." She put her hands on his shoulders, rotated him to look back in the other direction.

"Suddenly, one of the billboards fills in, mint green. And then another one eggshell. Another one canary. One by one the ads are covered over, and it morphs into this. All the visual noise becomes gentle and beautiful. The sun comes out. Just, a rolling wave of colors. And we slowly pull back and we see you standing on the roof of a building, with a paint roller in your hand, and you sigh or something. Maybe you smile. A job well done."

When she looked back at him her stomach dropped. It was that horrible feeling when a pitch has failed, but you only realize it during the silence afterwards. She thought she was hitting it out of the park, but really it was in the stands, out of play. And she was in the stands too, sitting there with her glove, and it was right to her but she still didn't catch it. She stepped on some guy's foot and she fell on her ass and got ketchup from somebody's garlic fries all over her arm. And from the look on Carter's face he might as well have been thinking about baseball too. She could practically hear the comical slide whistle of his boner going flaccid.

"This is an ad you want to do?" he asked.

"It's an ad I'm doing. It's already approved. All except for the part about you. But I know if we can prove that you were the founder of Rectangling they would want to use you."

"Nobody's using me."

"No, I mean, *you* would be using *them*. Think about it. You would get paid so much. Way more than the Pepsi thing. And then it would keep paying off. Every time the spot airs, you get residuals. And more than that, think what it does for

154

your future. It establishes you as an important artist, a historical figure even. It gives you credibility that you can parlay into other projects if you want to, or if you need the money."

She knew she had blown it. "Not interested," he grunted.

The walk back to the car was the worst part. Maybe she should've flung herself from that bridge. It would've felt about the same.

"I'm sorry," he said. "I really do like you. But I'm gonna walk home now. Don't take it personally."

She didn't protest as he walked away. She knew she never should've stopped here. She'd overthunk it. She was too in-her-head. Should've just followed her beastly instincts.

Such a sweet guy, too. So sensitive. Her friends would never believe it, that a guy who looked like that had rejected her because he was offended by her plans to monetize his art. Even a total purist you'd think would've hit it and quit it. *That was great, honey. But I'm an artist. Don't call me again.*

He stepped out into the street between two parked cars, and didn't see the one that was trying to pull out. Margaret held up a hand and opened her mouth, about to yell to him, but was too late.

It was okay, the car stopped in time. Carter looked unphased at first, but suddenly flew into a rage and started yelling at the guy, "motherfucker" or something, she didn't hear it clearly. The car backed up, slamming into another parked car, then burned out and took off. For a second she thought it had hit Carter, but it hadn't, and the next thing she knew he was holding onto the back of the car, dragging along behind it like a water skiier.

It was such a strange sight that her mind couldn't wrap around what it was for a second. It told her he was stuck, the car had hooked onto him somehow, and he was being dragged by it. But of course that wasn't what was happening at all. He was flipping out. He was attacking a moving car. On purpose.

*Holy shit,* she thought. *I almost hooked up with a maniac.*

# 9

CARTER COULD NOT *BELIEVE* he was turning down sex after this long. Oh God, he was so ready for it, too. He was really into Margaret, but that shit about the cell phone ad made him want to throw up. Until that conversation he didn't even know he *had* an artistic vision to sell out, but the suggestion of it was like a punch in the balls. Which was not something he was into.

He came out from under the freeway cursing to himself, not really watching where he was going. He stepped into the street between two parked cars before he realized that one of them was trying to pull out. The driver saw him in time and jerked his car to a stop. Carter held his hand up in a "sorry" wave, but the driver didn't look mad – he looked terrified. It was the guy!

"Motherfucker, I *knew* it!"

In a panic, the driver put the Camaro in reverse, stepped on the gas and crushed the back end into the Toyota behind him, giving it a little push. Carter still had to leap out of the way as the car tore into the street, tires squealing and smoking. As the driver tried to U-turn Carter ran after him. He looked at the license plate – crooked and loose from the collision – and had the presence of mind to know that he would never remember the number. So without thinking he reached out and grabbed onto it with both hands.

As the car pulled him part way down the block he danced his feet around to keep his balance, leaning backwards to put his weight into pulling the license plate off. As something snapped behind the right side of the plate his feet couldn't keep up anymore and he was being dragged, the top of his Bob Barkers scraping along the concrete. He'd have to let go if he didn't want to get killed, but he could feel that it was only connected by one bolt. The plate cut into both of his hands as he twisted it back and forth, trying to tear out whatever was holding it. Suddenly he fell flat on his face and skidded along the road, scraping his chest, his elbows and the sides of both hands bloody.

The whole thing was over in a few seconds, and he was left in the street with the wind knocked out of him. Margaret was standing above him.

"Carter! Are you okay?"

"I'm fine," he said. "I wanted to talk to that guy."

The Camaro was long gone. But he had the license plate. He stood up, put the plate under one arm, and wiped the blood from one palm onto his shirt like he was wiping off a little mud.

"I'll take you to the hospital," Margaret said. He wouldn't let her, and he could tell she was relieved by that.

Carter felt justified in making a scene as he stormed into the police station "Where's Detective Rogers?" he yelled. An officer he didn't know grabbed him by the arm, but a Sergeant named Cobbs came in from another room and said, "It's okay, let him go."

"Is Detective Rogers here? I need to talk to him."

"He's not here right now. Are you Carter Chase?"

"Who are you?"

"I'm Sergeant Cobbs," he said, extending his hand. "You wouldn't remember me, but we met once before, years ago. Is this about your brother?"

"Yeah."

"I know a little about the case. Follow me."

"There," Carter said, tossing the bent license plate onto the Sergeant's desk. "That's the prick I was trying to tell you guys about, the one who's been following me around. I guarantee you he's the guy that got my brother. White man in his forties, brown hair, driving a black Camaro, there's your license plate number. Exempt plates, what does that tell you?

What the fuck is going on here? And don't give me the runaround 'cause you don't know, I could've already taken pictures of that thing and made copies and sent it to various organizations and what not. You don't know."

Cobbs looked at the plate on his desk, frowned, exhaled. "Take a seat, please," he said, pulling a chair up to his desk. Carter sat down.

The Sergeant put on reading glasses and opened his laptop. "Give me a minute to go through the case file," he said.

There was a tense silence as Cobbs scrolled through, squinting a little as he read. Occasionally he would raise his eyebrows in mild surprise, or nod his head a little if something he read confirmed a suspicion he'd had. Eventually he looked up at Carter.

"As I'm sure Detective Rogers has already told you, there's not much we can do in a case like this. I know it's easy to believe the worst, but in most cases like this the person just doesn't want to be found. They just want to go off somewhere and sometimes they want to start a new life, but usually they come back and everything is fine. And you know, that's their right, there's nothing illegal about that. But it's upsetting to their loved ones who don't know what's going on with them, so I understand why you're worried.

"In this case there are good signs and there are bad signs. I asked Detective Rogers to check your brother's bank records. He found a checking account, a savings account, two credit cards, a debit card in Mark's name. Other than automatic billing, none of the accounts have been in use for months. No card swipes, no checks, no deposits. No large cash withdrawals before the disappearance. The last transactions were just groceries, restaurant bills, things like that."

"That sounds bad."

"It does, but if he's trying to hide, maybe he has some money stashed away somewhere. Or maybe he's using an account that we don't know about. Here's the other thing. He had automatic billpay for a cell phone plan, so Rogers checked the records on that, and the phone has been in use fairly frequently since the time of Mark's disappearance. All local calls. Let me show you the list here and see if you recognize any of these."

"Oh, those are all me. He left his phone in the house, I didn't own a phone, Abbey asked me to take it so she could get ahold of me."

"I was afraid it would be something like that. So that doesn't help us."

The Sergeant clicked through some more windows before giving up on finding anything significant and taking off his glasses. "Well, let's see about these plates," he said.

He picked up the phone on his desk, read the license plate number to someone on the other end. He listened, and something surprised him.

"Are you sure?" he asked. "That's... odd."

"What?" Carter asked.

"Give me a minute," Cobbs said, and left the room.

When he came back his demeanor hadn't changed one bit. "We'll look into it," he said.

"You'll look into it!?"

"That's all I can tell you."

"What the fuck is going on here?"

"We'll look into it."

So Carter took a cab back to the duplex, took a shower, brushed his teeth. He looked at porn but thought about Margaret as he jerked off.

# 10

HE WANTED TO pace around and punch things. It was hard to stay in one place and make hot dogs for people. He was off in his own world when it hit him that somebody was trying to get his attention from across the street. "Hey! Hey man! *Hey, Sidewalk Patrol!*"

He looked up, and it was that kid Jimmy, waving to him.

"Hi Minnie Mouse," Carter said, waving back. It cheered him up a little. *The kids look up to me*, he thought.

He was about an hour into his shift when Cobbs came up and ordered a kielbasa. He didn't recognize him for a second out of uniform, all bundled in winter clothes, with a hat pulled down to his eyebrows and a hood over that.

"I recommend the Mark Chase instead," Carter said. "It's my signature dog. I named it after my brother. My brother who's missing."

"Okay, that sounds good, I'll try that," Cobbs said.

"So how did looking into it go?" Carter snorted as he pulled the dog out of the baste and put it on the grill.

"You haven't been followed by anybody else that you've noticed, have you?"

"No. Should I expect to be?"

"I don't know. But nobody's watching you right now that you know of?"

"Not that I know of."

"Okay. I want you to listen very carefully. I'm breaking federal law by telling you this, so I hope you appreciate it. The man who followed you works for Homeland Security, he was trying to ascertain your relationship with your brother. Your brother isn't missing - he's alive and in custody at an undisclosed federal facility."

"What!? What did he do?"

"Don't ask questions. Just listen. Your brother is classified as an unlawful combatant. He has not been charged and will not receive a trial. He was picked up under a program called—well, I shouldn't even tell you what it's called. But he's a suspected terrorist."

"What!? How the fuck—"

"I'll tell you my understanding of it. The intelligence agencies have – and I'm not even sure which agency it is, now that I think about it – they keep these databases. They have files on everybody. I'm not talking about, like, John Lennon's FBI file, I'm talking about massive collections of mundane data. Anything they can get from your bank, your ISP, phone company, the places you shop. They've been doing this for years now. They went to all these corporations and convinced them it was their patriotic duty to hand over this type of stuff, and they just collect it all together and it sort of creates this information portrait of the person."

"So, what, they thought he was connected to somebody, or he was making a bomb or something? There's just no way. If you knew my brother you'd know it's a misunderstanding."

"Well, it's not even anything that straightforward usually. It's mathematical. You know when you see on the news that they foiled some terror plot, a guy was gonna set off a car bomb or something? When they catch that guy they have his file and they compare it to the other bad guys they've caught and the computer looks for patterns. So they have a profile of what a terrorist is like. It's not necessarily that they bought a bomb or something. It could be they, you know, they watch *Matlock* late at night and they buy frozen pizzas on Tuesdays with their Safeway cards and socks at Target on the weekend. Just whatever it is, it's an algorithm and if you fit it they believe you are or will be a terrorist, and that's what they have on your brother."

"What kind of shitty lawyer did he have to let this happen, and not even--"

162

"Well, the thing is they don't have to charge terrorism suspects, or put them on trial. Or even admit that they have them. So there's not really anything you can do. But I'm sure he'll be okay."

"He'll be okay!? How can you say that?"

"*You* did time, right? *You* survived."

"Yeah, but is he in an FCI, or is he in one of those places where they shine lights on you all night and stick things up your butt and all that?"

"I don't know, it doesn't tell you that on his file."

"You don't know Mark, but I do. And there's no fucking *way* he's a terrorist. I'm the fuckup in this family and even *I'm* not a terrorist."

"Well, that can only be a good thing then. If he's innocent then he can't really incriminate himself, can he? I mean unless he just gives in and starts telling them what he thinks they want to hear."

"I can't believe this shit. This is un-American!"

"Well... try telling that to America. Look, I'm sorry, there's literally nothing I can do to help you with this. But I thought you had the right to know. Although legally you don't."

Carter stared at the burning oil on his grill for a minute before deciding there was nothing he could do at this moment but scoop the dog into a bun and put the toppings on it. "Six dollars," he said. Cobbs paid him with a twenty.

"I'm gonna fight this, you know," Carter said, counting out the change and putting the twenty in the cash box. "This is bullshit. They can't do this. I'm gonna take it to the internet, I'm gonna take it to the media, I'm gonna take it to every fucking court there is, and I'm not gonna stop until they let my brother go."

Cobbs was pulling two ones out of his change to stuff into the tip jar. "You know, I'm sure I'd want to do the same thing if I were you, so I can't blame you. But honestly I'd recommend against bringing any attention to this. You have a record, so they'll use that to smear you. And if they have to they can easily shut you up for good."

"You really think they'd kill me over this?"

"Easier than that. Have you ever looked at a pornographic website?"

"What?"

"If you have, even one time, it's in the cache of your computer. Even if you delete it, they have computer forensics experts who can dig it back up. Not just whatever you were looking at that got you off, but every nasty ad that popped up on the side, every disgusting thing that you accidentally clicked on and then shut right away when you realized what it was. Maybe you didn't even see it, you were on a page full of thumbnails and you never scrolled down to it, but it loaded so it's in your computer's memory. All they have to do is find something where they can prove that the girl was one day under 18, and then they got you for possession of child pornography. Maybe you didn't even know it when you saw it but when people hear what you've been charged with they picture something different. And good luck explaining all that to a jury. So in my opinion you should just forget about saying anything about this to anybody. But it's up to you."

At that, Cobbs took a bite out of the dog. He nodded as he chewed it. "Good," he said, turned and began to walk away. "*Really* good. Thank you for this."

He got a few steps before he stopped and looked back at Carter. "That's not a—I wasn't trying to threaten you there. That was my honest advice." He felt bad, so he put the other two ones in the tip jar.

# 11

CARTER DIDN'T KNOW what he was doing here. Not just in this life, but in this pub where Barry was hosting the weekly trivia night. He'd begged Carter to come and said it would show him what his art was all about and it seemed kind of sweet to Carter that this guy actually wanted to be friends. He could use some of those, so he showed up.

He got there earlier than he meant to, sat by himself in the corner staring into his Jack Daniel's. He recognized his server as a frequent customer at the hot dog stand, and when she came to check on him she recognized him too. "Oh, those are the greatest. The Chase Dogs! I love them."

"We changed the name to the Indefinite Detention Dog."

"Why's that?"

"Long story."

It was a good thing he got there early, because by the time 8 o'clock rolled around he might not have had a place to sit. Most of the tables seemed to be filled with regulars. They all joked with each other, taunted the other teams. A few tables looked more intense, academic types taking the competition very seriously, as if they didn't know this was usually a bunch of questions about old TV shows and athletes. But this time would be different.

Barry sat down at a little table with a microphone and introduced himself. Carter was with a table of 30-ish law office employees who had looked upon him with pity and recruited him to substitute for their missing player. They told him they were best with sports and current events questions, he told them he'd be good if anything Civil War came up, but that he was out of touch when it came to pop culture. He didn't mention the reason why. He told them it was his first time, that he was a friend of Barry. They had seen Barry there before but said this was his first time hosting.

"Hi," Barry said over the P.A. system.

"Hiiiii," the crowd sang back.

"My name is Barry Winston, and I'm going to be doing something very different this week." Some people clapped and whooed with exaggerated enthusiasm. "Normally we do Trivia Night here, right? Well today we're doing the opposite. Today we're doing Importance Night."

To say that Barry's concept didn't go over well with the crowd would be an understatement. During the first few questions people laughed politely, but they quickly figured out that he was serious, and the place went painfully quiet.

Carter and his team did well in the history round – questions about Gandhi, Joan of Arc, Martin Luther King Jr., Yitzhak Rabin... all people who had died for what they believed. Carter contributed the answer to the question about John Brown's raid on Harper's Ferry. Of course he knew that one, he used to have a book about John Brown. The lawyers had never heard of the guy and were impressed.

By the third round the competitors were in open rebellion against Barry, booing and heckling his questions. By the fourth most of them, including all of Carter's team, had given up and walked out in protest.

Carter stuck around, both out of loyalty to Barry and curiosity about where this was going.

The traditional movie-themed seventh round seemed like it was probably less fun than usual. The questions were not about the movies themselves, but things that their makers had done in real life: Sam Fuller being present at the liberation of the German concentration camp at Sokolov, Paul Newman earning a place on Nixon's enemies list, Marlon Brando dropping out of the lead role in *The Arrangement* to dedicate his time to the civil rights movement, Jet Li turning down *Crouching Tiger, Hidden Dragon* because he promised his wife he'd take a year off if she got pregnant. The implication was that movies are trivial, family, activism and duty are

166

important. It struck Carter as kind of an anti-art stance for a performance artist to take, but he could dig what Barry was getting at.

The current events round was even more uncomfortable. The theme was "things your government does that you should know about." After a pointed question about indefinite detainment policies, Barry nodded at Carter, proud to have force-fed the handful of stragglers and the bar staff a pitcher of truth juice.

Carter didn't mind that much. He knew it was well intentioned. He'd surprised even himself when he told Barry what was going on with his brother. But who else was he gonna confide in?

"I knew he was in trouble, but I didn't know it was that bad," Barry had said.

"You knew he was in trouble?"

"I saw them come talk to him. I thought they were knocking on my door. I thought they were FBI or something."

"You saw them arrest him?"

"No, I don't know. I just saw them come looking for him."

"Why didn't you tell me this before?"

"I thought you knew. I thought we talked about it. Remember when we first met? I told you I didn't want any trouble."

It did no good to be upset about it now. Barry was a nice guy. As a literal card-carrying member of the ACLU – he thought it was funny to laminate the flimsy punch-out card they sent him and keep it in his wallet – Barry was outraged by what he heard, but he was also understanding about why Carter was keeping it on the down low.

Mason, when he heard, directed his rage in a different direction.

"That doesn't make any sense," Mason said. "We had cops supposedly looking for him for months, and they didn't know he was in jail?"

"I don't know if they didn't know, or they just didn't tell. It's one of those unlawful combatant things. He can't see a lawyer and he can't see the evidence against him. It's all off the record."

"So what did he do?"

"He didn't do anything."

"Obviously he did something, or why would they arrest him?"

"It was a computer profile thing. They got these databases. They decided he fit the profile of a terrorist."

"Are you kidding me? That son of a bitch, what happened to him to--"

"I'm not saying he *is* a terrorist, dipshit. This is Mark we're talking about. Do you know how these things work?" Carter gave him the whole spiel, about how they go through your emails, bank statements, web history. "So the guy said if some bomber watches *Andy Griffith* every night, and then he eats pizza afterwards, and if Mark does the same thing, the computer might profile him as a terrorist. He didn't do anything. He just fit the algorhithm."

"Well, then he should've thought about that before he fit the algorhithm."

"I wish I knew what it is. They won't tell us anything. I bet it was just some random pattern like that. If they even knew him—I mean, you'd think if it was gonna be one of us it would be me. I'm the one with the record."

"Yeah, maybe it's your fault. Did you recommend some crazy bomb-making book to him, and then he went and bought it on Amazon to shut you up, didn't realize he got himself on a watch list?"

"No, I doubt it. We didn't really talk about that kind of stuff."

But it got him thinking.

Abbey didn't blame anybody when she heard. She felt too helpless to even point fingers. It broke Carter's heart to see it. She talked about being willing to wait forever, then she broke down. She pointed out that by now she'd known Carter longer than she'd known Mark. If she remained loyal, and he ever got out, would Mark even want to be with her? They had gotten comfortable together, but they were really still getting to know each other before this interuption. What could she do? Carter didn't have an answer, and pretended not to notice that she was reaching out for emotional support. He didn't know how to give it. That wasn't his thing.

The final round of Barry's Importance Night was the kicker. The questions weren't even masquerading as a quiz anymore, they were more like essay questions. Profound, search-your-soul type of questions. "If you were to die tomorrow, would you be proud of the life you lived?" "Do you treat other people the way you want them to treat you?" "Are you really doing what you were put here for, or are you lazily sticking with the consequences of past decisions?" "What can you do to leave the world a better place than it was when you got here?" When he asked "What could you be doing right now to make your life better?" a woman snorted, "Leaving!," and then she did.

Carter was embarrassed to be wiping a tear from his eye, but no one saw it anyway. There was nobody left except some new people at the bar who were watching a basketball game, the bartender turning the volume up loud enough to dominate the space. Barry laughed into the microphone. "Looks like you won, Carter. Last man standing."

He waited for Barry to pack up his things. "Thanks, guys," Barry said, waving to the bar staff as he put on his coat. They pretended not to hear him.

"Well, *I* liked it," Carter said.

# 12

WHEN CARTER SHOWED UP for his next shift Tony's stand was cleaned up. It was still covered in old beat up stickers but most of the photos and other decorations that had been taped all over it were taken off.

"Hey, it looks kinda naked. What happened?"

Tony looked up at him with big sad eyes. "I want to leave your brother's picture, but I can't find it" he said.

"That's okay, I took it down."

"Why?"

"Don't worry about it. What's wrong, Tony? Are you okay?"

"We need to talk, Carter."

"Yeah, what's up?"

"It's time I close the stand and retire."

"Hey, that's great. Congratulations, Tony. More time with your wife, right?"

"Yes."

"Why don't you seem happy, then?"

"It's good. It's good."

"Come on, Tony. What's going on?"

"The city won't renew my permit. That's why I close."

"Oh, shit. Is it because of me?"

"Because of them," Tony said, pointing to the Mountain Dew logo on the wall. "We're in the way. Outdoor advertising company pay more than us. Tell me to lease building."

"That's bullshit, you can't afford that."

"No."

"And who the fuck eats a hot dog inside, anyway?"

"Exactly!"

"Well, I'm sorry. You're a good man, Tony. You've

taught me a lot."

"I didn't teach you apple sage marinade!"

"Yeah, well, teach a man to fish."

"To fish?"

"It's a saying. Forget it."

"Well I'm sorry, buddy. I still pay you this week at least. After that I don't--"

"No, don't do that. I'm fine. What about you? Do you need money?"

He didn't answer. The answer was yes.

"I'll give you money, Tony. I have it."

Tony waved his arms around. "No no no. No sir. I will figure it out. Now, help me pack."


He kneeled between their graves, wondering how to tell them about Mark. He couldn't keep putting it off. He wasn't gonna say it out loud though anyway, he was gonna think it, like a silent prayer. So they must be hearing him now. They must already know.

Barry's questions were still fucking with his head. For all he knew Barry didn't even mean it, he might've been just trying to bum everybody out. But in the vulnerable state Carter was in those things cut right to the bone. His life felt more aimless than ever, stuck in limbo. His goal of finding Mark was unachievable. He had no purpose.

It was the first one that he kept coming back to. No, if he died tomorrow he would *not* be proud of his life. He didn't want to die as the guy who stole Nikes, lived in his brother's house, lived off checks from Pepsico and got beat up a couple times. That was not a good way to be remembered. Or forgotten.

There were a couple good things he did. He made up a good hot dog recipe. And there was the art movement, the rectangle thing, he could be proud of that. He was the guy who turned down the phone company commercial. That was pretty good.

Would his parents be proud of him for that? No, they

wouldn't get it at all. They wouldn't know why turning down money was better than making it. They would've loved it if he was on a fucking commercial. It would've blown their minds.

He wanted to be something Mom and Dad would've been proud of. And there was more pressure now that he knew Mark could be gone forever. He was the last of the Chases, the only one representing the family. That's not counting Mason, because let's be honest, he didn't want Mason representing the family. He shouldn't be thinking that, though. *Sorry Mom and Dad.*

He tried to concentrate on what he wanted them to know. That he had tried, that it was the government that did it this time, the system. That it wasn't his fault, that there was nothing he could do.

He thanked Mom for the basketball. Said he was using it every day. That it was really helping him to deal with everything.

He thought about how sorry he was. About how much he appreciated how much they'd done for him growing up, even if it hadn't worked out. The sacrifices Dad had made, getting up early every morning, driving to the ferry terminal, taking the ferry to work, working all day, coming back, watching the news, falling asleep on the couch, doing it all over again. Working – the exact thing Carter had spent his life trying to avoid – so that Carter and his brothers would have food, clothes, electricity. Sacrificing his happiness for theirs, and never once complaining about it. Never seeming like he wanted to be doing something else.

He thought about Mom when they were in elementary school, how she would make sure they got the best teachers, get them transferred if she knew the one they got was an asshole. She'd go to his basketball games, pick him up at practice when Dad couldn't. They were there for him a lot. He should've been there for them. He thought about how bad he fucked up, wondered why he turned out so bad, wondered if Pepsi Smooth came in two liters or just the cans and the smaller bottles.

It was hard to concentrate with Mom's monitor going. Now she was sacrificing herself the way Dad did. Providing for Carter, keeping a roof over his head - Mark's roof – that he probably didn't deserve. All this at the expense of her own dignity, a crass defilement of her final resting place. When she was alive he abandoned her. When she was dead he disgraced her.

She probably didn't care so much about the monetization of her burial site. She wasn't as cynical as he was. And it wasn't like the ads were brainwashing anybody. People already knew about Pepsi. They were gonna drink it whether Carter was getting paid or not. But it was kind of tacky. Mom and Dad deserved better than that. He owed them better than that.

From the looks of it, though, business was booming. In fact, maybe it was the nice weather, but it seemed like even more visitors crowded around Krijole's grave than the last time he was here. The tourists were starting to catch on to this hot spot, and the mood was more upbeat. More singing. More laughing. More of a celebration of the man's life, or of being young.

Sensing someone hovering behind him, he turned around. A fairly young but grey haired man with a dog on a leash was taking his picture with a phone.

"What the fuck?" Carter yelled.

"Sorry, I didn't mean to intrude. I just felt bad for you."

"Why? 'Cause some asshole was taking my picture?"

"All these kids hanging out here having a party, and you're obviously mourning somebody, it's gotta be frustrating."

"Yeah, sometimes."

"So I wanted to scan your QR Code there, order something through your link so your people get a cut. That's all."

"Oh. Thanks."

His dog was shitting. It was on somebody else's plot,

between graves. The man looked appropriately embarrassed, pulled a plastic bag out of his pocket and scrambled to clean it up. Carter figured he was okay.

"I could use some Pepsi Gear anyway," the man smiled. "Have you tried Pepsi Smooth yet?"

"No. What is it?"

"I'm not sure. I guess it's Pepsi, but more smooth?"

"Okay."

"Or it might be one of those ones that's like diet, but with more sugar so it tastes better. I can't remember. I heard it's getting good reviews online, though."

"Oh. Cool."


"What can you do to leave the world a better place than it was when you got here?" If Importance Night had been last week, Carter's answer would've been to find Mark. This week he knew that wasn't gonna happen. What he could do, he thought now, is get the fuckin Pepsi ad off his mom's grave.

Was he really doing what he was put here for? It was hard to say. What was Mark taken *away* from here for? Was there really a purpose to anything? No, it was just fuckin random. Maybe all he could do is fill in the holes that the universe created. If he couldn't get Mark out he had to *be* Mark. He'd already adopted his home, his lifestyle. He was no substitute for Mark, but he would try to be like him, be responsible and stay out of trouble. At least after he was done with Dante.

That's what he had to do. He had to quit fucking around, do something that would make the parents' graves proud.

# 13

MARGARET COULDN'T BELIEVE IT when they told her Carter had been calling for her. She didn't think she'd ever talk to him again. She'd blown it, and after that weird incident with the car she was kind of glad she did. But she called him back and here he was apologizing and saying he was interested in taking part in the campaign. Maybe as a consultant of some kind. Or whatever she needed.

He seemed genuinely sorry. He said he was going through a lot with some family tragedies and his perspective was changing about what he wanted out of life. She was pretty sure he was serious and not just regretting turning down the sex offer.

She had just one question for him. "The billboard that you painted over. What color was it?"

"The color my brother picked out to paint some of his walls. Fresh Green I think it was called. Or Spring Fresh Green."

She didn't tell him, but she'd been going out to other artists to act as advisors to the design team. None had bit yet, but none had turned her down on the spot like Carter had. She asked about him – none had heard of him, but they all agreed that the idea stemmed from a billboard on top of a duplex that was painted over light green.

Oh boy. This was going to be awkward. But she told him she would make it happen. She had to – his participation would really legitimize the campaign, and give both herself and the firm some credibility, make them feel a connection to the art world. *Yeah, we're creating advertising for corporations, but this is Carter Chase, the founder of the Rectangling movement. We're not hacks.*

Bob Garrett, the director of the Evergreen Valley

Funeral Home, was also surprised to get a call from Carter. When Mistalynn told Bob who was on the line the name sounded familiar, but he had to look it up to remember him.

It was unusual to be contacted by a client this long after the fact, but not unheard of. Sometimes they feel guilty about penny-pinching a loved one's monument and want to replace it with a fancier one. Sometimes they just want to thank you. Sometimes they need another grave for another deceased loved one. Pretty much all of these calls make him uncomfortable. But that's the job.

Mr. Chase's concerns were about the affiliate program. Yes, he was receiving his checks, no, he did not need direct deposit. He had changed his mind about sponsorship and wanted to terminate the contract.

Bob knew, and the file confirmed, that this was not possible. The client had signed on with Pepsi for 5 years with optional extensions. According to the contract, only the advertising party could end the agreement prematurely. Mr. Chase's only option was to call the customer service number on his check stub to see if they could help him.

The customer service number couldn't help him. First it was a maze of numbered menus – if you are calling from the U.S., press 1. If you are an advertiser press 1, if you are a publisher press 2, if you do not know the difference between an advertiser and a publisher press 3. Please identify yourself by entering your social security number followed by the pound sign. This call may be monitored for quality control purposes, to agree to continue press 1, to start over press 7. Blah blah blah, and then he's put on hold for a while, and then they tell him they can't get him out of his contract, he has to log on to such and such to apply for a whatever.

When he tried the website it was the same runaround. He found an option for renewing his contract, but not one for ending it. When he tried to submit a form for customer service it told him that during business hours he would have to call the toll free customer service number that had sent him here in the first place.

Carter didn't know how to shop for clothes, but he knew he needed some new ones, especially when it came to footwear. He couldn't start a new life wearing his Bob Barkers, but his feet were bigger than Mark's, so he couldn't wear any of the shoes left in the duplex.

He went and talked to Nasir at the Men's Wearhouse, who sold him a pair of black Rockport dress shoes. The name seemed familiar – maybe it was a classy name brand, maybe he'd heard it in a rap song, he had no idea. He got some nice slacks and some button up shirts in different colors, but said no to more ties.

The meeting was with Thom, not Margaret. Thom seemed eager to take credit for landing Carter on the campaign, which didn't seem fair, but at least Carter would avoid the social discomfort of working closely with Margaret. Oh jesus, so many things that would've been better if he'd just went home with her that night.

It was a lunch meeting. Thom probably thought he'd have to prove he was down with the common man, go to some down home diner or something. He was surprised when Carter suggested Shear Elegance.

"Oh, of course," Thom said. "I should've remembered you were at Leto that time I first met you. So you know your food."

"Yeah," said Carter. "I'm a bit of a, uh, food enthusiast."

Carter had the cured arctic char, Thom the roasted hake. Thom kept ordering silly looking drinks for Carter as a joke. "Could you bring my friend here a Lemon Bessie Blue?" Carter kept drinking them because it made the guy laugh.

"So tell me," Thom asked. "You turned Margaret down at first. She thought you considered this – I probably shouldn't be saying it – she thought you considered this selling out. So what changed your mind?"

"Just thinking about my parents. They did shit they prob'ly didn't want to do so they could provide for me. I wanted to do something for them. Something that would've impressed them when they were alive."

"That's really great. But you don't have to feel bad about what you're doing. Believe me, I understand. The advertising world – it's bullshit, right? This is the last place in the world where I thought I would end up. I'm an old punk rocker, man! You believe that?"

Carter shrugged.

"We're just like you, man, we're a bunch of freaks, outside thinkers and creatives. Personally I'm not an artist, I couldn't draw to save my life! But I love art. I support art. And what I want is your vision, and I'm going to put the full resources of Mind Bandit behind that vision, and I'm going to share it with the world. That's what I do."

They set it up for the next day. Carter would come in, get a tour of the place, fill out the paperwork, see where his office would be.

Thom smiled and shook his head as he signed the check. "Great taste in restaraunts, too! This is going to be great."

"Yeah, good to work with a fellow foodie," Carter said.

# 14

IT WAS A DIFFERENT setup than last time he came to the Rossi Building, unless he'd just barged past security that time without realizing it. He wasn't sure. This time a guard in the lobby stopped him and asked his name. Thom had told him to text when he got there, and he'd been too embarrassed to admit that he didn't know how. He tried talking the guard into letting him in, but no go. So he called up to the front desk. When he got through to Thom and explained the predicament, Thom asked him to give the phone to the guard.

By the guard's expression it looked like Thom was chewing the poor guy out for not letting Carter through. "Yes sir," the man said, turned the phone off and handed it back to Carter. "Right this way, sir," he said with forced politeness.

"My fault, man. Sorry," Carter said.

Thom met him at the top with a laugh and a manly handshake. "Sorry about that. I like those security guys, but they don't know shit about art. Follow me." They headed down a wide hallway lined with details from their various campaigns blown up onto huge five foot by five foot foamboard signs. They were appealing designs – vivid pop-art inspired graphics of pretty ladies, samurais, astronauts, animals. Artfully messy, retro but in a modern sort of way. Out of context he couldn't identify what products or services they represented until he got to the simple old-fashioned cartoon man wearing the stethoscope and the crown.

"Doctor-King," Carter said.

"Yeah, we did that," Thom said, glancing down at Carter's shiny feet. "Hey, I like your shoes."

"They're Rockports," Carter said. Thom was wearing brand new looking Puma skate shoes to compliment his business on top, cool on the bottom tie-and-jeans combo.

The actual workspace was very open and well-lit, with lots of windows. The layout was fairly similar to that place where Mark had worked, but it felt really different because it was decorated in a more aggressively hip manner. The furniture was all painted a dark maroon, the walls and ceiling left bare and utilitarian like a warehouse, the cement floor carefully stained to create the illusion that it had once been used as a garage. Or maybe painstakingly dismantled and transported from an actual garage? Hanging from the ceiling in the center of the main room was a huge, weathered, wooden display that must've been from an old magic show, depicting a man's jeweled, turbaned head with glowing, hypnotic eyes.

Most of the desks weren't walled off, so they seemed more like work stations than cubicles. Designers and editors stared at banks of large monitors, surrounded by sketches, reference photos and color swatches. They looked up and smiled as Thom brought Carter around and introduced him to everybody. Dawn and Danielle both remembered meeting him at Leto, and he pretended to remember too.

"This is where we're going to put you, if it's okay," Thom said as they came to a big desk facing the window. "Are you a Mac guy?"

"Yeah. Sure."

"Good, that was my guess."

The view was awe-inspiring. Carter stopped out in front of the desk to get a better look.

Thom laughed "See, I understand how you think," he said. "That's exactly what I want you to do. I want you to look out onto that city and I want you to imagine yourself painting over it all. Making it your own."

As if they were worried the window seat wouldn't be enough to butter him up, somebody had put sort of a gift bag on his desk too, overflowing with promo items and gift certificates from the agency's various clients. Carter pulled out one of the Doctor-King bars and put it in his pocket.

182

Thom pointed out a conference room where several people were discussing a presentation. Margaret was leaning back casually in her chair, facing the other way. She looked over her shoulder just in time to see them outside the window and she did that excited shriek and wave that some young women do when they're surprised to run into a good friend that they haven't seen in a while. Good acting.

"This is the kitchen over here, for when you need a snack," Thom said. It had a refrigerator, a microwave, a retro style toaster, a high end espresso machine, a dual head milkshake mixer and two tables with napkin holders and condiment racks like you'd see in a greasy spoon. One entire wall was covered in an armor of plastic cartoon character lunchboxes. "And you gotta see The Lounge. This is one of the places you can go to kinda relax your mind and get your creative juices flowing."

The Lounge was like a caricature of somebody's childhood basement, with shag carpeting, glittery popcorn-textured ceiling, a brand new couch with patches on it to simulate rattiness, bean bag chairs and wooden end tables decorated with glass grapes and piles of vintage TV Guides. A skinny balding dude sat cross-legged on the floor playing old video game cartridges. The huge TV screen was hi-def but framed by a gaudy old wooden entertainment center. Another guy was in the corner digging through a big box full of old action figures, searching for inspiration.

"A little more laid back than you expected up here, isn't it?" Thom asked proudly.

"Yeah, I guess."

"Am I blowing your mind or what?" "Yeah, it's pretty cool."

In an alcove just past The Lounge, Carter noticed another flight of stairs up. "I thought we were on the top floor?" he said.

"That goes to the roof," Thom said. "You play ball at all?"

"Yeah, you mean basketball?"

"Yeah. We have a hoop up there."

This was the first thing that really impressed Carter. It might actually help him while working here. He could go up and throw the ball around when he needed to get his mind straight.

"Can I try it out?"

"Yeah, sure. Let's see if the ball is up there." He led Carter up the stairs.

"To be honest," Carter said, "I haven't really played against anybody in a long time, I just shoot."

"Well, maybe this will change that." The door opened out onto a rooftop half-court. Not a ramshackle one either. Other than the size and some weather damage it was pretty deluxe.

"I don't know if it gets as much use as it used to," Thom admitted. "We used to have more serious ball players on staff. We'd even go out for drinks after work, come back for a game. Can you believe that? We'd willingly come back to hang out when they're not even working!"

"Well, it's pretty nice," Carter said, admiring the set up. It had smooth flooring almost like a tennis court, and a regulation hoop that Carter envied. He wouldn't worry about breaking it or tipping it over, like the one he'd bought for the backyard. The court was contained by a high chain link fence with netting on top, but one corner on the hoop end had a big tear in it.

Noticing Carter eyeing the hole, Thom laughed. "They didn't really think about snow piling up on there. It collapsed during the storm last year. Or... two years ago? I can't remember. Was it last year or the year before we had that snow storm?"

"I don't know, I missed that," Carter said.

Thom turned serious. "Yeah, we should get that fixed. You don't wanna--" He mimed shooting a ball up through the opening.

Carter's stomach dropped. He walked over to the fence

underneath the hole and looked down to the traffic on 5$^{th}$ Avenue.

"Looks like the ball isn't out here," Thom said. "I haven't been up here in a while. I guess nobody plays that much anymore. But a guy your height, we can get some competition going."

Carter tried for a polite response, but it never left his lips. He just stared down and gripped the fence.

"You, uh-- you okay, man?" Thom asked.

"I think I know where your ball is," Carter said.

"You do?"

He wondered about the specifics. Did it actually hit her straight on? Probably not. They would've figured that out from the body. More likely it smashed the windshield, distracting her, so she didn't see the car stop in front of her. Did she get a chance to see what it was? Did it hit the street first and bounce? Is that what would happen from this height, some gigantic bounce, or would that have popped it? Maybe it was a direct hit.

*Of course* Mom hadn't bought him a basketball. It wouldn't make any sense. The ball wasn't a gift, it was a clue that had gone ignored. There was no last message from his mother after all, no "keep practicing" or even "keep your eye on the road." You can't really keep your eye on the road after something falls out of the sky and explodes glass in your face.

It's just like with Mark. It's all completely random, just coincidence, nothing more, no meaning. If fate has it out for you, if you're unlucky, if you're in the wrong place at the wrong time, there's nothing you can do. You're fucked. Accept it. What else can you do?

<u>to do</u>
1. ~~find Mark~~
2. ~~money~~
3. revenge?

# THREE

# 1

JASON FLEMING WAS in the back counting his till for the night when Patty came to get him. "Some guy's asking for you, Jason," she said. "He says it's important."

Jason sighed, carefully placed the uncounted portion of bills sideways on top of the till, and locked it all up in the safe.

"Oh my *God*, man," he whined when he came out and saw who it was. "How many fucking times are we gonna go back and forth on this, Carter?"

"I'm not here for a rematch. I just want to tell you something."

"We have a bouncer tonight. And you know you're not allowed in here."

"I just want to warn you, you can't trust Dante. I learned that the hard way, a couple times."

"Wow, thanks for looking out for me, man. That's really sweet of you."

"He told me about Ian Blair and all that."

"I don't know what that is."

"Isn't that his name? The drummer guy he hangs out with now. I forget the name of the band. I thought he was retarded but Dante says that's just the way they dress."

"You're wasting your time. I don't even know who that is you're talking about."

"Well, Dante seems to know him pretty well. He showed him your shoe collection in the storage space."

"What?"

"The guy collects limited edition shoes like you do, only he has a lot of money from touring so he can just buy them from guys like you instead of camping out on the sidewalks himself. Dante hooks him up. From your storage space."

"Bullshit."

"I swear to God, he was wearing Kris Krijoles when I saw him. Where else would he get those? And he's the same size as you, apparently."

"You have to leave now."

"You're size 11, right? That's what Dante told me. I thought you would be bigger, Dante said 11. Anyway, I thought you should know."

Jason pulled out his phone and started composing a text.

"Could I get like a Jack and Coke or something?" Carter asked.

"No! Get the fuck out! You know you're not allowed in here."

"Okay. That's fair."


As Carter watched Jason Fleming's black Mustang pull up to the front of the storage space he breathed a sigh of relief. He'd called everything right: the conversation *would* cause Jason to go check his shoe collection, he *would* go get Kerry first, giving Carter enough time to beat him there on the bus, and most importantly the shoes *were* at Lake View Self Storage, the same place Dante had recommended to Carter's brothers years ago. The next step was to figure out which unit they were in.

That part wasn't as easy. If it had been in the first row he could've spotted it from where he was standing across the street, but he saw the car turn out of sight. He ran around the block behind the lot, which was somewhat elevated, but it wasn't high enough to see in there. And he didn't want to deal with the razor wire coils on top of the fence.

After about a half an hour he saw the car leave. He waited a few minutes, then walked up and rang the buzzer.

"Hey man, sorry to bother you. I'm trying to catch my friends Jason and Kerry Fleming. I don't know their pass code. Do you know if they're in there?"

"There's nobody in here right now."

"Well, can I come in and talk to you please? I wanna rent a space."

It was the same guy that was working the last time he was here, the poor guy that Mason had argued with.

"Hey man, I don't know if you remember me," Carter said, "but I was in here a while back, I lost my space due to a non-payment issue."

"Well, I'm sure I told you then there's nothing I can do about it."

"I know, that's okay. I lost it fair and square. But I wanna give it another shot, right, and my friends – I must've just missed 'em – my friends were gonna show me which one they were in so I could try to get the space next to them. For convenience."

"Which unit is your friend in?"

"I forget. Over on that end somewhere. I forget the number."

He walked over to his computer. "The last name's Fleming?"

"Yeah, if it's under their name."

"Yeah, there's a Jason Fleming. But I can't really... I don't think I can give out that information. Unless you could prove it somehow that you know him."

"How am I supposed to prove it?"

"Okay, I'll give you part of the number to see if you can guess it. Thirty..."

"Thirty?"

"The number is *thirty*..."

"31?"

"Yes! There's a Jason Fleming in #31."

"That's him. So could I get the space next to that?"

"No, I don't think so," he said. He typed something in. "I could get you this one, facing it. There's a vacancy there." He turned the screen around and pointed to a unit in the next row.

"Well, that doesn't work."

"It's not really that far of a haul, honestly."

"I know, but... Well, what about this side?" Carter pointed to the other side of the same structure Dante's was in, the unit built back-to-back with his.

"You'd rather have the other side than just directly across from it? This one is directly across from it."

"I know."

"Well let's see, that's #41? No..." He typed something. "Yeah, no, that unit's not available yet. It's delinquent, actually, so it probably will be vacant, but not until it goes up for auction and then gets cleaned out."

"Can I get on a waiting list for it? Reserve it for after the auction? I'd like to get in there as soon as possible."

"No, we don't like to do that because we never know if the bill will get paid at the last minute. That happens sometimes. Easier for us that way."

"But 41's connected to my friend's space?"

"Yeah, they're back-to-back."

"There's a door between them?"

"No, they just share a wall. You'd actually have to go all the way around here to get to your friend's, so it's not really what you're looking for. I'd go with this other one."

"Nah, I want #41."

"Sorry man, wish I could help you."

"What day is the auction?"


Back at the duplex the deliveries were still arriving. Every day or two another few books came from different used book stores around the country. Like many publications these days *John Brown* by W.E.B. Dubois was no longer printed as a hard copy, but some of the major cities still had used bookstores, which trafficked in that sort of thing. He'd tear them from their mailers and carefully stack them up on the living room table. There were 22 copies so far. Different editions: some of the boring one with just text on the cover, a couple tinted red with a photo of Brown set over a silhouetted tree, but mostly the one with a clean-shaven Brown holding up his right hand, consecrating his life to the destruction of

192

slavery.

Carter also ordered a pair of earbuds. He'd been listening to *Sergeant Pepper's* more and more, and found out he could stream it on his phone from drpepper.com.

And there were the materials, mostly purchased online, some at the hardware store, all with Carter's real name and debit cards. Each ingredient in a separate transaction, not wanting to be *too* obvious, but deliberately leaving a trail. Yes, I, Carter Chase, did purchase this fertilizer.

It didn't really matter anymore what anybody thought about him, what anybody knew he was up to. He wasn't gonna be timid about looking stuff up on the computer. It was a weird sort of rebellion, Googling phrases like "how do i make bomb" and "easiest bombmaking instructions" and "order bomb supplies." He even set up a separate login on Mark's computer so this would all be under his own name. Fuck 'em. This'll be over soon enough.

Whenever he heard a car in the alley he'd look out the window, waiting for that black car to pull up again, or maybe even an SUV. For somebody to kick the door down and put a bag over his head. But they never came, so his plan progressed.

He really didn't know what he was doing. The bombs he'd made as a kid were simple ones without detonators. Now, of course, there was more information available. Details and tips were more scarce than he'd expected, but not entirely absent. He learned about different types of pipe bombs, some with electronic detonators, some just with spring-loaded mechanisms that lit matches (seemed too risky). He kept getting distracted by unrelated matters, like when he found out about "bat bombs" used in World War II. They actually dropped bombs full of bats that flew into the nooks and crannies of Japan and started fires that were deadly to a place with so many wood and paper-based structures. Great idea! Too much trouble to start buying bats, though.

The John Brown book mentioned that Brown and his men would drink "creek water mixed with a little ginger and a spoon of molasses." Carter tried to make his own version, minus the creek part. It didn't taste delicious or anything, but he liked drinking it. It felt cleansing somehow. Made him feel righteous. Helped him prepare.

Barry seemed pleasantly surprised to find Carter on his doorstep.

"Hey man! Good to see you."

"Good to see you too, Barry. I wanted to tell you about something real quick."

"Sure. What's up?"

"Well, how's your art going?"

"Oh, slowly but surely. I'm still working on ideas for what to do next after Importance Night. I want to make sure it's a worthy follow up."

"Oh, yeah?"

"Yeah, I was really happy with how that one turned out."

"Then I wasn't the only one who liked it."

Barry laughed.

"Well, Barry, you know how we saw those billboards down the street that got painted over, and you said they might've got the idea from ours?"

"Yeah, I meant to talk to you about that. It's a whole movement now!"

"You know about the rectangles?"

"Yeah, Rectangling. I read about it on Art Forum."

"Okay, well here's the thing. There's this advertising firm downtown, they're doing a major campaign for... phones or something. I don't know what it is. But they wanted to pay me a bunch of money to help with it, as the Father of Rectangling. I decided not to do it, it's a long story. But I sent them a letter and told them I misled them, it was really the performance artist Barry Winston who I got the idea from."

"Why did you say that?"

"I'm not an artist, man. You are. I don't know if they're gonna contact you, but if they do I think you should take the

194

money. You might think it's selling out or whatever, but look, you could pay for the kid's college. You could stop working, spend more time with the kid, more time with the art. I already had a little money, I just wasted it on expensive food. I wouldn't do anything good with the money. You would."

Barry never expected such open kindness from Carter. He was unusually sensitive to instances of male bonding, so his eyes started to water a little. "I don't know what to say, Carter." He noticed the book that Carter was clutching.

"Oh yeah, I wanted to give this to you," Carter said when he noticed Barry eyeing it in his hand. "*John Brown* by W.E.B. Du Bois. Your history round reminded me of it. You should read it if you haven't already."

"No, no I haven't. Wow, thanks. I'll get it back to you as soon as I can."

"No, keep it. I got more."

"Well, thanks brother. I really appreciate this."

"No problem. You're a good guy, Barry. Glad I knew ya."

"Yeah. See ya later, Carter."

Before Barry shut the door Carter remembered something else. "Oh yeah, one thing. Very important. Tell them that you barely know me. We're just neighbors. Not even that – my brother was your neighbor. We're not close."

"I don't understand."

"Trust me. It's better."


Abbey seemed very confused when she received her copy of the book. "I don't... I don't usually read non-fiction stuff like this. Is it good?"

"Of course it's good, why else would I give it to you?"

"It's a good read, though?"

"Well, it's old, it's a little dry, but the subject is really interesting. There's a better book I read about John Wilkes Boothe, and the manhunt to catch him. That's a guy who gave his life for a cause he believed in, but it was a terrible cause. John Brown was on the right side. That's why I like this book."

"Okay. Yeah, I should probably read more historical stuff. It'll be good for me. So you're doing a lot of reading now?"

"I'm taking the time for a number of things that weren't important yesterday."

"Like what?"

"I'm joking. That's just a line from a song. 'Fixing a Hole.'"

"Fixing a hole?"

"Just a line from a Dr. Pepper commercial."

They paused to enjoy the summer mango caprese salad with truffle salt. For some reason it was the sides that excelled at Mary Mary's, never the entrees. "This shit is *good*," Carter said, chewing with his mouth open. "Different though. They changed the recipe, didn't they?"

"Not that I've noticed."

"Huh. My taste buds have been weird lately, I think. Things taste different." He looked around. "This is where we first met, remember? Back when it was called nomi."

"Of course I remember that."

"Fitting, I guess."

"What's fitting?"

"I don't know."

Abbey sighed. "Carter, this is really hard for me. I can only imagine how hard it is for you. But we're both going through this. If we need to talk about it, we should talk to each other."

"Have you known me to be a guy who talks about it?"

"Once or twice."

"Well, I don't need to talk about it. I'm good."

"If you're good then why did you want to meet me? You *need* to talk. You just don't know how to start."

"I don't need to talk."

"Okay, that's fine," she said sarcastically. "If you're not comfortable talking to me about it, you can talk to other people who know what it's like. You can talk to Mason."

"Oooh, that's cold!" The laugh sort of threw off the

momentum of Abbey's plea. She didn't know how to keep pushing it. "Look, I appreciate it, Abbey. But I have it figured out. There's nothing to talk about at this point. I just want to enjoy a good meal with a good person." He didn't say "one last time," but he thought it.

# 2

THE AUCTION WASN'T really what he'd pictured. The fast-talking guy like at a cattle auction was there, but not the rich people holding up paper signs to signal their bids. He probably shouldn't have worn his suit.

There were around ten bidders, plus associates, and they were serious. They obviously knew each other and what they were doing. They would line up while the auctioneer unlocked the door and lifted it open. Then they'd take turns looking inside for a minute. They weren't allowed to step inside or touch anything, but they all had flashlights to shine into the corners and get a better look. They scanned for labels, noted the sizes of boxes, looked for identifiable tools or equipment. One guy had a little reporter's notebook like Carter had, he was jotting down numbers and adding them up, value estimates, maybe.

The first locker up for bidding was half-filled with neatly stacked rows of boxes and went for $430. Carter figured the bidders knew something he didn't, because he assumed those were mostly tax returns and dishes. But the bidding seemed to get lower as the morning went on. One locker just had some beat up trikes and some garbage bags that were probably filled with ratty stuffed animals. That one went for $5 and probably wasn't worth it. Carter couldn't decide if it was sad or happy. You can't pay your bills, you're losing everything, but it's a bunch of garbage anyway. Or, you can't pay your bills, you're losing everything, *and* it's a bunch of garbage.

Unit #41 came up fifth. So apparently the owner had *not* come through with the rent in time. That was the good news. The bad news was what was inside: a couple tool chests, a motorcycle that looked like it was in pretty good condition. Things good enough to make the bidders optimistic about the contents of the various boxes and trunks stacked along the sides.

Carter raised his hand first, then let the two fat guys in the front get into a bidding war. They smiled and joked with each other, might even be friends, but each was too competitive and stubborn to let the other guy win. When they got to $500, Carter stepped in and raised it to $1,500.

Everybody turned around, surprised by this intrusion. The bidding didn't usually get that high, but now their minds started reeling, trying to figure out what this new guy knew about the contents of that unit. "You a motorcycle guy?" Tweedle Dee muttered. And then, "Sixteen."

"Three thousand, then," Carter said.

The fat guys looked to each other, like *somebody needs to do something.* "Don't look at *me*," Tweedle Dum said. "I'm not going that high!"

"Thirty-one."

"$4,000."

A lady in a baseball cap started to laugh in disbelief. "Who *is* this guy?"

"Going once," the auctioneer said.

"You know it's cash, right?" Dee asked Carter condescendingly. "You really have that much cash on you?"

Carter pulled a comically fat roll out of his backpack.

"Going twice."

"Hold on, Fred," the last bidder said.

"You know I can't do that, Bill," said the auctioneer. "No time outs in an auction."

"Question of procedure. The bidding is above two-thousand, that means I get two hours to go to the bank, correct?"

"Yes, two hours from the close of bidding to get the cash and find me."

Bill breathed deep and exhaled slowly.

"Three times."

Everyone watched Bill. He shook his head. "No. Kate would kill me."

"Sold for $4,000 to the gentleman in the back."

"This is your first time, right?" the man said as he stapled the payment and deposit receipts to a few pages of xeroxed text.

"Yeah," Carter said.

"Okay," the man said, handing Carter the papers. He pointed at a number handwritten near the top. "There's your code for the front gate, and a reminder of the policies. Everything out in 48 hours, do not use our dumpsters or garbage cans, sweep with a broom afterwards. That's serious, you need it to be clean. If there's even a piece of string left in there you won't get all of your deposit back. All right?"

"No problem."

"Okay, well, congratulations, you have fun now."

"You too."

Lake View Public Storage didn't rent U-Haul trucks like a lot of storage facilities did, but a neighborhood dealer was conveniently located within walking distance. Carter rented a 10' truck and took a trip to the hardware store. He'd looked through the tool boxes in the unit and didn't see anything he thought would do the job. He wasn't exactly sure what *would* work though, tools never having been his thing, exactly. He almost sprung for an air metal shear, not realizing it had to be hooked up to an air compressor. When he figured that out he switched to a cordless shear, plus charger and battery (sold separately). He had to stop by the duplex so he could plug it into the wall for a few hours, then he headed back to Lake View. By that time it was dark, which was better anyway.

He backed the truck up close to unit 41 and opened the back door, like he was loading up. There was no padlock on the gate to the unit, because it was his responsibility as new owner and he hadn't bothered. But he'd gotten one at the hardware store for later. He raised the gate to just below his height, not all the way up, to make it harder for any passerby to see inside. He stacked some of the lighter boxes on either side to block the view even further.

There were heavier boxes at the back of the unit. Out of curiosity he cut open one of the ones on the top. It was filled with random engine parts and other heavy shit. Great. His left arm was feeling weak, he was hoping he wouldn't have to do a bunch of heavy lifting. But he had to, so he did.

Once he'd cleared a door-sized opening to the corrugated metal back wall of the unit, Carter crouched down with the metal shears and started cutting a line from the bottom edge up. It wasn't as easy as the instructions made it sound, but after a couple messy tries he started cutting a fairly straight line, then another, then a slash across. He had a hard time cutting all the way through, but when he gave it a hard kick one side peeled off and it bent inward like a door opening just a crack.

He shined the flashlight through the opening. His path was blocked by stacks of shoe boxes on the other side. He reached in and pushed hard, knocking a box out of the middle and toppling the ones above it. Then he pushed out the remaining boxes, chipping away at the wall of shoes until there was room to crawl through.

The Nike Brothers really knew how to pimp a storage space. The collection of shoes stacked at the back seemed to be duplicates or ones they didn't care about as much. The prize winners were behind glass in jewelry-counter-style trophy cases, perched on perfect shoe-holders they must've bought from a Foot Locker or something. The other wall had shelving units holding boxes of shoes from floor to ceiling, neatly stacked and labelled. In the middle were a leather chair, a love seat and a small coffee table with empty beer cans on it. They must hang out here and just look at their shoes!

Carter didn't want to ruin the place. He just came for the Kris Krijoles. He spotted one pair in the case, which fortunately wasn't locked. While he was opening it he noticed a light switch, which he flipped. The counter was wired into a portable generator in the corner so it could light up. Now he could put the flash light down.

The shoes on the wall racks were carefully organized, which didn't surprise Carter, knowing the Flemings. There were laminated signs tacked to some of the rows designating different styles of shoes: running, soccer, action sports. The basketball section was the biggest and where he found the Kris Krijoles. He noticed the labels were organized alphabetically from top to bottom, so shoes of the same style were all together.

He pulled them out and started loading them through the hole in the wall back into unit 41. He thought Dante had sold off most of them until he noticed a whole bunch more in the overflow section he'd made such a mess of on his way in.

As he awkwardly carried shoes by the armload into his U-Haul he couldn't help but laugh. Couldn't believe he was stealing these fuckin things again.

When he finished transferring all the Krijoles he could find he neatened the stacks, turned off the light, climbed through the hole and bent the metal back as close to its original position as he could manage. He stacked the heavy junk boxes back where they had been, hiding the damage to the wall from his side, at least. He was worried if the storage people spotted it right away they might call the cops on him. But by then it should be too late anyway.

He left all the shit in the unit, because he wouldn't be needing the deposit back. The shoes didn't even half fill the truck. Maybe he should've gotten the cargo van, it would've been easier to drive. Since he had all that room in the back he thought about taking the motorcycle, but he didn't know what kind of repairs it would need, or have time to learn how to ride it. They'll probably just auction it again next month anyway. One of those fat guys'll know what to do with it.

# 3

CARTER WOKE UP feeling pretty good. The headache wasn't as bad as usual – crunchy around the temples, but nothing sharp. His left arm felt a little weak again, but not numb.

He made the bed, which he didn't usually do. He took out the garbage and the recycling, and cleaned all the dishes in the sink. Mentally he felt relaxed, but when he suddenly had to rush to the bathroom and take a big dump he knew his stomach wasn't on the same page.

He did his burpees to get the blood flowing, then shot some hoops. He still missed more lay ups than he considered reasonable, but his free throws were on point. He took a shower and drank two big glasses of the John Brown ginger-molasses water, and then he felt ready so he changed into Kris Krijoles and started loading up the truck.

He sat down at the bar at the Fox Sports Grill and put his bag down next to the stool. He looked at the menu and didn't see what he wanted.

"Will you be ordering food?" his server asked from behind the bar.

"Yes."

She opened her writing pad. "What can I get for you?"

"Look, I don't want to be an asshole, but can I order off menu?"

She took a moment to try to hide the disdain in her voice. "What is it you want?"

"There used to be a hot dog stand down the block, but they got shut down. I just need a hot dog real bad, and I don't see one on the menu. I'm willing to pay a ridiculous amount." He pulled a stack of twenties out of his wallet and put it on the bar. "You can split this with the chef, or charge me whatever you want and the rest is tip... whatever sounds fair to you."

"The hot dog stand, you mean Tony's, right? I used to go there sometimes," she said. "Didn't you—"

"Yeah, I worked there for a while."

"What happened, he retired?"

"Yeah, sort of. Forced out of business, really."

"Oh, that sucks."

"Yeah, a lot of things do."

"There's not really anywhere around here to get a hot dog anymore, is there?"

"No. There's Thai food, burritos, Subway, that steak house. I didn't want to go to Cheesecake Factory. You guys have 'grill' in your name... I'm sorry, this is a shitty thing to do, I normally would never do this."

"Well, I can't promise anything, but I'll see what I can do."

Once everything was cleared with the chef, she asked about condiments. He thought he would have to explain what Mark Chase style was. "You mean with the horseradish and caramelized onions and everything?"

"Sauerkraut, sharp cheddar..."

"Okay, I'll tell him."

"And I'll have that to go, if it's okay."

He left a copy of *John Brown* under the stack of cash.

Carter stood right where he had so many times, in front of Comcast's Mountain Dew billboard, on the former site of Tony's Gourmet Hot Dogs, eating his Mark Chase dog, Fox style, and watching the skateboard kids across the street, rolling around a little radio blaring some kind of extra-obnoxious rock. He noticed a Kris Krijole patch on the back of one kid's jacket. It made him smile even before he realized it was his little friend Jimmy with the Minnie Mouse skateboard.

It was an odd combination of flavors on this dog, but it was impressive that they'd even made it. It was on an Italian roll that comes from their Spicy Italian Sausage Sandwich, but it seemed like an actual hot dog. And they even had sauerkraut! Why the hell did they have sauerkraut in that kitchen? He didn't remember a reuben on the menu. Maybe somebody had to run to the deli for some of these ingredients. Maybe his assumptions about the Fox Sports Grill had been unfair. Of course, he never would've gotten that type of service without bribing them. Isn't that how it works in this world? He who has the most wealth gets the most hot dogs.

He balanced the remaining half of the dog in between thumb and forefinger while wiping mustard off his other hand with a napkin so he could use Mark's phone to call Margaret. She seemed as wary as she should be of his call but did agree to meet him during her lunch break at one o'clock.

When he was down to the last bite of hot dog he smooshed it against the Mountain Dew logo and smeared it across, making a line of mustard and relish. He wiped his fingers on the napkin as he jaywalked over to the skateboarders.

"Hey, kid," he said.

"Which one?" a couple of them asked.

"Minnie Mouse. Jimmy."

Jimmy spun around, acted aloof. "What's up, Sidewalk Patrol?"

"What are we listening to here? Is this a recording of actual angels in Heaven playing their beautiful music? How did you get this?"

"Funny."

"Sorry. I wanted to ask you about Kris Krijole, though. You like Kris Krijole, huh?"

The kid looked over at the patch on his shoulder. His friends laughed.

"Yeah, so what?"

"You get that patch after he died?"

The other kids chimed in again. "No!"

"He was into them way before it was popular," said a kid with filthy blond dreadlocks.

"Let me ask you: what do you like about him?" Carter

knew he was acting like a local news reporter working on a clueless human interest story, but he didn't care anymore. He was coming from a place of genuine curiosity.

"I don't know. Everything. What are you asking me?" He pushed off on his board.

"I want to know what he means to you. What is it, the music, the lyrics?"

"I don't know, they're good songs."

"You're a smart kid. There must be something."

"I think the lyrics—the lyrics are angry but his voice to me, I think his voice sounds sad. I don't know."

"It makes you sad?"

"No, happy. He feels the way you feel sometimes."

"I wish I had something like that," Carter said.

Jimmy didn't know how to respond to sincerity coming from Carter. "Next question," he said.

"What size shoe do you wear?"

"What the fuck!" The kids all laughed.

"Tell me the size, I'm in a hurry."

"You're fuckin crazy, man."

He stared at Jimmy's feet, trying to estimate. "Are you guys gonna be around here for a little bit?"

Ten minutes later Carter returned with a Nike shoe box in his hands. He tried to give it to Jimmy, but the kid brushed it away. Carter sat it down on the ground and stepped away.

"If they don't fit it's your own damn fault. I gave it my best guess."

The other kids opened the box and couldn't believe it. Brand new and everything. The kid with the dreads noticed the paperback book tucked beneath them.

"What's this for?" he asked.

"Don't worry about it."

"Oh shit, he's wearing them too," dreadlocks said, pointing to the Kris Krijoles on Carter's feet. The kids passed the smaller pair over and into Jimmy's hands. He admired them, smiling big, despite his best efforts.

"You're giving me these? Why?"

"Too small for me."

"Why do you have these?"

"Long story. But I'm happy to get them to someone who appreciates them."

"Thanks man." For a moment his eyes looked different. Carter had never seen Jimmy with his guard down.

"No problem."

"You want some money for those?"

"No."

"You better not say I owe you a hand job or something."

"Ah, fuck no! Jesus, kid!" Carter put his hands up in innocence and backed away about five more feet.

"Good."

"I could get you some weed."

"No. But I'll tell you what, you want to repay me, answer one question for me."

"Oh no, here we go, some child molester question."

"No, man. I just want to know. You're on your skateboard there, you got your dead rock star you love, you like getting in fights with adults, you're a little hellraiser, right? And then... a picture of Minnie Mouse! What the fuck?"

"You already asked me that!"

"Well, your answer was shit."

"What's wrong with Minnie Mouse?"

"'Cause you're supposed to put something cool on your skateboard. Minnie Mouse is not cool. It's the most mainstream thing in the world. The most bland. And girly too."

"Exactly. You can't be cool for liking Minnie Mouse. You can't even like Minnie Mouse ironically. Most people look at that and think I'm a dipshit. But if they can see it and still think I'm cool that proves they're not superficial."

"So it's a test?"

"Yeah."

"Okay."

Carter figured if he told the kid he was cool then he passed the test, but he couldn't say something like that. He just nodded and walked away. Then, "Hey, I just thought of something."

"What's that?"

"Do you want a motorcycle? I could get you a motorcycle."

"What?"

"Ah, forget it. It's probably not there anymore."

# 4

HE DIDN'T HAVE TO look at his watch to know that one o'clock was rapidly approaching. He recognized the lunch hour foot traffic. That meant it was time to call Dante.

"Hey Dante, it's Carter."

"What the fuck did you tell the Flemings!? They changed the lock on the storage space!"

"Oh shit, I'm sorry man."

"I thought we were cool!"

"That's true, we *were* cool, you told me we were."

"Now they're telling me I took the Kris Krijoles! What the fuck? And why are you calling me?"

"Well, it sounds like I'm calling at a bad time. I just wanted to say I was sorry about everything."

"Fuck you!" Dante hung up. Carter called back, but it went to voicemail.

"Carter again, Dante. We must've gotten cut off. Sorry about that. Look, I'm headed to an important business meeting right now at the Mind Bandit advertising agency, top floor of the Rossi Building downtown. So I can't talk to you right now, but I'll catch you later. After my meeting at the Rossi Building, 5$^{th}$ and Columbus, ad agency on the top floor. Peace."

Getting close to the final stage. He walked over to the parking lot where he'd parked the U-Haul. When he first got there he was thinking maybe this was the lot he had robbed when he was a kid, but he realized now that it wasn't. That would've been a couple blocks north, maybe where there's a parking structure with condos above it. A shame to see a historic landmark like that go away.

Now was the riskiest part of the plan, and the least necessary. There was a very good chance that he wouldn't even try. It all depended on whether or not Jason Fleming was working a day shift at The Dock, and if so whether or not his car was parked in a good spot to creep up on without somebody getting suspicious.

Jason seemed to work long hours, judging by how many times Carter had seen him in there. And he's definitely been known to work at this time of day. Carter just had to roll by and try to spot his black Mustang. If it wasn't there, no loss, he'd move right on to the big finale. But if it was there there was gonna be some fun. There was gonna be an exclamation point on this thing.

It was there.

Jason was talking to a customer about the first round draft picks when he heard the bang. The wall of liquor bottles rattled and clanked for several seconds, and when they settled down two or three car alarms were going off in the surrounding blocks. Everyone, even old Vic Clements, got up and headed outside to see what was going on.

In a city you hear loud sounds – metal doors and dumpsters being slammed, cars backfiring, things like that – that can be confused with gunshots or explosions. This was not one of those. This was unmistakable. Something fucking blew up. That something turned out to be the front end of Jason's beloved 2014 Ford Mustang GT. The damage actually looked small compared to the sound they heard – you'd think the whole thing would've gone up. Instead there was this foot-wide puncture wound on the hood spewing flames and smelly black smoke. The windshield was shattered into a tile mosaic that was mostly white, the color of the airbags inside. He dropped to his knees in anguish, but his co-workers lifted him and pulled him back in case the fireworks weren't over yet. It was a few minutes before he thought to pull out his keychain and stop the alarm from blaring.

He just kept thinking *I know who did this.*

212

# 5

COBBS WAS AT his desk scarfing down his morning yogurt (Greek, blueberry) when he had to take a call from a young woman desperate to talk to Rogers. Another one. This was the punishment Cobbs got for finally suspending the lazy asshole: having to take on his workload. Which turned out to be bigger than he expected.

But it was good that he took this one. The woman on the phone was named Abbey, she was the girlfriend of Mark Chase, the missing person who'd turned out to be a detainee. She'd had a conversation with Mark's older brother Carter that she couldn't shake. He'd given her a weird book, was acting very strange and talking about dying for a cause. She didn't know what to do.

"Did he say what he was upset about?"

"His brother. He's still missing."

"He didn't say anything more than that, though?"

"No."

"Okay. Well, I know Carter, I might be able to have a word with him. Can you verify his address for me?"

Cobbs figured it was most likely nothing, but he had to cover his ass. It had obviously been a mistake to give out classified information. This was always his problem: caring too much about honesty and doing the right thing. Misleading people didn't come naturally to him. He couldn't stomach lying to this guy who just wanted to find his brother. But of course, as he'd infamously told the officers passing around a joint at the Christmas party, just because you disagree with a law doesn't mean you can violate it. He'd fucked up, it was a dumb mistake, and at this point all he could do was make sure Carter Chase kept his mouth shut about it.

Chase didn't answer the door. The neighbor, a friendly hippie type, did answer his.

"No, I was knocking on *this* door."

"Oh, okay."

"That must happen all the time, must be a pain."

"Yeah, it's a design flaw."

"Well listen, have you seen Carter, who's staying here?" The guy was flustered, didn't know what to say. "Do you know him?" Cobbs asked. "Carter Chase?"

"No. I mean yeah. Just as my neighbor's brother, though. That's all. I don't--"

"It's okay sir, this is not an investigation. Carter isn't in trouble. At least not with me. A friend was worried about him, wanted me to check on him. That's all."

"Oh no, is something wrong?"

"I don't know. I hope not. Looks like he's not home. Any idea where I can find him?"

"No, I don't know. I saw him shooting hoops this morning, but I guess he left."

"Does he still work at that hot dog stand downtown?"

"I don't know. I guess so."

"Okay. Thank you sir. You have a nice day now."

The hot dog stand wasn't there anymore. Or at least not today, and he didn't see it packed up anywhere like it probably would've been if it was closed for the day. For a second he had a feeling like he wasn't sure where he parked, came expecting his car but turned out to be on the wrong block. But Cobbs had a good memory for geography, and he knew this was the right location. Now there's nothing but a big Mountain Dew billboard with yellowish brown crap smeared across it.

Since he'd already parked he decided to stay on foot. He called Sue at headquarters and got Chase's contact number from the report. When he called it there was no answer, it went to voicemail. The recording didn't sound like Carter, and the name he said was Mark, the brother.

214

"Hello, this is Sergeant Cobbs. I'm trying to find you. It's nothing bad, I just want to talk to you about something. Give me a call back at this number if you get this. This message is for Carter."

He probably didn't really need to specify that he was calling for Carter. He knew Mark would not be able to check his voicemail for quite some time.

What now? He had no idea. He'd tried residence, work place, he didn't have anything else to go on. If only he could get in touch with that fed that had been spying on Chase for months. Surely that guy would know his hangouts. But Cobbs wouldn't have the foggiest idea how to get in contact with him on short notice, they really didn't have that sort of inter-agency relationship. Even if he did it would be a terrible idea to consult them on this, considering the trouble he could get in for what he'd told Carter Chase.

Maybe the stand had moved? It was lunch hour – a lot of the office drones were out and about, getting their coffee, or bringing takeout back to their cubicles. He stopped two men in ties and trenchcoats.

"Excuse me, do you know where to get a Mark Chase dog?"

"They went out of business," one of the men said.

"They did?" said the other one.

"I remember they used to be right here. I was hoping they just moved," Cobbs said.

"No, I think the guy retired. Or he couldn't afford the permits or something."

"That's a shame," said his friend. "Those things were good!"

"They were," Cobbs said. "Thanks anyway, guys."

The people who worked around here knew Carter's food, so they must've known him too. He'd have made friends and connections. When the stand went out of business, he might've found work somewhere else in the neighborhood. It was worth walking around some more, looking in windows. So he did.

It had been forever since he'd done this kind of detective work. He liked it, but he also felt rusty. Kind of helpless.

Shit. The brother's girlfriend. He hadn't asked her where Carter worked. He needed to call her back for more leads. He checked the numbers in his phone before remembering he'd taken the call in his office. Mr. Attention To Detail, not bothering to write down a phone number.

He called headquarters.

"Do a favor for me, Sue. There was a call on Rogers's direct line this morning, I took it at my desk. I need you to check the Caller ID, give me the last number on there."

"What's the name?"

"Abbey something."

"You have a pen ready?"

He did, but as soon as he started writing the number down, something clicked. Chase's phone records. He'd looked at them when he was trying to find the brother. They were all local calls, he remembered, because that could've been a good sign if it had really been the brother making the calls. Cobbs tried to picture the list. He didn't have that kind of memory. But he remembered one odd thing he'd noticed at the time. A couple of the businesses that had been called had almost the same address, just different suite numbers. Didn't seem to mean anything, but it stuck in his head. One of them was initials, and then Counselors? Consultations? JMJ Consulting. Something like that. The other one he hadn't known what the words meant. Something about brains, or minds. Mind Reader. Mind Buddy. Mind Bandage.

It wouldn't matter what the name was if he could only remember the address. He was thinking it was downtown somewhere. He wanted to say it was around here, even. That would make sense. Businesses Chase knew from selling his hot dogs. What street was he on, 4$^{th}$ Avenue? And the hot dog stand had been on 5$^{th}$.

5$^{th}$ and Columbia, it was somewhere around there. He

was pretty sure. Must be in the Rossi Building. That's right up here. He could go there and ask about Carter, it was the best lead he had. There was a side entrance around the corner, but he thought he should go around to the front. In the lobby they'd have a directory, he could look for the JMJ consulting firm and the Mind Bandage, or whatever it was. He'd recognize it if it was on there.

But he stopped in his tracks, because that was Chase on the sidewalk, crouched down over an unzipped athletic bag, tinkering with something. He had his back turned conspicuously, trying to shield whatever he was doing from prying eyes. Cobbs caught a glimpse of a box inside the bag, and Chase was messing with something inside the box. What was it?

It was silver and round. Cobbs smiled – for a second he thought it was a tall boy. No, it was longer, thinner. It was a length of metal pipe. He was pouring a handful of something into it. Then screwing a cap on the end.

What the fuck? It couldn't be.

Cobbs had his hand on his sidearm.

"Carter! Carter Chase!"

Chase stood up, but he didn't turn around. He didn't hear Cobbs. He was wearing earbuds. He had the box under his left arm now, the empty gym bag wadded up in his hand, dribbling a basketball with the other. He dropped the bag in a garbage can and kept walking.

Cobbs followed Chase around the corner, watched him enter the revolving door to the lobby. Was this what he thought it was? It seemed so improbable. But he had to assume it was. He had to call this in.

He looped back to the corner, away from the windows, didn't want Chase to see him. Called dispatch. Backup on the way.

But he couldn't wait. If this was real, this was his responsibility. He had to go in there.

Tiptoeing through the revolving door. Hate these fucking things. Runs through the lobby, weapon out. Security guard sees him. He yells, holds up badge.

"Big guy with a basketball! Where'd he go?"

"Uh, top floor! Mind Bandit!" the guard says, panicked.

Into the elevator. Guard tries to go with him.

"No, stay here," Cobbs says. "When they get here tell them I went up."

Elevator ride takes forever. Heart beating hard. Picturing the worst. When the doors open he hears commotion down the hall, runs toward it, no hesitation. People crying.

"Carter Chase!" he yells. Follows where the fingers are pointing. Stairway to the roof.

His responsibility. Not waiting for backup. Swings the door open. Chase standing there, holding the box. Hostage with him, some space between them. Clear shot.

"Put it down!" he yells. "Come on, Carter! Put it on the ground!"

# 6

AS CARTER MADE his march to the Rossi Building he had to put the earbuds in and listen to *Dr. Pepper's Lonely Hearts Club Band* to relax. He knew this was what had to be done. He knew no other way. Still, his heart was beating out of control. It was like that first convenience store hold up, except for this there would be no easier second time.

When Carter first figured out that his Mom had been killed by a rogue basketball, he took it to mean that life and death were a big non sequitur joke, a cruel tossing of darts. But after some time had passed and the depression lifted he stopped seeing it that way. He started to realize that life wasn't all random. There was a math to it. There was a chain of events, a cause-and-effect. The ball may have fallen from the sky and taken Mom for no reason, but the series of coincidences that led Carter back to that basketball court where the ball came from was too complex to consider accidental. If that junkie kid hadn't tried to rob Tony when Carter was standing there, Carter wouldn't have worked at the hot dog stand. If Carter hadn't worked at the hot dog stand he wouldn't have gotten to know Margaret. If he hadn't gotten to know Margaret he wouldn't have been offered the job at Mind Bandit. If he hadn't been offered the job at Mind Bandit he wouldn't have been shown the roof of the Rossi building. But all those things *did* happen. The ball flew out that hole, down to the front seat of Mom's car as she drove down 5th Avenue, and then Carter's life retraced the ball's arc right back to the source.

What happened to Mark was the same. It wasn't a roll of the dice. It was an algorithm. It was a pattern of data. What Carter had to do was change the data back, shift the math. He had to prove that the algorithm wasn't looking for Mark. It was looking for Mark's brother, the guy that actually *is* a criminal, the guy that actually *did* build a bomb. Or two. But bomb #2, the pipe bomb in the box in the gym bag with the basketball, didn't seem right yet. It looked right, it felt wrong.

The junkie kid! The kid that sent him on this path to understanding. The kid with the bags of coins, caked in filth and chunks of tar, collected from sidewalks, fountains and sewers, from days of spare-changing downtown, desperately trying to trade it for currency his dealer will accept. He was on the other side of the street walking the other way.

"Hey, kid!" Carter yelled, pulling the earbuds out and hanging them over his shoulder, like he'd seen people do.

The kid looked at him, seemed to recognize him, looked away.

"Bring that change over here."

"Fuck you."

"I'm serious. I'll buy your change."

The kid hustled over. "Oh, thanks man. Thank you so much. Here, I'll count it in front of you." He poured some out on top of a newspaper rack and started spacing them out by denomination.

"You're the hot dog guy, right? What happened to your stand?"

"Mountain Dew. Look, I'm in a hurry, let's use the honor system. How much you think you got there?" He took out his wallet.

# 7

CARTER GOT LUCKY and the lobby security guard recognized him from last time. "You're here to see Thom again?" he asked. Carter didn't even have to drop the name himself.

"Yeah," Carter said.

"Right this way, sir."

"Thank you."

He pushed the button for the elevator. The guard called to him from down the hall. "Coming from the gym?" he asked.

For a second Carter thought he was commenting on his sweatiness, 'cause he'd ditched the gym bag in a garbage can outside. He put a hand to his forehead. He'd just mopped it with a napkin before coming inside, and it wasn't too bad yet.

"Oh, this," Carter said, holding out the basketball he had under his arm. In his other hand was the box. "It's from the half court on the roof," he said. "I came to bring it back."

When the elevator doors opened on the top floor, Carter was inside bouncing the basketball. The sound loudly reverberated through the hall as he dribbled down past JML Consulting and the wall displays of Mind Bandit's greatest hits.

As he came into the office, heads turned at their work stations, smiling at him. It was a funny thing to do, dribble inside. They didn't seem that shocked to see him. But their faces changed as they heard his voice and picked up that something was off about him.

"I brought your ball back," he said. "I thought you would want it. There's a little blood stain in the creases if you look closely, but as you can see it bounces great."

Thom came out from his office to see what all the commotion was. "Hey, Carter. What's—what's going on?"

Tucking the box under his arm, Carter threw Thom the ball. Thom caught it.

Carter looked up at the vintage sign hanging from the ceiling, the sorcerer or hypnotist or whatever he was. He shook his head. "You guys seem like such nice people. Don't you feel bad doing this stuff?"

"I don't understand. What's wrong, Carter?"

"Don't you see that you're a part of it? We're not people anymore. We're just data. Clicking our screens, buying products, buying files, creating a profile so you can sell us more shit, unless we buy the wrong shit, and then we get locked up."

"I don't think I follow you, but we can—"

"And another thing. The Doctor-King bar! Are you kidding me? You gotta change the meaning of Dr. King? Nothing is sacred anymore. It's terrible."

"I'm sorry Carter, I don't know what you're talking about. Maybe we could—"

"Martin Luther King! I'm talking about Martin Luther King, the leader of the civil rights movement! That's what Dr. King means. Not a candy bar! You're erasing his name, and everything it stands for, to sell chocolate."

"Okay, I hear you, Martin Luther King. Let's stay calm. Why don't we go into my office and talk about this?"

"I'd rather go up to the basketball court."

"Okay, Carter. Whatever you want. Let's go."

Danielle – or was that one Dawn? - looked concerned. "Thom, no."

"It's okay."

Carter looked around, making eye contact with each of them. "Look, I know somebody's probably calling security already. But I want you to call the police, and I want you to tell them that I have a pipe bomb." There were gasps as he opened the lid of the box and showed them the device.

Carter felt stupid marching him up to the roof, holding that thing, pointing it at him like it was a gun. Thom kept holding his hands up, even though he hadn't been asked to.

222

When they got up there Thom turned around slowly. He looked more sad than scared.

"What is this, Carter? We didn't do anything to you."

"You did more than you know."

"If you want to work on the campaign again—"

"I don't want to work on the campaign. I want you to fix your net there." He cocked his head in the direction of the hole.

"You want me-- I mean, yeah, yeah, whatever you want."

"Don't worry. You'll be safe. As soon as they get here…" Carter trailed off as he stepped over to the fence and peered down to the street. "I'm sorry about all this."

He stayed quiet for a minute as he watched. No police cars at the front of the building yet. He didn't think they'd bother to sneak in the back. He hadn't heard any sirens yet, either.

Nothing to do now except wait. He'd prepared everything as best he could. Only time would tell if any of it would work.

He hadn't seen Margaret in the office, so at least that part of the plan was a success. Right about now she was pissed off that he'd stood her up. Later she'd feel even worse. But he didn't want her to have to see this.

Thom mentioning the campaign made Carter wonder about it, and whether or not they'd taken his suggestion to involve Barry. As he started to ask about it he was interrupted by the sound of the door bursting open behind him. He hadn't realized they were there yet. He turned and saw that it was Cobbs, all by himself. He was yelling, and then the gun went off.

Cobbs heard himself yelling, seemed like it was someone else. Carter looking at him. Something wrong in his eyes. Not complying. Not comprehending? He has to shoot. Has to shoot. He shoots, center of the chest. Drops him.

Watches the box fall. Pipe pops out. Oh shit. Bounces on the ground. Metal sound. One end pops off. Coins spill out.

"Oh fuck oh fuck oh fuck!" the hostage yells, running to the fence, trying to create distance.

Don't be stupid. Don't touch it. He touches it. Picks it up, dumps out more change. For shrapnel? No, for weight. Attention to detail, make it feel real. It's not a bomb, just a pipe. A fake.

He was alive? Coughing. Or laughing. Eyes glazing over. "What did you do, Carter?" Cobbs asked, checking the suspect's pulse. No pulse. Too good of a shot.

Before John Brown was hanged, he said, "This is a beautiful country." Before Carter Chase was shot he said, "Hey, did—," ignored a command to put the bomb down, and then fell over. You know, maybe it was better for Barry anyway that his name didn't come up in all this.

As Carter slumped to the smooth surface of the basketball court he laughed at himself, gurgling blood. *Way to give yourself up, dumbass. You hesitated too long.* His head was curled under his body, staring at his feet as his vision went blurry. The light reflecting from the shiny surface of his Kris Krijoles turned into stars. They felt good on his feet, but he regretted it now, dying in Nikes.

# FOUR

# 1

ACCORDING TO THE acquaintance of the suspect, Carter Chase had been staying in a duplex leased to his younger brother Mark Chase, who was also her boyfriend. This was corroborated by the property owner as well as information in a missing persons report filed by the acquaintance.

The officer involved in the shooting, Sergeant Cobbs, had a history with the suspect both before and after his incarceration. Cobbs was one of the first officers to arrive at the suspect's home, despite protests from commanding officers. He made the others wait for the bomb squad before entering. The residents of the adjoining home, a couple with a young daughter, were evacuated and put up in a downtown residence inn. Upon entry there were concerns about an odor that might have been from explosives or chemical booby traps of some kind. The robot spotted no danger, and the fumes were found to be caused by recent painting that had been done in a bedroom and hallway. The home was unusually clean, free of clutter and looked to be freshly vacuumed.

While they waited they got word about the U-Haul truck. It had been found with its tires slashed in an alley downtown, and was found to be rented in Carter Chase's name, on his debit card. With the scare in the Rossi Building and the car bombing less than a mile away there were understandable concerns about the contents of the vehicle.

Cobbs recognized the address. "That's behind Niketown, right?" he asked. He thought about going over there, but decided to stay put. His superiors would likely be there, because it was a more populated area and closer to headquarters. He didn't want to be sent home yet, and knew he was pressing his luck as it was.

Bomb making materials were found only in the garage, unassembled and safely stored, and the home was declared clear in just over four hours. The FBI guys got to go in first, then the locals.

Detective Wood, who had been assigned the earlier missing persons case, helped gather the evidence. Along with the materials from the garage, officers confiscated a personal computer, a survival knife, a baseball bat that appeared to be bloodied, and some mail.

"Are we missing something?" Wood asked the Sergeant. "No guns? No ammo? Doesn't make sense."

"I don't know. Maybe he didn't like guns."

"He sure doesn't anymore."

"Fuck you."

"Hey, don't feel bad about it, Cobbs. You did the right thing. He was gonna blow those people up."

"With what, a pipe full of dimes and pennies? I'm not even sure how much gum he could've bought."

"Other bomb worked. The one on the car."

"Yeah, if that was him. But there was no one in the car. We don't know that he was trying to kill anybody."

"Well, the guy's a weirdo, we know that much."

"I guess so. Seemed okay when I met him, though."

"You saw the bookshelf, right?"

"What bookshelf?"

"In the living room there's a bookshelf with ten or fifteen copies of the same book on it. Those were the leftovers. He gave a copy to the next door neighbor, maybe others."

"What is the book, *Catcher in the Rye?*"

"No."

"*Hop On Pop*? Don't keep me in suspense."

"It's called *John Brown.*"

"Like the abolitionist?"

"I don't know. Guy with a beard."

"Huh."

Cobbs wondered if he should feel guilty about all this. He remembered that he'd actually met Carter Chase as a young man, before he'd pleaded guilty to breaking into a shoe store. The memory was hazy, but there was something he'd admired about the kid's straight up refusal to implicate anyone else, including the weasel who'd ratted him out. He didn't seem like a mad bomber, then or now. But clearly it was the information about his brother that had set him off. Now Cobbs *really* knew he shouldn't have told him. Or at least he should've played down the utter hopelessness of the situation.

When Captain Scott arrived he let Cobbs know how displeased he was about his texts being ignored. "The assistant chief is on his way, it's time for you to go home. You know how this works. Get some rest. Talk to a therapist. Go up to Victoria for a weekend. You're outta here."

It was actually a pretty good idea. Cobbs had always wanted to go up there and see the dragonboat races, but he could never get Cindy to renew her passport. Now that they were separated there was nothing holding him back.

Assistant Police Chief Simmons ran a small news conference in the morning. He started with a prepared statement about the basic facts of the three incidents leading up to the police involved shooting of suspect Carter Philip Chase, a felon, freed earlier this year on compassionate release grounds. One, the bombing of a parked car on 1st Avenue. No one was hurt. Two, leaving a suspicious vehicle in an alley, a rented moving truck with its tires slashed. No explosives found inside, but a considerable amount of stolen property. The third incident was the bomb threat and hostage taking on the top floor of the Rossi building. The suspect was shot and killed by a police Sergeant who happened to be in the area at the time of the incident. No one else was harmed.

Bomb making materials and instructions had been found at the suspect's place of residence, he said. No motive was known. "But we can all count ourselves lucky that the suspect was not able to carry out any further attacks," he concluded before opening the floor to questions.

"Sir, can you tell us more about why Mr. Chase was released from prison?"

"I understand, I'm told it was a compassionate release,

he was diagnosed with a terminal brain tumor. That's all I know about that, you'll have to talk to-- talk to the warden I guess."

"Chief, you referred to stolen property in the moving van? Moving truck, rather?"

"Yes, it was filled with shoes, Nike shoes, we have identified them as stolen merchandise from the Nike's shoe store, which the van was parked behind. Mr. Chase had been incarcerated for, uh, a break-in incident at the Niketown store downtown."

"Have the shoes been returned to Niketown?"

"No, they've been taken into evidence."

"What type of shoes were they, sir? What style?"

"I'm not—I don't have that information. We're-- there's gonna be a press release that we'll give out later."

"What sort of evidence do you have that the suspect was involved in the car bombing?"

"Uh, there was both forensic and physical evidence. I won't go beyond that."

"Sir, we're hearing that the stolen shoes are associated with the musician Kris Krijole. Have you found any other evidence to suggest that the crimes were inspired by this music?"

"I don't know anything about that."

"Can you comment on reports that there were other terrorists involved?"

"It is still a very active investigation. Three persons of interest were arrested at the scene. At this point they are not considered suspects, but it is still a very active investigation."

"These are the three men that Mr. Kamaka, the security guard, said were friends of the suspect, trying to get to the top floor to meet him?"

"I can't comment on that."

"Can you comment on the reports about what the suspect said? They say he was yelling about--"

"Yes. Witnesses have told us the suspect was saying... he was giving a sort of a rant about, something about Martin

Luther King. Dr. Martin Luther King."

"Do you believe this is a racially motivated crime?"

"We are talking to his, to the administration at the facility where he was incarcerated, trying to find out if he was involved in any white supremacist gangs. I won't go beyond that."

# 2

COBBS WAS TIRED and needed coffee. Abbey wanted to see him, so he told her to meet him at the new Dunkin' Donuts that just opened up on 5$^{th}$ in that spot that used to be a restaurant, Mary's or something like that. She said she knew the place and that it was "strangely appropriate." Normally he would be sensitive about perpetuating the cops-eating-donuts stereotype, but he was trying to be more laid back while he was on his leave, like his friends told him to. Go with the flow. Anyway he wasn't even having donuts, he was having a Hot & Spicy Breakfast Sandwich & Wake Up Wrap.

He would've waited for her to get there before he ordered, but she showed up 16 minutes late and he felt self conscious just sitting there. When she walked up to his table he rushed to swallow the big bite he was taking out of the wrap and self consciously wiped his mouth with a napkin. "I'm sorry. I didn't realize how hungry I was. Do you need anything? My treat."

"No thank you."

"Coffee, or..."

"No thank you."

She sat down across from him and looked down at the table. Her sad eyes barely hid behind the tiny lenses of her sunglasses. He was still getting used to that trend.

"You were supposed to help him," Abbey said. "Not kill him."

"I'm sorry, Abbey. I wish I hadn't." It was all he could say. He looked her in the eyes – in the lenses – to show that he was sincere. After a bit she broke eye contact and looked around at the mostly untouched decor.

"This is weird," she said. "I used to come here when it was a different place. It looks so different."

"Yeah. But I'm glad they're finally opening Dunkins around here," he said. "I grew up on the east coast."

"I've never actually been in one before. What kind of donut shop sells sandwiches? What's that all about?"

"You've never had their sandwiches? Oh God, you *have* to try them!" he said, genuinely enthusiastic, and not just for the change of subject. "You want a bite? It's spicy," he said, holding his out for her.

"No thank you."

"Selection's not as good, but quality-wise I'd say they're on par with Jack in the Box. And their coffee is the absolute best. I love Dunkins."

"Huh."

"Not for the donuts."

"I know," she said.

"You know, I honestly liked him," Cobbs said after a while, breaking the awkward silence. "And I felt for him, the situation with his brother. But he was threatening those people. He said he had a bomb."

"I know."

"They said he told them to call the police. He *wanted* a confrontation."

"I know."

"So what was I supposed to do? I would've rather arrested him, talk it out with him, but he wouldn't put the thing down. I didn't have a choice."

"I know."

"You know, so what are we discussing here?" He could feel himself losing his cool, tried to dial it back. "I don't blame you for being upset. I can sit here and you can tell me I'm a bad person if you want. But what else do you want out of me? I don't know how to tell you how sorry I am. Do you think I'm proud of what I did? I have to live with this for the rest of my life."

"And so do I. I'm the one that called you. I'm the one that knew something was wrong and didn't know how to help."

234

"You tried. You did more than a lot of people would've done. There was no way to know what would happen."

"I know," she said. "I know." She took the shades off, finally, and nervously tapped them against the table. "That was here, actually," she said. "This was the last place that I talked to him. In fact... this was the first place too! I mean, I had talked to him on the phone before that, but then we met in person here."

"Right here?"

"Out there," she pointed out the window. "They had outdoor seating then."

"When it was Mary's?"

"Mary Mary's. But it was called nomi then, I think. Pretty good place. He embarrassed me because he was complaining about the food being expensive and then he just pulled out a candy bar that he brought and started eating it."

Cobbs laughed.

"Did you see on the news - or I guess you would know it anyway -- they said he was talking to them about Martin Luther King?"

"Yelling at them. I don't know what that was about."

"I think I do. There's a candy bar called a Doctor-King bar."

"Sure. Yeah, Mind Bandit, the firm there, they had done some advertising for Doctor-King. But they didn't know why he was bringing it up."

"One thing I had to learn about Carter, he really believed that some things should remain sacred, that things should have meaning. To him, the name Dr. King should always be about the historical guy, Martin Luther King, and what he stood for. Civil rights or whatever."

"I don't get the connection," Cobbs said. "The Doctor-King is the guy on the label, he's like a king of doctors. It's a totally different thing."

"I know, but to Carter it was... he found that offensive for some reason. Forget it. All I'm saying is, we can't let Carter's death be meaningless. People have to know he wasn't just some nut."

"You said he was talking about dying for a cause?"

"Yeah, that's what he said he liked about the book he gave me."

"That was the John Brown book? W.E.B. Dubois?"

"Yeah."

"He had a whole shelf filled with that book. Apparently he was giving them to everybody he knew."

"Did he give one to you?"

"No," the Sergeant said, not having thought about it before. "I'm not sure why not. That's a good question." He turned on his phone and texted Sue at headquarters:

*"any packages 4 me"*

Normally he'd never abbreviate like that, it made him feel like a moron. But he was on leave.

"So if it wasn't just suicide by cop, what was it? What cause did he think he was dying for?"

"I can only guess," Abbey said, "but I'd say it was for Mark. That's all he ever cared about when I knew him, was getting his brother back."

"Yeah, I guess that would make sense. We think he has a bomb, he has hostages, he makes his demands, 'let my brother go.' He was smart enough to know they'd never let him out for that, but it damn sure would've brought attention to the situation. And he was running out of time to do that. He was desperate."

"He never told me he was sick. I don't think he told anybody."

"He didn't have many people to tell."

"That's true."

Cobbs' phone slid a few inches across the table as it vibrated. He glanced at the text from Sue:

*"yes 1 package 4 U"*

it said. Then a second text:

*"return address Carter Chase"*

# 3

"THE BUREAU OF Transportation Statistics Field Office" looked innocent enough, as if it were some sort of field office for a bureau that collects statistics about transportation. But Cobbs had been assured that the building was being used as a front for another federal agency. It better be, or this appointment (and trip) would be a waste of time. He only had so much administrative leave until the inquest. And he was already missing the Dragonboat Festival.

It was extra vacation time, basically, but he didn't take it lightly. Everybody told him the same things: *you did everything right. You made a judgment. There was no way to know the bomb wasn't real. That guy was a nut. Who knows what he would've done? You probably saved lives.*

Cobbs couldn't brush it off that easily. He'd met Carter Chase. He'd known where his mind was at. He'd even seen him do it before, offering himself up, taking the fall. He should've figured out what he was up to.

More than that, Cobbs worried that he'd implicated himself in a system he didn't want to be a part of. When he told Chase about his brother's indefinite detention he thought he was separating himself from the policy, doing his part not to support it. He warned Chase about how the government could shut him up, but the government never had to, because *he* did it. He shut the poor guy up for good.

Abbey was right. He had to do something to make things right. There was no way he could just walk away.
He had to help Carter succeed.

Pierson himself came out to the lobby to get him. "Sergeant Cobbs?" he asked.

"That's me."

"Pierson," the man said, offering a firm handshake.

Cobbs followed Pierson back to a small office cluttered with Washington Redskins memorabilia.

"Have a seat," Pierson said, gesturing to a chair in front of his desk. Cobbs sat, looking around at the various posters and pennants.

"Football fan, eh?"

"Baseball too. Originally from Cleveland," Pierson said, pointing to a bobblehead of the Cleveland Indians mascot on a shelf.

"Oh, I didn't catch that," he laughed. "Yeah, Redskins *and* Indians. That's unusual."

"Why is that unusual?" Pierson asked. "I grew up in Cleveland, then I moved here. Those are my teams."

"Oh, I didn't mean anything," Cobbs said.

"That's okay." Pierson reached into a cooler and took out two bottles of water. "Water?"

"Sure. Thank you."

"We're not allowed to waterboard anymore, but we have a lot of these left over."

Cobbs didn't know how to react to this guy.

"It's a joke," Pierson said. "For humor. Lighten up."

"I'm sorry. It's funny. I just have a lot on my mind."

"I know you do. I've been briefed. Listen Sergeant, I know you've come a long way to talk to me here, to tell me your theories of why this Mark Richard Chase is innocent, but before you get into that I need to tell you that this is very insulting to my agency and to myself personally."

"Sir, I don't—"

"This is my office. You let me finish. Now, I don't know what they told you, but we are not an agency that makes a lot of mistakes. Our model does not leave room for human error. Do you understand what it is we do here?"

"Somewhat."

"Somewhat. So why do you believe that you, a city cop, can tell us how to do our job? Are you an expert on statistics? Are you an expert on databases? Are you a profiler? Have you studied terrorist patterns and behaviors? Do you have a security clearance? Do you even *somewhat* know anything?"

Cobbs hadn't opened his bottle of water yet, but he held off because he thought this would be an awkward time to do it.

"You don't have to answer any of those questions. The answer is no to all of them. So that's all I need from you," Pierson said. "How 'bout you?" he asked, pleased with himself. "Do you have any questions for *me*?"

"Sure," Cobbs said as he reached over and flicked the top of the Chief Wahoo bobblehead. "Did you ever consider using the Bureau of Indian Affairs as your front agency?" Then he twisted the lid off the bottle and took a swig.

The bobblehead jittered back and forth, vibrating the other objects on the shelf. Pierson took a drink too. He leaned back in his chair, looking at the ceiling. All the sudden he snorted. "Indian Affairs," he mumbled, smiling. "All right. That's pretty good. I'm going to give you this round." He laughed before turning serious again, but not as cold as before. "This detainee. Mark Richard Chase. Can you tell me how you knew we had him?"

"We had a missing persons case on him," Cobbs said. "Your people were tailing his brother, Carter Chase…"

"We do that sometimes with the relatives of suspects, to assess whether or not they're involved."

"Well, Carter Chase spotted your agent who was following him and brought me the plate number."

"I hear he brought you the whole plate."

"That's correct, he did. So I looked into it and I found out that the car belonged to your agency and that you were following him because his brother was your detainee."

"That information shouldn't have been available to you."

"Well, I've made some friends over the years."

"I'm sure that you have, otherwise you wouldn't be in here meeting with me. Especially about something like this."

"I'm not trying to tell you how to do your job, sir. I'm just trying to do mine. I always tell my officers to do all the reading, do all the homework, dot all the i's, cross all the t's, don't be lazy. That's why I'm here. My job isn't finished until I've made my case to you, sir. I believe Mark Chase is innocent. "

"Well, that's impossible. I can see why it might not seem that way from the outside, but this a very good program with an extremely high success rate in capturing potential terrorists before they strike."

"How much of an investigation could you have done on this guy? I noticed you don't take computers or phones into evidence."

"We do sometimes, but we don't usually *need* evidence. That's not really the business we're in. I couldn't say offhand if we did it in this particular instance. I'd have to look at the file again."

"I'm telling you you didn't, because they were still in his home. We took them as evidence in an investigation involving his brother, Carter Chase."

"The bomb scare. And you're the officer who shot him, correct?"

"Yes sir."

"Well, I apologize for that. As you know we'd been monitoring him. After the license plate incident, when he made our agent, we assigned a drone to him, but it can take some time to get the legal clearance on something like that. It appears he took advantage of that processing window."

"See, that's my point. *Carter* took advantage of that window. Not Mark. You have the wrong Chase. They've gotta be a similar profile. Same family background, obviously. And Carter ended up living in the same house that Mark had, using the same phone and computer. But *Carter* is the one who acted. He's a felon, he has a violent temper, experience with explosives, he also had more weapons and bomb making materials at home at the time of his death. He had a relationship with Mark, but not a close one, because he'd been

242

incarcerated for years. I know you have your algorithms and profiles and everything, and I'm not questioning their success. I'm just saying they were pointing you to Carter, not Mark."

"You said it yourself, Carter Chase was in prison the whole time. The data that led us to Mark Chase was all his own, it came from his purchases and bank activity and a number of other factors. You're right, the profiles would've led us to Carter Chase as well, but we didn't get a hit on him until last month. We got Mark Chase over a year ago."

"So Mark's purchases figured into that data? Let me show you one of those purchases," Cobbs said, reaching into his bag and pulling out a book. "This is *John Brown*, by W.E.B. Dubois."

"Isn't it pronounced *dew-bwah*?"

"No, it seems like it would be, but it's *dew-boys*. It's weird."

"Huh. I always thought it was *dew-bwah*."

"It's not. But you know who John Brown was, correct? He led a raid on an armory, tried to start an uprising, and was hung for it. Technically a domestic terrorist. Probably a red flag in your program, right? Make the buyer look like a radical? It couldn't have helped his case to have it on record that he bought a biography of American history's greatest domestic terrorist."

"Probably not. But that's just one point of data in the whole portrait."

"Carter thought buying this book might've goosed his brother's profile. He sent me this copy at my department. Showed up a couple days after I killed him. Read what it says." He opened the book to the title page and handed it to Pierson.

"To Cobbs," Pierson read out loud. "My brother bought me this book on Amazon. Apparently that's illegal now. Best wishes, Carter."

"This was one of the books Carter asked his brother to get it for him while he was in prison. Mark bought all of Carter's books. We found an e-reader in Mark's desk, he didn't really buy paper books, except the ones he bought for Carter. Before the bomb incident Carter was giving copies of this to his friends. He ordered dozens of them, this was at the end of last month."

"And that's when he showed up in our database."

"Exactly."

Pierson rested a pointer finger under his lower lip, his eyes looking off to some far away thought, and exhaled. He was seeing it now.

"It's true, terrorism suspects tend to buy physical books rather than e-books, that could be one point against him. And it is possible that the content of that book would figure in. Since he purchased it from a seller on Amazon that could also be a factor, if the seller was a known associate of other suspects, or had had any transactions with them. Those elements, combined with other possibly incriminating data, in aggregate... it's an intriguing notion."

"Okay, good. So we're both intrigued. But how does this help an innocent man who's locked up with no charges, no chance of a trial?"

Pierson kept thinking about it, his eyes distant. He pulled on his bottom lip, nodding repeatedly like the bobblehead. He raised his arms in the air, stretching, then sat up straight. "Well, shit. I'll tell you what. I can't promise anything. I don't know if there's anything I can do. But I'll look into it. I really will. I'll have them run his phone conversations and emails through our scanners again and see what we can find. And if I'm convinced he's really innocent, that some analyst wasn't doing his job and let a false positive get through, then... I don't know. I'll shoot off a few emails."

Cobbs exhaled. He knew this was the best he was going to get. Better than he could've expected. He jumped to his feet.

"Okay, thank you sir," he said, shaking hands again. "Go Redskins. And Indians."

"You know it."

# 4

MASON HADN'T LEARNED many lessons from his late brother Carter, but he had to give him one thing: the Pepsi ad on Mom's grave was a masterstroke. It had been more dumb luck than smart business, but what did it matter? It worked. So when it fell upon Mason to take care of Carter's funeral arrangements he knew he wanted to sign up for the same affiliate program. Unfortunately Pepsi wasn't taking on new accounts, he was told, so he had to settle for a lower paying protein bar sponsorship.

When Abbey found out about the ad she tried to talk Mason out of it, but he didn't care what she thought. Even Dana had some misgivings. It seemed to her like Carter would've wanted an old school ad-free grave. But Mason argued that if Carter disagreed with affiliate programs he wouldn't have been collecting those checks from Pepsi. He convinced himself that was a solid justification and not just an excuse.

Mason was more of a milkshake guy, but the Pro-Bars appealed to him. Similar to a Doctor-King bar, but with more caffeine. They sent him a couple boxes, one in peanut butter and one with goji berries. 22 grams of protein, not bad. He wasn't sure what to do with so many, though. Since he didn't bother to read the letter they came with, he didn't figure out until later that he was supposed to pass them out at the funeral.

There weren't many people to pass them out to anyway. The pallbearers were himself, Mark's neighbor Barry Winston, Tony from the hot dog stand, and three burly young men on loan from the cemetery staff. The only other mourners were Dana, Abbey, Barry's wife and kid, Tony's wife and a punk kid named Jimmy. "Kris Krijole's over there," Dana had told Jimmy, pointing to the other grave. "This is a private event."

"I'm here for Carter Chase," the kid said. "I'm a friend."

"Oh," Dana said, surprised. "I guess you're in the right place then." She didn't even want to know what the relationship was there, so she didn't ask.

They had the service at Verizon First Methodist, figuring it must've been Carter's church since he'd used it for Mom. In fact it felt like kind of a rehash of her funeral, except more intimate because none of the extended family had shown up. They'd all been invited, but maybe they couldn't afford two trips in two years, or who knows, maybe the controversial way Carter went out had scared them off. He didn't blame them.

The burial part was short and sweet. The pastor rushed through the prayer and had to shout over the noise from the Kris Krijole fan drum circle. Security clearly hadn't clamped down on those kids as much as Mr. Garrett had led Mason to believe. He hoped if he complained he could get a partial refund, or at least a coupon.

A few times since the shooting Mason had laid awake at night thinking about childhood: building forts in the park, going fishing with Dad. He wondered what was different about Carter, why he didn't grow into adult responsibility the way he and Mark had. Why he couldn't get a real job or stop stealing and fighting. And he wondered if there was anything he should've done to help him find his way. Now, at the service, he felt like he'd already taken care of the necessary soul searching, and was ready to move on. It surprised him how emotional the others were. Abbey was a woman, of course, but Barry seemed even more broken up.

There was a nice moment – a very brief one – when the drummers and the pastor paused at the same time, and a peaceful quiet fell over the cemetery. As luck would have it a technical error caused the muted speakers on Mom's marker to suddenly kick in at full volume, blaring an incongruously upbeat pop R&B jingle for an awkward minute while one of

246

the borrowed pallbearers messed with a hidden touch screen menu trying to find a manual override option.

Barry bristled at the screw up. "To do this to Carter, of all people," he muttered. "They're killing him all over again."

Mason patted him on the arm reassuringly. "It's fine," he said. "My brother *loved* Pepsi Smooth."

In the months after the funeral, things really changed around the family plot. For one thing it became less crowded as Krijole's visitors began to level off a little. Sure, most days he got handfuls of curious tourists, but not the legions of dreadlocked campers he used to attract. It was an interesting dilemma for advertisers. On one hand Mason suspected it was Krijole kids who kept desecrating the graves, including Mom's, by painting rectangles over their monitors. On the other hand, less kids meant less hits, and less earnings.

But it didn't matter to Mason anymore. He'd never really profited from the Krijole foot traffic like Carter had with Mother's grave. And his expectation of morbid tourists interested in Carter's grave itself hadn't panned out either. Clearly he'd overestimated his brother's level of notoriety. For most of the public, the story of Carter Chase came and went in one news cycle.

The earnings were modest, and then the Pro-Bar advertising department abruptly excercised their right to terminate the contract, no explanation given. Mason emailed several times and never got a response. Later he found a 1-800 number for the company and started hassling their telephone representatives, often bringing up the First Amendment. After weeks of this an apologetic letter arrived from a publicist. She explained that the Pro-Bar company had been receiving complaints and boycott threats ever since a wire service ran a story about their advertising at the resting places of controversial figures. "In order to protect the image of our family-oriented line of products we have decided to re-evaluate our sponsorship policies. We do not wish to pass judgment on your loved one, but merely to be more selective

247

about our choice of burial advertising as part of our responsibility to our stock holders. We're sorry for your loss. Thank you for your interest in the Pro-Bar brand."

Mason tried to explain all this to Mark during his first cemetery visit after the government saw fit to let him go. Mark wasn't listening. He was skinny and weak, his eyes dull. He was still getting used to the air and the sunlight. Most of all he was overwhelmed by all this happening at once.

Back at the facility, they'd all been happy for him. Interrogators had figured out pretty quick that he was nobody, then they left him alone. Every once in a while some agent would come in to see him, tell him *sorry bro, it's out of my control.* It was a shock when they pulled him out of his cell and presented him the offer. His head was spinning and then they told him about Carter.

Abbey held Mark's arm delicately. They were unsure of each other, both of them more traumatized by their two years apart than bonded by their few months together. When Mark dropped to the ground Abbey gasped, thinking he'd lost balance again, but really he was kneeling down to give thanks. He knew what Carter had done for him.

A couple in their twenties walked by holding hands, the first Krijole visitors since they'd gotten there. The two sat down quietly by their hero's grave and started ritualistically laying out clippings and other mementos.

"We had to take Mom's off too," Mason said, pointing at the discolored rectangle on her marker. "See that there? Yeah, that was the monitor. I found out what happened was one of Carter's checks got sent back marked 'deceased,' and they must've done a Google search on the name, found out about the bombs and everything. So they wouldn't let us re-up."

"Can we just be quiet?" Abbey asked. "You can tell him about this later."

"He needs to know this. It would've been his money too. We would've split it. He could've used it."

It was true. Mark didn't feel ready to go back to work,

even if they'd take him. Worse, in order to be released he'd signed an agreement forbidding him from suing anyone involved with his incarceration and relinquishing all ownership of his life story. Government lawyers had already negotiated book and movie deals with Viacom, but he wouldn't be involved.

"They're so stupid," Mason continued. "They shouldn't be so worried about being associated with a guy like Carter. People like edgy stuff like that. I was telling the guy at the funeral home that. Nothing wrong with a rebellious image, don't you think, Mark? You used to do PR."

Mark looked up at him and shrugged.

"I mean, obviously the funeral home guy doesn't have a say in it, though," Mason conceded. "And I guess they must know what they're doing. They're Pepsi."

A light wind blew through the trees. The Krijole fans, who had been laying on their backs looking up at the sky got up, took one last look at the grave marker, and went back to their car. Not much later, as the sun was going down, Mark, Abbey and Mason left too.

Shadows fell on Mom, Dad and Carter. With no visitors around to set off the motion detectors, none of the nearby monitors were activated, and all was quiet. At last they could rest in peace.

CPSIA information can be obtained at www.ICGtesting.com
Printed in the USA
LVOW12s1045040514

384356LV00002B/343/P